Dragon
Curse

Also by Lisa McMann

» » « «

LISA McMANN

THE UNWANTEDS QUESTS

Dragon Curse

Aladdin

NEW YORK   LONDON   TORONTO   SYDNEY   NEW DELHI

ALADDIN

An imprint of Simon & Schuster Children's Publishing Division

1230 Avenue of the Americas, New York, New York 10020

First Aladdin hardcover edition September 2019

Text copyright © 2019 by Lisa McMann

Jacket illustration copyright © 2019 by Owen Richardson

For information about special discounts for bulk purchases, please contact Simon & Schuster Special Sales at 1-866-506-1949 or business@simonandschuster.com.

The Simon & Schuster Speakers Bureau can bring authors to your live event. For more information or to book an event, contact the Simon & Schuster Speakers Bureau at 1-866-248-3049 or visit our website at www.simonspeakers.com.

Book designed by Karin Paprocki

The text of this book was set in Truesdell.

Manufactured in the United States of America 0719 FFG

2 4 6 8 10 9 7 5 3 1

This book has been cataloged with the Library of Congress.

ISBN 9781534416017 (hc)

ISBN 9781534416031 (eBook)

Contents

To readers, writers, and dreamers

Dragon
Curse

A Hasty Decision

Aaron Stowe, head mage of Artimé, stared hard at Drock as the small group of mages and dragons flew toward the castle Grimere in the land of the dragons. The dark purple dragon was known to be troubled. He was the least reliable by far of all of Pan's brood. Yet he was the only one making sense right now.

"You must listen to me," said Drock in a low voice. He dropped back in flight so his face was next to his mother's flank, near where Aaron and the other humans rode. "You and your party should leave my mother's back and climb onto mine. I will take you home." He glanced around at Pan and

LISA McMANN

his siblings. All of them had glazed eyes and were intent on heading toward the Revinir and the castle. "It's a dragon curse. She's calling to us with her roar. They're all being controlled by the Revinir, but I . . . So far I have resisted it. I'm the only one."

"But—" said Aaron. A moment ago he'd urged Pan to turn around, and she'd ignored him. And . . . this was *Drock*. If Drock was making sense, did that mean that Aaron might be the confused one? He turned to watch as hundreds of dragons flew toward the castle Grimere, coming from all directions. Drock was right. The Revinir had to be controlling them with her roar. Calling to them, as Drock said. It seemed clear by the way the dragons in their party were all acting, and had been acting lately.

Aaron thought it through again: The Revinir was controlling Pan, the ruler of the sea, and her children. Most of them, at least. Was it possible that Drock could be somehow unaffected? Or . . . could the difficult young dragon be leading them into a trap?

Getting away from hundreds of fire-breathing dragons didn't seem like a trap.

But switching dragons in midair wasn't exactly an easy task. At least they weren't flying over the gorge between the worlds anymore, but a fall to the rocky ground from this height would be just as deadly.

Aaron's face shone with sweat. His lips were pressed tightly into a gray line. "I don't know what to do," he muttered, and turned to Henry. "What do you think?"

"I don't know either." Henry was anxious too. He glanced at Sean and Scarlet and two of his children, Ibrahim and Clementi, who rounded out their party. They all seemed uneasy. Uncertain. And they all desperately wanted to find their fellow Artiméans on the rescue team, who were seemingly lost in the land of the dragons, and bring them to safety. They'd been traveling days to do so! Turning back now seemed like a lost opportunity, a waste of precious time. But there was nothing that felt safe about moving forward into this situation.

Sean leaned in. "This doesn't look promising at all. I know we want to find our loved ones, but we won't last more than a minute against the Revinir and her new dragon army."

"I agree," said Scarlet, then lowered her voice to a whisper. "But how do we know Drock is trustworthy?"

"Hurry!" said Drock, trying to fly steadily close to his mother without knocking into her. Pan seemed not to notice him or what he was attempting to do. She and Ivis and Hux and Yarbeck soared straight and true toward the castle, like all the other dragons. Right into the heart of danger.

Aaron's blood pounded in his ears. He felt light-headed. Dragons were not something to mess around with. And the six mages, no matter how powerful they might be, wouldn't have a chance against this mob. He ripped his fingers through his hair, agonizing over the options, then absently checked his pockets, feeling for heart attack spells. He had plenty of them and was prepared to fight. What if the Revinir was holding the rescue team captive? What if they were in that castle somewhere? What if they were so close to them—could they really turn around now? Kaylee was among the ones they sought. What would she think if she knew he'd done that?

Aaron regarded Drock again. The dragon's eyes were clear. He was the only one engaging with the Artiméans, responding to them. And despite the young dragon's salty disposition, he was the only one Aaron felt like he could trust in this moment. Instinctively Aaron knew something was wrong here, and it was obvious Pan wasn't acting like an ally. Their missing loved ones might be nearby, but there was no way this group could take on the army of dragons without being killed. Most of them anyway. Aaron had to be wise in his role. The people of Artimé were counting on him to make good decisions. To bring this rescue team home alive. To be a good, smart leader, even if he didn't want this job. Besides, he couldn't stand the thought of Frieda Stubbs and the other dissenters having even more ammunition against him—they'd made his life miserable enough without that.

The head mage swallowed hard. Holding on to Pan's neck, he crawled along the dragon's back and beckoned to his team to follow. "Let's go with Drock," he said. "Back home. Before it's too late."

A Tinge of Gray

By the time Fifer and Thisbe Stowe and the others in their party were exploding out of the volcano into the dingy gray light of a strange world, it was far too late to turn back. They burst up and flew wildly in all directions, then slammed hard into the murky water surrounding the volcano.

Fifer hung on to Thisbe for all she was worth, knowing that her sister was currently stuck in the throes of one of the Revinirroar episodes that rendered her nearly paralyzed. Left alone, Thisbe would certainly drown. Once Fifer could catch her breath and wipe the slime from her face, she called out to Simber.

Simber, who'd stayed in the air upon his emergence into this world, shot over to the twins and plucked them out of the water, then brought them to the edge of the volcano. He went back for Kaylee, Samheed, and Lani while Talon collected Seth and Crow. Some of Fifer's birds managed to untangle well enough to go after Carina and pull her ashore.

Once everyone had been collected and brought back to the volcano, all of them in varying degrees of pain from the violent expulsion, they sat stunned and dripping dirty water. They tried to clean off, taking in their surroundings as they did so.

Fifer, the acting leader of the team since Alex had died, looked to Simber to see if he wanted to discuss what to do next, but anger was etched in the cheetah statue's face. Clearly he needed a moment, so Fifer stayed near Thisbe instead and tried to hold in her own frustration about the mistakes that had led them here. Thisbe's reaction to the Revinir's call had definitely cost them. Fifer glanced at her sister, who was still knocked out from it.

The iridescent scales that peppered Thisbe's arms and legs caught the dim light. Fifer saw that the scales lay flat now, but she had seen them stand up before. She took a moment to study them, wondering how they felt, then tentatively ran her forefinger over Thisbe's forearm. The scales' edges were sharp, but not enough to cut her. They were admittedly beautiful, like natural jewelry—almost beautiful enough to tempt Fifer into drinking some of the dragon-bone broth, which had caused them to appear. Not that she had access to it, so it wasn't really an option. Besides, would any human really want to have permanent scales? Did Thisbe hate them? Resent them? Or . . . maybe she loved them. The dragon-bone broth had definitely given Thisbe some otherworldly, mystical powers, though they appeared to be small and as yet undefined. Fifer nibbled on her lip, reluctantly admiring the scales. When Thisbe stirred, Fifer took her hand away and turned again toward Simber, gauging his level of crankiness. He still seemed extra mad.

Eventually Thisbe groaned and sat up, not quite sure what had happened. The look on Fifer's face made her afraid to ask, but she did anyway. "Where are we? Is Sky here?" Thisbe winced and looked all around, feeling guilty. This was all her fault. The grim silence confirmed that Sky was nowhere to be found in this depressing place.

Once the last of the waves created by the volcano's

emergence ricocheted off the shores of the distant mainland, the lake around them became eerily still. Hordes of insects gathered and buzzed just above the surface. Occasionally a mysterious ripple stirred the water.

On the mainland, a thick layer of mist hovered over a city of ancient ruins. Kaylee clambered partway up the volcano and peered toward it. "No people over there," she reported. "At least none that I can see from this distance." But she spotted all sorts of bushes along the shoreline bearing colorful fruit, a stark contrast to the rest of the world. "There's potential for food if we need it," she added. "I don't know about this water, though." She wrinkled her nose at the dank lake and sniffed her sodden clothes. "We shouldn't drink it unless we get really desperate, and even then we'll have to boil it." There was nothing resembling firewood anywhere on the rocky volcano.

"Maybe there's a well on land," Carina said, pointing to the ruins. "Or a freshwater river."

"We'rrre not going anywherrre," said Simber in an angry growl. "We'rrre staying herrre all togetherrr until this volcano sinks and takes us with it."

Fifer glanced nervously at the stone cheetah and stood up.

LISA McMANN

"It's going to be fine," she declared with confidence she didn't feel. And though it felt natural to be in this leadership role, her voice wavered. "It's just a small setback."

"It was a huge mistake," Simber roared. "I should have nev-errr let you talk me into it."

"I suppose the alternative was better?" snapped Fifer. "Splitting up?" She knew the cheetah was right, but she didn't like admitting it. She felt flush with guilt, even though it wasn't *her* fault that Thisbe had stopped guiding them in the middle of everything with absolutely no warning. "We'll be out of here in no time. It's . . . it's just a glitch."

"Glitch, smitch," Simber said under his breath. Fifer ignored him.

"I'm sorry, everybody," Thisbe said, feeling frustrated and downcast. She flexed her aching joints and got slowly to her feet. "I didn't realize that the Revinir's roar could affect me out-side of Grimere." Remnants of frightening images still flashed before her eyes and hovered at the edges of her mind. Her heart sank. It was terribly worrisome and depressing knowing that the dragon-woman's range was so broad. Her roar had traveled all the way into the volcano network that led to other worlds!

Would Thisbe ever be able to get away from it? Wouldn't there be any relief once they made it home?

Fifer's mouth twitched in frustration. She wanted to lash out, to blame her sister outright so that Simber wouldn't be so mad at and disappointed in *her*. But she knew Thisbe couldn't help what had happened. And lashing out would make Fifer feel even worse in the long run, so she kept quiet and sipped sparingly from her canteen. They didn't know how long they'd be here before they'd get sucked back down. And then what? Which portal would they try next? How long would this go on before they found their world? This wasn't nearly as easy as Thisbe had made it out to be.

Tense hours passed. Gray clouds hung low above them, heavy and stifling. They could scarcely see the mouth of the volcano they'd been thrown from because it was shrouded in mist. A bit of the top of the volcano still smoldered, leaving a growing layer of smoke trapped in the atmosphere to intermingle with the clouds. It was hard to take a deep breath. There was no wind, just the occasional ripple on the water. No one noticed any movement on the mainland.

Simber let go of some of his anger, and eventually he and Fifer talked quietly, trying to come up with a plan. Thisbe brooded by herself, thinking all sorts of troubling thoughts, like the fact that she was the cause of this problem. It was obvious that Fifer was annoyed with her, and Thisbe didn't blame her. She knew Fifer would soften up eventually, but it didn't make her feel better. Perhaps because of the depressing setting, Thisbe's mind strayed to thoughts of Alex's death. About how she hadn't been very nice to him the last time she'd seen him. This kind of guilt plagued her whenever she was feeling down, and it wouldn't leave her mind now.

Seth stayed near Thisbe at first, ready to help if she needed anything. But she didn't seem to want to talk to him. After a while he went to the water's edge and peered at the surface. He noticed the occasional ripples and squinted at them, trying to get a better view in the dim light. "I think I saw a fish," he said, looking over his shoulder to where the others sat. It was never too soon to scope out food options—he'd learned that much over the past many months.

Carina got up and joined her son. "Where?"

Seth pointed to where he'd seen a ripple, but it was gone. "Just wait," he said. "There will be another one."

They waited patiently. Carina pulled a long, heavy fishing line out of her rucksack and began to untangle it. "I'm not sure I want to eat a fish that lives in water like this," she muttered, "but I suppose we can't be choosy under the circumstances." She knelt and looked around for anything that resembled a worm to bait her hook.

A movement and a small splash a few feet out caught Seth's eye. "There," he said, pointing. "Nice and close. Did you see it? It's big."

Circular ripples spread out from the spot where Seth was pointing.

Carina tossed her line toward the area, then wrapped the other end around her arm several times to give her some leverage in case the fish was as big as Seth seemed to think. She held the string slack with both hands and waited.

Seth leaned over the water, looking for the telltale flash of a silvery fish belly.

With a loud surge, a giant, bug-eyed eel rose up, its huge jaws agape. It clamped on to the fishing line and slammed its body into Seth, knocking him off balance on the uneven, rocky ground. The eel squealed and sank, pulling Carina in with it and dragging her under the water. Seth's feet slipped on the damp rocks, and he fell in after her.

Another Try

Samheed and Lani charged for the shore—they'd seen eels like this one before. "Get back!" Lani shouted to the others. "Move away from the edge!" As Talon came flying over, Samheed dove in and grabbed Seth. He yanked him, sputtering and coughing, to shore. There was no sign of Carina.

"Mom!" Seth cried as he scrambled up the rocks. "Somebody get her!"

"I'm trying!" said Talon, flying over the area and peering anxiously at the water. He'd seen one of his best friends, Lhasa the snow lion from Karkinos, get snatched up by one of these

LISA McMANN

giant deadly eels. Luckily, Kitten had been able to save her fellow feline with one of her lives, or Lhasa would be dead now. As Simber joined him in flight, Talon rose to get a broader look, searching intently for any sign of movement as the surface went still again.

"What can we do?" Kaylee asked, grabbing at her empty sword hilt, momentarily forgetting that she'd lost her sword in the moat around the castle Grimere. She stood back helplessly.

"Simber, do you see anything?" Fifer called.

"Therrre!" growled Simber, and jaws agape, dove without hesitation into the lake. Talon charged after him, staying just above the violent splashing that ensued. The eel's tail flipped above the water, swatting at Talon. The bronze giant deftly caught the end, sinking his steely fingertips into the flesh. He wrapped his legs around it and flapped his wings wildly to keep from getting pulled down. He hung on with all his might while the eel batted him around, slamming him over and over against the surface of the water.

"He's whipping him around like a pool noodle!" Kaylee shouted.

Nobody else knew what a pool noodle was, but this was

no time for inquiries. Thisbe, Fifer, and Seth edged closer to the water despite the warnings. Seth went from clutching his drenched shirt to clutching his head in disbelief and anguish. "Mom!" he yelled again, though it did nothing to bring her back.

An agonizing minute passed. Where was Simber? Had he been crushed by the giant serpentlike fish? Had Carina been able to get a breath before she'd been pulled under? Was she even still alive and struggling to untangle herself, or had the eel squeezed the life out of her? How long could Talon hang on to the slimy creature's tail?

With every violent twist of the eel, Talon wrenched toward the volcano. Soon the Artiméans could tell that Talon was slowly pulling the eel out of the water and closer to them. Samheed watched for a moment, then looked around frantically. Seeing Fifer's bird hammock spread out, he lunged for it. Grabbing the longest rope, he ripped it loose from the fabric. "Come on, everybody!" he called. Coiling the rope, he bounded partway up the side of the volcano with Lani rolling over the rocks in her magical contraption behind him. Kaylee followed. "Everyone!" Samheed said again. "Up here! Talon, try to come this way!"

Confused, Fifer and the rest followed Samheed up the side of the volcano. Stopping on a large ledge, Samheed partially uncoiled the rope and handed the loose end to Lani. Then he cast a magic carpet spell and climbed on it. He commanded the carpet to move to Talon and uncoiled the rope slowly as he went out over the water.

"What's he doing?" Fifer demanded once she and the others reached the ledge.

"Everybody grab on!" Lani handed the slack end of the rope to the ones behind her, then locked her wheels and gripped a new spot a short way up it and leaned precipitously over the edge.

"Oh, I see!" said Thisbe. "We're going to help pull Talon and the eel."

"Precisely," said Lani. "Everybody hold tight and plant your feet behind rocks. Get ready to reel them in. Just don't yank too hard, or we'll pull Sam off the carpet."

They stood in a line, positioning themselves behind boulders for support, as Samheed inched closer to Talon.

Talon yanked and strained, moving little by little toward Samheed and the volcano.

"Hurry up," Seth muttered, his normally pale cheeks red with exertion. He knew his mother could hold her breath for seven minutes, like most of the humans here, but time was ticking. And if she hadn't had a chance to get a breath before the eel yanked her under, she would be in big trouble by now. Seth's own breathing was shallow and quick, and he felt an old familiar panic swelling inside his chest. He gripped the rope tighter, his hands beginning to tremble.

"She's going to be okay," Thisbe whispered comfortingly from behind him. She recognized the panic signs and understood what was happening to him. "Focus on something and take slow, deep breaths."

Seth gulped and nodded and tried to breathe more slowly.

"Come on, Talon!" Samheed shouted, jiggling the end of the rope. "Almost there!"

Finally, with a huge lurch, Talon reached for the rope that Samheed held out to him. But the eel began to slip from his other hand, so he grabbed on again. Neck outstretched and mouth open, Talon lunged and grabbed the end of the rope in his teeth. The eel switched and twisted, yanking Talon and hauling Samheed off the magic carpet, but the theater director hung on and dangled from the rope until his magic carpet caught up to support him.

"Everybody pull!" Samheed shouted to the others on the side of the volcano. "As hard as you can!"

They pulled, and slowly they began to reel in Samheed and Talon. Once Samheed was above the side of the volcano, he hopped off the magic carpet and helped the others pull Talon and the eel and whoever else was still attached to the submerged end onto dry land. Everyone stared at the rope as they strained, pleading silently that Carina would soon surface.

With its tail fully out of the water, the eel fought harder than ever. But Simber soon appeared, his jaws clamped around the eel's throat and his wings flapping wildly. A second later Carina surfaced, even more tangled in the fishing line that was hanging from the eel's mouth. She drew a few ragged breaths before being dragged back under.

"She's breathing!" Thisbe said, giving Seth an encouraging look. "She's going to be fine." She pulled on the rope as hard as she could—she wasn't about to let Seth lose his mother. Not if she could help it.

Seth nodded, unable to speak. But he felt a little better.

As they strained and pulled Talon and Simber and Carina toward them, the volcano shivered. The still water on the opposite side of the volcano tremored. But because everyone was singularly focused on the rescue, none of them noticed it.

The volcano trembled again, then shook harder and plunged swiftly downward. The Artiméans screamed. Fifer's birds scattered into the air, while everything and everyone else was swallowed up by a heavy rush of water.

No one let go of the rope.

No one let go of the eel.

Everyone but the falcons went together into the volcano network with no warning and no plan and no idea which portal to exit through and no clue if Carina and Simber were still attached to the other end of the eel.

But someone else knew. A sleek, smooth, brown-and-purple-polka-dotted sea monster had been circling the volcano network on a continuous loop on a mission from Sky, who'd sent her in search of this very group to guide them to the right volcano. But Isobel the sea monster wasn't expecting them to be dragging one of the horrid, deadly eels with them. She nearly passed them by in her hurry to get away from it, but she knew these humans were important—maybe even more important than her fear of eels. Isobel guided herself toward the front of the team near the twins, as far from the eel as she could get. Thisbe caught sight of her and, with a joyous look on her face, alerted Fifer and Seth, indicating they should all follow the sea monster. Isobel took the lead, steering the group away from several portals until finally aiming for one very specifically.

Oh, please, let this be home, thought Thisbe.

Oh, please, let my mother be okay, thought Seth, struggling even more to breathe now that he was in the shallow pod.

Oh, please, let this strange monster thing get me out of this mess, thought Fifer.

As they followed Isobel, Fifer felt in her gut that this time she wasn't making a mistake like she'd done before. With confidence, the leaders aimed for a bright, fiery ring and went through it, exploding out and flying through the air. And then they landed in the familiar clear, cool waters of their own world. They were home.

But they were still in a mess of trouble.

As soon as Talon and Simber emerged from the top of the

volcano, the two began flapping their wings, holding a strong grip on the giant eel, straining to keep the thing out of the water so they could control it better.

Carina dangled by the fishing line a short distance from the eel's mouth. But now that she could breathe, she came to her senses and tried to untangle herself. Frustrated and getting nowhere, she grabbed hold of the line and concentrated, then whispered, "Dissipate."

The magical fishing line vanished into thin air. Carina dropped to the water below. Talon and Simber forced the eel back into the volcano's gaping maw, hoping to contain it at least momentarily while they collected their team.

As they attempted to do so, the volcano spat out one last round of passengers—the huge flock of Fifer's falcons, who had immediately plunged after their leader. They dragged the torn hammock with them. Red and purple feathers flew everywhere. The birds appeared bedraggled but unhurt.

Simber dodged the squawking blast and loosened his grip. Sensing it, the eel yanked free of its captors and dropped hard onto the side of the volcano, then bounced into the water and slithered away, nursing its wounds.

At long last, everyone had made it to the land of the seven islands. Battered but alive.

As they all swam to the volcano's shore, Isobel, who didn't normally like being touched by humans, dove underneath Thisbe and Fifer and lifted them up to ride on her back. Then she went to gather Carina as well. She brought the three of them to safety and climbed on shore, knowing Sky would want her to take care of them. Isobel worried over the group for several minutes as they recovered and squeezed the water from their clothes. Then something caught the sea monster's eye. Isobel bounded several yards away and looked sharply out to sea, detecting something.

"What is it?" asked Thisbe.

The sea monster pointed a flipper, but Thisbe couldn't see anything.

Several minutes later, Thisbe could just make out a bony spike slicing the water, and a person holding on to it. Soon a familiar voice called to them. "The Fifer! The Thisbe!"

Everyone turned to see Spike Furious speeding toward them. Standing on the whale, gripping the spike, was Sky. Tears of joy and relief spilled from her eyes. Rather than go home to Warbler, she'd remained with Spike in the area and waited for the volcano to emerge, hoping to see Thisbe arrive safely with Isobel. When Spike drew close, Sky dove off and scrambled ashore, grabbing Thisbe in a tight embrace, never wanting to let go again. Then she tackled her brother and the others.

Isobel looked all around. Satisfied that she'd completed her task, she slipped unnoticed into the water and disappeared.

Not yet visible on the horizon, but coming swiftly from the west, Drock the dark purple dragon sniffed the air sharply, picking up a new but familiar scent. Somewhere ahead of them were the three young mages he'd come to know in the dungeon—the ones that Aaron was seeking. The memory of them freeing him from his muzzle and giving him new wings was sharp and clear. Seth's scent, in particular, which was laced with anxiety and a good variety of cheeses, was more distinct than any other. Drock would know that boy's smell anywhere after the stressful time they'd spent together. He knew the goodness level in that one was very high. They'd come to an understanding in that dungeon stall—they were more alike than different in those difficult moments.

Drock thought he could detect a similar level of panic from Seth as he'd noticed that day in the dungeon—or perhaps the boy lived in this constant state of anxiety always, which would be regrettable. The dragon pushed onward toward the scent.

Soon the tip of the volcano appeared on the horizon. Drock squinted, searching for the children, wanting to be certain before he said anything. He sped faster. When he finally caught sight of the flying cheetah up above the volcano, he craned his neck to look at the riders on his back. "Aaron," said Drock with a rare bit of warmth in his voice, "it is good we left the land of the dragons. I think we've located the ones you seek."

Together Again

The volcano-hopping group couldn't see Drock coming, nor did they expect him. With a lengthy journey ahead, an eel in the waters, and no telling when the volcano would sink again, and with Spike there to help transport people, they kept their greetings brief and all headed to Warbler Island, going at top speed aboard flying and swimming creatures. Everyone was ready for a proper reunion and some much-needed food and rest.

Copper, the ruler of Warbler and mother of Sky and Crow, had been alerted to the approaching eclectic group. She and several other Warblerans were waiting to greet the visitors

LISA McMANN

and offer a warm meal. And while she'd hoped to see some Artiméan friends returning home, she hadn't imagined she'd see Sky among them. When Copper realized Sky was there on Spike's back, she nearly fainted from the shock. Word spread quickly, and the island exploded with the amazing news that Sky was alive and well.

Sky ran onto the beach and fell into her mother's awaiting arms, and Crow followed when he made it to shore. The three were reunited again.

When Sky and Crow finally let go of their mother, they returned to the others who'd trickled to shore by now. Sky took the opportunity for a less hurried greeting this time, smiling through tears as she accepted condolences from her friends over the death of Alex and their apologies for not knowing how to begin to look for her and for assuming she was dead.

Soon Copper's chefs were serving up a feast on the beach for the entire crew.

The Artiméans ate heartily, but there were many questions and much to talk about. Before they could begin to share their stories with Copper and the other people of Warbler, Spike, from the water, alerted them to an approaching dragon flying toward them. Simber confirmed it. Soon even the humans could see the speck in the sky.

"Who is it?" Fifer asked Simber.

"It's Drrrock the darrrk purrrple," said Simber, frowning. "He has passengerrrs." Wondering why Drock would be coming from that direction and who his passengers might be, they waited impatiently for him.

As Drock drew near, Simber detected who his riders were. Despite his concerns over seeing Drock without the other dragons, he let a rare smile escape and refrained from announcing the identities of the passengers to the others, thinking they would be more delighted to discover them with their own eyes. Soon the six mages on board stood up in the hollow of the dragon's back, peering anxiously around the beast's neck at the group gathered on Warbler's shore.

Kaylee shaded her eyes with her hand, then exclaimed, "Oh my God! Aaron! It's Aaron!" She dropped her plate of food and ran for the surf. The dragon glided down and skidded across the water. Then his tail began to churn, propelling them forward. Kaylee turned back and hollered, "Everybody! Henry's here too, and Sean! And Scarlet! And Ibrahim and Clementi! I can't believe it!"

The battered people from Thisbe and Fifer's group felt new energy surge through them. Thatcher, Carina, and Seth all exploded to life and ran into the surf to greet their loved ones. Crow, straining to catch a glimpse of Scarlet, followed a bit tentatively, then abandoned his shyness and broke into a run when he saw her dive off Drock's back and start swimming toward him.

The two people in the slowest-moving relationship ever recorded reached each other, waist deep in waves. They faced one another for a second, then relinquished all decorum and embraced, holding each other like they never wanted to let go. Then Scarlet pulled back, took Crow's face in her hands, and as seawater streamed down them, she planted a kiss firmly on the young man's lips. Crow looked shocked for a second. Then he gathered Scarlet up in his arms. With a grin he kissed her back.

Fifer cheered at the sight of her beloved former caretaker looking so perfectly happy. But Thisbe's eyes were elsewhere. She caught Aaron's eye, and a lump formed in her throat. Aaron put his hand to his heart in silent gratitude at seeing her. Then Thisbe and Fifer ran into the surf and skirted Crow and Scarlet, who were kissing *again*, and joined Kaylee in hugging Aaron. Thisbe couldn't stop her sobs, and after a moment Aaron let go of the others and picked her up as if she was a little girl. He held her as they cried together. Fifer watched her brother and sister, her eyes filling with tears. But she didn't worm her way into the embrace. It had been a very long time since Thisbe and Aaron had seen each other.

Thatcher tackled Henry and their children in a huge group hug. They staggered through the water to Lani, who'd gone as far into the water as her magical wheeled contraption would take her. Henry broke away and threw his arms around his sister, and they all continued slogging to shore.

Samheed had stayed behind, waiting with Simber and Kitten on shore. They'd opted to watch the dearest loved ones reconnect first before joining in. Samheed wore a bittersweet expression as he took in the scene: Aaron was wearing the robe of the head mage, and he looked so strikingly like Alex in it. Samheed glanced at Simber, then tipped his head toward Aaron. "So it was Aaron who brought things back," he said. "Not Claire."

Simber nodded. "It appearrrs to be."

Samheed no longer held a grudge against Aaron—those feelings had subsided years ago. But the two had never been close. Samheed had always been much warmer and friendlier toward Alex—once they'd become friends, that is. And while Samheed could say with a fair amount of confidence that he trusted Aaron, he felt a slight prickling at the back of his neck seeing the man in Alex's robe. "I'm not quite sure how I feel about it, Sim."

Personally, Simber was glad to see Aaron in control as head mage. But he heard the hitch in Samheed's voice and eyed the man carefully. He knew the history between the two as teenagers. Simber had felt similarly about Aaron in the past as well—they all had.

But the cheetah possessed information about Aaron that Samheed didn't: Aaron was potentially immortal because of the magic seaweed that the scientists had used to save his life many years ago. And for Simber, the thought of never having to lose another head mage again was a great relief. Beneath Simber's stony, gruff exterior was a soft heart. He wasn't sure he could go through it again. And he'd grown fond of Aaron over the years. "He'll make a good mage," Simber said carefully.

"I know. It just seems . . ." Samheed didn't finish. Although he was thrilled to see everyone, he was feeling sort of down about it. Now that they were all reunited, he had an even greater urge to get home and have things return to normal. Back to the theater. Back to teaching students. And maybe pretending like everything was okay, even though he knew it would be a long time before he could say that. He missed Alex deeply.

He wasn't sure what was prompting his negative feelings about Aaron—perhaps it was just the surprise of discovering he'd become the new mage instead of Claire. As Aaron broke away from his family members and came onshore to greet the rest of them, Samheed tried hard to shake off his uneasiness.

It was just that Aaron *looked* so much like Alex with that robe on. Samheed's heart throbbed painfully, but he attempted a grin and embraced Aaron. Then he took a few steps back as the new head mage and Simber exchanged an awkward hello. Feeling entirely out of sorts, Samheed kept walking backward to give the two privacy and allow Aaron to talk with his new right-hand statue. As Samheed turned away, tears pricked at his eyes and momentarily blinded him. He stumbled in the sand and moved more quickly as a huge wave of grief washed over him. Seeing Alex's identical twin wearing the robe was truly jarring. All of Samheed's worst memories of Aaron came flooding back: The time Aaron pretended to impersonate Alex in the first battle with Quill. The time Samheed first learned of Mr. Today's death at Aaron's hand—they'd told him and Lani just moments after Alex had risked everything to rescue them from Queen Eagala. And there was Aaron's absolute heartlessness with his parents and family when he was leader of Quill. Yet Alex had kept giving Aaron chance after chance after chance.

And now Alex was gone, and that same person who'd committed all those horrible acts was in charge of Artimé. It was shocking to think of it like that, but those were the facts. Samheed continued to flee the celebration gathering, reprimanding himself. He should feel excitement—they'd found Thisbe *and* Sky, and they'd be home soon. But he couldn't shake the troubling thoughts. Surely he wasn't alone in thinking them. Many people disliked Aaron because they didn't know all the intricate details of how Aaron had come around to being a good and worthy person.

Eventually Samheed waded out into the water, not far from Drock, who appeared to be brooding too and not inclined to talk. Samheed dove under a wave, trying to clear his head. Trying to talk himself out of this funk. Aaron had been bad once, but he'd changed. And he'd sacrificed a lot for Artimé. Samheed knew this intellectually, but his heart still yanked around inside him. Was Aaron right for Artimé? Could he be effective as a leader after the choices he'd made? After the history he'd had?

Samheed couldn't shake the doubts, though he vowed to himself to try. He owed it to Aaron. After all, Aaron had totally turned his life around and had played things right for over a dozen years. He'd apologized profusely for his wrongs, and he'd done everything in his power to make up for his misdeeds. Claire had forgiven him—that was a big moment. Kaylee had fallen in love with him, and she was one of the smartest people Samheed knew . . . though it was true she'd never known him when he was a horrible person. Aaron had even moved away from the island of Quill, showing no interest in ever wanting to be involved in the politics of Artimé—either with the magical world or against it. So why was Samheed so apprehensive about this appointment?

He floated on his back for a few moments, searching for answers, until he heard Lani calling for him. He flipped up and waved to her, then wiped his face and sloshed toward the shore so he could greet Henry and the others. And hopefully soon he'd be able to push the harsh feelings toward Aaron away for good.

Home at Last

T he new arrivals ate heartily while Thisbe recounted the story of her time in the catacombs and her escape, as well as her time spent with Sky. Then Fifer told Aaron and the others about her group's agonizing journey, their battle with the Revinir and its tragic ending, and the search for Thisbe. Aaron listened silently to the tale of his twin's death. His face was gray and etched with grief, and he was unable to speak for a long while. When it came time to share his team's story, Aaron nodded at Henry, asking him to do it. The young healer shared how things had gone down in Artimé from the time the world had turned gray.

LISA McMANN

Henry skimmed over the parts where Aaron had been challenged by the growing group of people who didn't think he should be leading Artimé. He briefly mentioned one of the altercations, in which Aaron had felt that his son, Daniel, had been threatened.

Samheed frowned and glanced at Sean, who caught his eye with a grim look. Was there more to this than Henry was letting on? As uneasy as Samheed had been feeling, he wasn't the least bit surprised that some other people back home had been vocal about Aaron being in charge. Not everyone had forgiven the young man—not everyone knew him as well as the group gathered here. So their judgments were sure to be skewed. Could that hurdle ever be overcome? Samheed turned his gaze toward Lani, who seemed sympathetic about what Aaron was going through.

Lani threw Samheed a warning look, as if she anticipated what Samheed might be thinking. She knew him well.

Samheed looked down, abashed. He was well aware that he tended to leap to anger and suspicion, though now he was much better at controlling it than when he'd been a teenager. Back then, Lani had been a good foil to his frequent billowing frustrations, so he sometimes looked to her to help him gauge his levels of emotions and see if he was being reasonable. At this moment, Lani didn't appear troubled at all that Aaron had taken the role of head mage rather than Claire. Samheed's frown flickered and dissipated. Perhaps he'd just have to get used to this idea, even though the news had not been what he was expecting. It would no doubt grow easier to accept in time. He hoped the loss of Alex would too.

Talk turned to the future and what, if anything, they should do about the Revinir. Thisbe opened her mouth to speak her mind about the situation and her intent to go back as soon as possible. But Crow and Carina and Lani immediately stated that they were relieved to be away from the foreign world. "I'm not eager to return any time soon," Carina said. The others agreed.

Thisbe closed her mouth and listened, a consternated look on her face. Being back in familiar territory had clearly given some of them new perspectives.

"I'm ready to be home too," said Fifer. She was exhausted—physically, mentally, and emotionally.

"I need my bed for a good long time," Seth remarked.

LISA McMANN

"And then," said Fifer with a yawn, "once we're rested, I think we need to have a celebration."

Thisbe's eyes widened. She couldn't stay silent any longer. "What?" she exclaimed. "Celebrating *what*, exactly?"

"A masquerade ball," Fifer said decisively. "To celebrate our return! Like what the grown-ups did when they came back from their adventure. Only we'll do it with costumes, too."

Thisbe's lips parted in confusion. "A . . . a *ball*?" Had they all forgotten that Alex had died on this mission? A celebration seemed terribly out of place. And a waste of precious time. They needed to prepare to fight the Revinir!

As several of the others voiced their exhaustion from traveling and fighting and their interest in Fifer's idea, Sky remained silent next to Thisbe. The two exchanged a bemused glance, as both were aghast at the thought of celebrating at a time like this. Neither of them felt like having a party, for a multitude of reasons. The mere fact that Fifer had suggested such a thing felt like a huge betrayal to Thisbe after how she'd said so valiantly just recently that she would go back to the land of the dragons with Thisbe to help rescue her people. *Their* people.

Thisbe's scales caught the firelight. She folded her arms

over her chest and pressed her mouth firmly in a determined line. The others would come to their senses after a good night's sleep back in Artimé, and then they'd all be back to planning the next move against the Revinir. At least Thisbe hoped so.

Feeling hurt and outnumbered, Thisbe and Sky didn't voice their disagreement. Not now. But there was no doubt in Thisbe's mind that she would be returning to Rohan and to Maiven Taveer. To rescue Dev, if he was still alive, and the other black-eyed slaves. To end the spell that, according to Aaron's account, seemed to have affected many hundreds of dragons from worlds away. It was the same spell that affected Thisbe and would continue to plague her until she found a way to stop it. It would be her life's goal. It had to be. She couldn't live like this, never knowing when the next roar would strike. Her scales quivered at the thought.

Not to mention her people needed her. And she needed them, too.

Certainly the Revinir knew Thisbe was hiding out somewhere. Once the dragon-woman had control of all of the land of the dragons, what would stop her from venturing here to look for her?

LISA McMANN

Had *everyone* forgotten about these things? Had they lost their minds? A *costume ball*?

Thisbe noticed Ibrahim and Clementi weren't exactly cheering the idea either. Instead they were throwing concerned glances her way. Thisbe smiled grimly at them. She didn't know them very well—they'd been newly declared Unwanted and were still finding their way around Artimé when Thisbe, Fifer, and Seth had originally snuck away on their first quest to save the young dragon captives. But they'd listened in horror to Thisbe's passionate tale, and they seemed to understand the reason behind her strained silence. Maybe it was because they'd so recently been through that scary time in Quill and sent away from everything that had been familiar. Or perhaps they were a little bit disappointed to turn back from the mission they'd been excited to join. Whatever their reasons, they tapped their chests lightly to indicate they were with Thisbe. Their dedication made Thisbe sit up a little taller. It was nice to have people on her side.

And Sky was with Thisbe too, of course. She squeezed Thisbe's hand, and her face was as troubled as the girl's. Even Samheed shot a curious look at Thisbe to see what her reaction

was to the conversation. Her favorite instructor seemed to understand something wasn't quite right about this.

Their support was affirming. They'd figure out how to deal with this problem once they got home. Even Thisbe needed a little bit of comfort before steeling herself for the next journey.

Eventually the party planning tapered off. Exhaustion overtook the group, and one by one they drifted off to sleep on the sandy beach.

The next day Sky and Crow bade their mother good-bye. Soon the entire entourage was on their way home to Artimé, riding on the most unusual assortment of creatures: one dark purple dragon, one stone cheetah, one whale with a spike, and dozens of falcons carrying a hammock. It was quite a picture.

Thisbe didn't like heights, and she hated birds, so she rode with Sky on Spike Furious. Most of the ride she brooded from her spot on the whale's broad forehead, her arms and legs partially encircling the bony spike and her cheek resting against it as she watched for her home island to grow larger. Occasional bursts of ocean spray kept her awake, and the wind sliced through her hair. Sky held on to the spike from the

LISA McMANN

other side. The three led the way, with the dragon and cheetah and falcons following by air. Sensing Thisbe's mood, Sky rode silently too, thinking about everything that had led them to this moment and how the two had grown so much closer through their despair and grief over Alex's death. There was an air of melancholy with both of them, despite being reunited with the others and each other.

"Are you okay?" Sky asked Thisbe when Artimé was large in front of them and Spike began to slow down.

"Not really," said Thisbe, turning to study her. "Are you?"

Sky was quiet for a long moment, then shook her head. "No." She choked back an unexpected sob, and tears mingled with the sea spray on her cheeks. Her heart was broken, and her bones ached. Nothing would ever feel okay again.

By nightfall the group made it to shore and were home at last. Fifer climbed out of the hammock and onto Artimé's lawn. She was feeling very strange, and a bit like a hero, though there were few to welcome her at this late hour. She'd become an important leader in her time away and was beginning to wonder what leadership in Artimé would look like now that she was home. It was a grown-up feeling she'd never experienced before on this island, and she liked it. Perhaps now people would forget that she used to be a dangerous child and put their trust in her. Look to her for advice.

Before going inside the mansion, she turned to find Simber so she could check in with him as she usually did before going to sleep. But instead of reporting to her like he'd done since Alex had died, he was talking quietly with Aaron. Fifer almost called out to Simber, but then she realized the two were talking about leadership things and plans for the next day. Her lips parted, and a cold feeling rose in her chest. She took a few uncertain steps toward them, but Aaron and Simber didn't notice her. After a moment, unsure what to do, Fifer dropped her gaze and glanced around self-consciously. She spied Sky and Thisbe walking arm in arm, Thisbe's scales shimmering like tiny stars in the moonlight. With a sigh, Fifer followed them into the mansion.

The twins moved about their apartment without talking. Fifer was weary and didn't feel like sharing her confusing thoughts. What had happened felt bad. And embarrassing, too—she'd apparently been demoted and replaced without a word from anyone. Obviously she'd expected the head mage to take over once they returned home, but she'd thought she'd at least have some sort of transition time or be kept in the loop now that she'd proven herself. Or, at the very least, thanked for getting everyone home safely. But there'd been none of that. It wasn't something she wanted to bring attention to. She didn't think her sister would understand, anyway . . . or care. Thisbe had been brooding and verging on quarrelsome since Fifer first mentioned wanting to have a celebration. Feeling miserable, Fifer crawled into bed and faced the wall.

As for Thisbe, the comforts of home were a welcome sight. But her mind whirred, and she wore a grim expression, growing more determined than ever to put a stop to the Revinir and her roaring spell and return the land of the dragons to its rightful rulers. It was going to take a miracle, and Thisbe had no idea how she would succeed, especially now that Fifer and Seth were being less than enthusiastic about helping. But she feared this war wasn't even close to being over. No one, no matter where they lived, was safe.

An Uneasy Feeling

Weeks passed. Aaron tried to dodge Frieda Stubbs and the dissenters, while Thisbe and Fifer wrestled with their individual issues and rarely saw eye to eye when they tried to talk. Thisbe desperately wanted everyone to work toward going back to the land of the dragons to fight the Revinir and save her fellow black-eyed slaves. But Fifer wasn't enthused about it. She didn't want to admit that her apparent demotion made her feel out of sorts and even less motivated to go on another quest, but that was the truth of it. What else was she supposed to be in charge of now but the costume ball?

LISA McMANN

Besides, Fifer thought that Thisbe needed to lighten up. Sure, Thisbe was part dragon now and had a special attachment to the land of the dragons that Fifer wasn't feeling. But the Artiméans had been through a lot, and they needed a break. She wanted Thisbe to slow down and let everyone recover after the harrowing months they'd endured.

Frustrated, Thisbe gave up arguing. She spent her days working with Florence, the Magical Warrior trainer, so she could finally learn the traditional magic of Artimé and earn her component vest. She wanted the vest for the layer of protection it offered, but mostly she craved access to the important magical components she would need on her return to Grimere. She couldn't go back without them. True, the magic might not work on the Revinir, who was half dragon now, so Thisbe was also thinking about how to take her down in other ways. But Artimé's magic would work on the awful soldiers who willingly served the dragon-woman. And she might learn something in her training with Florence that could help the slaves escape, which would be better than nothing.

While Thisbe doggedly worked to catch up to her sister's mage level, Fifer and Seth planned the extravaganza for all of

Artimé. They determined it should be held on the upcoming Day of Remembrance, which was also known to the Unwanteds as the annual day of the purge, when the Unwanteds were sent out of Quill. It was a time when many people of Artimé celebrated their birthdays, especially if their official birth date had never been noted.

Ibrahim and Clementi would be turning fourteen. Seth, who'd been born in Artimé and had an official birthday, would be fourteen soon after the costume ball, so he'd be celebrating early. And Thisbe and Fifer, who'd been born in Quill and didn't have a specific birth date that anyone had made note of, would be marking their thirteenth birthdays at long last. Thirteen was a special year for most children in Artimé, because it signaled the start of their magical-warrior training and working toward getting the coveted component vest.

Fifer had already secretly trained with Florence before the rescue mission and had been given her component vest and access to all the magical components. That was why Thisbe had some catching up to do. She was determined to learn everything possible in the least amount of time. Plus she continued to work on her natural fire-based magic, going to the jungle or the lagoon in the evenings by herself to find secluded boulders and dead trees and sandbars to blow up.

That left little opportunity for her to get together with Sky and her new allies, Ibrahim and Clementi, who seemed unwavering in their intent to help her. But it was critical that Thisbe take the time to do some brainstorming with them about what would actually work against the Revinir. Once the costume party was over and Thisbe had completed her magical-warrior training, they'd all have more time to figure things out.

Even when Thisbe wasn't preoccupied with determining how to defeat impossibly powerful enemies, she didn't find joy in parties. The music was often too loud, and there were so many people around all talking at once until the noise level became overwhelming. It was exhausting. And she still didn't think Fifer's costume extravaganza was appropriate after all the difficulties and grief they'd gone through. It felt wrong to celebrate like this after Alex's horrible death. Besides, no one knew what had happened to Dev. Was he even alive?

But Aaron, who seemed uncomfortable in his role as head mage, had mentioned to Thisbe that he thought the party was a good way to "unite the island and go forward together," despite the new situation. Thisbe was learning that this way of speaking was code for the dissenters being disruptive and harshly critical of him—which she'd witnessed firsthand since they'd returned home. Frankly, this group of people who had come out of nowhere seemed horrible.

The dissenters didn't act particularly enthusiastic to see Thisbe and Fifer home again either—they hadn't forgotten that the twin girls used to be a menace to the people of Artimé, and often threw suspicious glances their way. Thisbe wanted her brother to succeed, so she didn't confront any of them, even when they seemed to be talking about her and Fifer behind their backs. Instead she found herself taking out her annoyances on Fifer. The two argued more than either wanted to. But they couldn't seem to stop. Things were tense in the room they shared.

The unpredictable, paralyzing roars from the Revinir didn't help and only confirmed that the Revinir was still trying to get Thisbe and Drock to obey. The call kept Thisbe even more motivated to improve her power and abilities, so she could fight against the Revinir. It was so disheartening that those roars could affect her from this distance. There was no escaping it.

Fifer was sympathetic at first, but Thisbe often dropped to the floor and writhed around at inopportune times. Knowing Thisbe would come out of it eventually, Fifer's level of concern for her sister's episodes lessened.

Nobody else but Drock could hear that frightful noise, and it shook both him and Thisbe. "This nightmare is far from over," Drock said one day, staring worriedly to the west.

"Is she coming?" asked Thisbe. She checked her scales, which were lying flat on her arms and legs.

"Not yet."

"Maybe it's not us she's after."

Drock closed his eyes. "Perhaps." But neither believed it.

Drock, being the only dragon left in the seven islands, stayed close to Artimé rather than spend his time by himself at the island of dragons. Without the support of his family, Drock was lonely, and he struggled more and more to ignore the Revinir's call. It seemed to be getting stronger every time, or at least it felt that way. The only thing he had going for him was that it didn't leave him completely debilitated, as happened with Thisbe. On top of the physical repercussions, the roar reminded Thisbe that the awful monster-woman was alive and well and in control of hundreds of dragons and a number of black-eyed children.

There was something about the roar that made Thisbe miss Rohan. He'd been nearby to help her through it the first few times. And he'd been so gentle about it, unlike Fifer, who seemed increasingly annoyed every time it happened. It was almost like Fifer was beginning to resent that Thisbe had this affliction. Once, when it happened during one of Fifer's costume-ball planning sessions, Fifer got really frustrated at Thisbe. "I'm starting to get tired of this drama," she muttered, as if Thisbe were exaggerating the effects.

"I'm not making it up," Thisbe said when she could speak.

Fifer frowned. "I know." After a minute she added, "Sorry. I was just in the middle of something."

Fifer hurried away but questioned herself about why she was so annoyed by Thisbe and her dragon issues. Was it because of the bond Thisbe had with that land now? She had such a sense of purpose. Fifer was a little bit torn about which land she was supposed to be loyal to. Of course she felt strongly about Artimé, but that had lessened slightly after she'd been cast unceremoniously out of leadership—what would happen once the ball was over and she lost all of her responsibilities? But Fifer definitely didn't feel strongly about the land of the dragons after her unhappy experiences there. And it didn't seem fair that Thisbe did. She cared so deeply about people Fifer barely knew! Maybe that was the heart of what was causing her so much internal turmoil. Their lives, once inseparably intertwined, had unraveled and gone in different directions. Fate had forced them apart, and Thisbe had changed drastically from it, while Fifer felt much the same as before.

Tears pricked Fifer's eyes. Thisbe didn't seem to mind their newfound differences, while it was breaking Fifer up inside. Maybe she should try to care less too, but it was hard when she felt like she was missing out on something.

Oblivious to Fifer's mental war and mixed feelings, Thisbe worried about Rohan, wondering if he was okay. Or even alive. Her stomach flipped and twisted painfully whenever she thought about him. She felt helpless. Surely he'd use his seek spell if he needed her. But what if he was trying to, and he just couldn't do it? Even if he did manage to perform the spell, by the time Thisbe could get there, it would most likely be too late—and

she wasn't in any position to help him until she completed her training. These things kept her tossing and turning at night in her bed across the room from Fifer. In contrast, Fifer seemed to sleep like a log and have no cares except for planning the party. How was it possible that one twin could be so carefree when the other carried around the weight of the world?

Shortly after Thisbe had arrived safely back in Artimé, she'd looked at the gift Rohan had given her. It was a piece of paper-thin bark from a birch tree, folded in half. When Thisbe opened it, a diorama of a cave popped up from it, made from tiny sticks and curls of birch bark. Thisbe identified the all-too-familiar scene immediately. Cutouts of three people were sitting on logs inside the pop-up cave—Thisbe, Rohan, and Sky. A fire was burning, and there was a fish on a spit above it. Rohan had used berries and stones to add striking red, purple, and brown colors to it. It was beautiful, though smeared a bit. Definitely unlike any kind of art she'd ever seen in Artimé. Upon opening it and studying the intricacies within, Thisbe had begged Florence for a preserve spell component so it wouldn't tear or get wrecked. Thisbe pulled out the diorama whenever she felt like nobody understood her. It was comforting to be reminded that there was one person who did.

Little changed as more days passed. It still felt strange to be back in Artimé. Things were different. And the wedge between the twins continued to grow.

Added to that, Thisbe didn't like the looks from dissenters and others who kept asking about what had happened to her. They weren't exactly unkind, but Thisbe didn't really *know* these people very well. All the skeptical eyes on her made her uncomfortable. One day Frieda Stubbs stopped Thisbe coming out of the dining hall.

"Have you killed anyone lately?" asked Frieda.

"Wh-what?" Thisbe stammered. "No! Of course not."

It was horrifying, and Thisbe couldn't stop feeling disturbed by it. What kind of woman would say such a thing to anyone? She ran up to her room, and from that point she became more elusive, staying in her room whenever she wasn't training. And trying to slip past people so she wouldn't get stopped so often and have to retell things that were, frankly, horrible to have to relive.

But she had to eat, and it was lonely taking all of her meals via tube in her room. After a few days ruminating over Frieda

Stubbs, Thisbe decided she didn't want to hide from anyone, bully or not. So she abandoned that practice and reluctantly met up with her sister for lunch and dinner most days, even though Fifer seemed uncomfortable about discussing their return to the land of the dragons. It just didn't seem important to her now that they had left that conflict behind.

Others joined them for meals. Thisbe tried to tell herself that things would be back to normal again soon. She, Fifer, Seth, Ibrahim, and Clementi often had lunch together in the mansion's dining room. Usually Fifer and Seth dominated the conversation, which centered around their party-planning progress. Ibrahim and Clementi, who hadn't experienced any kind of celebratory tradition, listened with the kind of awe that most new Unwanteds had in common. Despite having lived in the glorious mansion in Artimé for nearly a year, the lavishness of this world was hard to get used to after growing up in Quill.

Thisbe sat mostly silent and withdrawn, eating quickly so she could get back to her lessons with Florence. Hopefully soon she would earn her component vest, though Florence hadn't mentioned it lately.

"What are you going to dress up as?" Seth asked Thisbe.

LISA McMANN

"What's that?" said Thisbe, startled out of her thoughts.

"I asked what you were going to wear to the costume ball."

"Oh," said Thisbe. "I have no idea. I haven't even thought about it." She paused. "Maybe I'll go as me."

Fifer rolled her eyes, frustration boiling up. Thisbe wasn't even pretending to be interested in Fifer's party. "She's been a bit difficult lately," she explained to the others in a teasing voice, "being part dragon and all. You'd think such a dramatic actor like her would be more excited about costumes."

Thisbe stared at her sister. "Fifer, seriously. Leave me alone about it."

"There's not much time before you'll have to come up with something," Fifer pointed out.

"There's also not much time before I need to go and save *our* people in Grimere."

Fifer looked away uneasily. "I just . . . I've been thinking about that," she said, "and I feel like we all need a longer break from fighting for a while."

"What. About. Dev?" Thisbe said icily.

Fifer continued to steer her gaze anywhere but at Thisbe. "I think we need a little time."

Thisbe stabbed at her plate. "I knew it," she muttered. "You're totally backing out, aren't you? You don't care about anyone. You promised!"

"Thisbe," Fifer said, her voice pleading now. "You're the one who—"

"Come on, come on," said Seth, trying to placate them. "Whenever you two fight, Seth loses." It was true. In the past when Thisbe and Fifer couldn't control their magic, Seth had taken a few unintended hits.

The twins sat in stony silence.

Clementi and Ibrahim exchanged a nervous glance. The two girls had rarely fought in their presence, so it was strange to witness it. Clementi spoke up hesitantly. "Thisbe, I was wondering if I could join you in your private session with Florence sometime so I could get some extra training. For when we go back."

Thisbe shoved one last bite of food in her mouth and threw her napkin on her plate. She looked up. "Sure, I'd love that," she said, chewing. She swallowed, and her shoulders relaxed slightly. "Today after Magical Warrior Training class." She drained her drink, then glanced at Fifer and Seth and added in a sullen voice, "You're all welcome to come, you know."

LISA McMANN

Fifer's face flushed. She picked up her conversation with Seth about the costume ball as if she hadn't heard the invitation. Seth seemed to be really uncomfortable about it.

A shadow passed over Ibrahim's face. "I'll join you too, Thisbe," he said. His angular jaw was set firm, his deep brown eyes troubled.

"Thanks," said Thisbe. She was eager to spend more time in the company of these two new Unwanteds. They were both smart and creative and really good with magic. And they seemed steady in their support of Thisbe's goal. Maybe they'd be her new favorite people, because Fifer and Seth definitely weren't at the moment. She shoved her chair back and tapped her tray, making the plate and utensils fold up smaller and smaller until they disappeared with a pop. "Thanks," Thisbe said again, feeling slightly better. "See you there." At least she wasn't going to have to do *everything* alone.

Impossible to Beat

Thisbe, Ibrahim, and Clementi spent part of each day thereafter with Florence, learning extra things like the adults in the advanced class were learning. Florence didn't want Thisbe in the advanced class quite yet, until she'd mastered the nonfatal spells. Though that seemed odd, since Thisbe already knew more than one way to kill someone if she had to. Obviously, the girl was very talented. But Florence explained gently that she still made some of the other Artiméans nervous because of her reputation as the more dangerous and destructive of the magical twins. They were worried for their lives, though they meant no offense.

LISA McMANN

It didn't seem to matter what they intended—Thisbe was offended. She'd learned to control her magic, but no one here had seen it. She tried not to care too much that people in Artimé still feared her. In fact, she wished people in Grimere would take up the practice of being scared of her—that would make things easier! Instead she focused on one thing: taking down the Revinir. But how? The way to do it was completely eluding Thisbe.

One day during their private lesson, when Thisbe, Ibrahim, and Clementi were resting after a particularly strenuous work-out with Florence, Thisbe brought up the topic.

"I think we need new, more powerful magic," Thisbe said. "If none of our spells work against the Revinir, we have to come up with something that will."

"That sounds good in theory," said Florence. "But how will we know what will work if we can't try it out until we're face-to-face with her?"

"It just has to be . . . huge," said Thisbe. "Super powerful. More powerful than anything anyone's ever created before."

"Spells like that are dangerous to have around," Florence said quietly. "We had one before. It's called obliterate." She shared with them the story of the single component that Alex had created when trying to take out Gondoleery Rattrapp. It was a spell that had obliterated a whole vehicle in Quill and had almost reduced Matilda, one of Artimé's dear gargoyle statues, to a pile of rubble. Not to mention that Sky had been close to where the spell landed—a few steps closer and it could have killed her. "That's not something we want to have happen again," said Florence. "We've lost enough friends and family."

Thisbe nodded somberly. She'd read that story in one of the books Lani had written. It was a sobering thought that Alex, even as good a mage as he'd been, had been so close to making an irreversible mistake. Why, if he'd made a mistake like that, had he been *so* hard on Thisbe and Fifer?

"I think the dragon aspect is the biggest problem," Clementi said. "Dragons have their own mysterious magic that we don't really know much about, since they're so secretive. Not to mention enormous."

"And if all of the dragons in the surrounding worlds are under the Revinir's spell," added Ibrahim, "which is what it looked like to us, we'd need new spells that would work on them, too, in case they aren't friendly to us like Pan and her kin are."

LISA McMANN

Thisbe blew out a frustrated breath. "Look. There's a chance I can hurt the Revinir with my fire magic if I can find a spot where her scales are thin. But I highly doubt I can totally destroy her with the magic I've got right now. Obviously the boom spell is powerful, and it works great on people and creatures our size. But I don't think it will work on the Revinir now that she's a huge half dragon. It might not affect her at all! It's like she's got some sort of spell-repellent ability or something. Samheed told me that none of our spells affected her, not even the triple heart attack. The components just bounced off."

"We definitely don't want anyone to go there until we know we can destroy her," said Florence. "That would be foolish. You're right that we need totally different ammunition than what we have now. But it's going to take some time to make spells that are much stronger than what we've used in the past. We need things we haven't thought to try before." She scratched her ebony-colored head and shifted the quiver of arrows on her back. "I'm having trouble thinking of what could work on her, though. The way you describe her is frightening. I'm . . . not sure we can fight her and win. Not at this point." She hesitated, then looked earnestly at Thisbe. "I hate that you are so determined to go, and in such a hurry. I just . . . I don't recommend it."

"I have to go," said Thisbe, eyes flaring, scales standing up, and a tiny plume of smoke coming from her nostrils. It was a strange sight—the smoke only seemed to happen when Thisbe felt an especially strong sense of impending danger or urgency about the future. "So I need your help. Don't give up on me!"

Florence studied her. "I won't stop you," she said grimly. "Besides, you're of age—you can do what you want. And believe me, I'm excited about getting rid of that monster once and for all. Even if no one else will say it out loud, I know Artimé is in danger as long as she's alive. She definitely knows where to find us if she wants to. It's imperative that we take her out of power. Permanently this time. I just hate that you think you're the one who's got to do it."

"I'm the best equipped. And the only one who is anxious to do it."

"True." But Florence still looked troubled. "I'm going to try to delay your trip until I feel good about it, though. And I'm nowhere near that point yet."

LISA McMANN

"I guess that's fair." Somewhat reassured, Thisbe glanced at Ibrahim and Clementi. "Do you have any ideas about how to beat her?"

"Not really," Clementi said. "But after hearing all the stories about what happened over there, and witnessing what went on here while you were gone, I think I know one thing that desperately needs to be improved in Artimé's magical system."

"What is it?" asked Florence.

Clementi glanced at Ibrahim. He nodded like they'd discussed this before. "We need to upgrade the seek spell," Clementi said.

"Or build a new one," added Ibrahim. "One that actually delivers a message, so people can understand what the other person needs. For a communication spell, it seems woefully lacking. It was really frustrating for Aaron and Henry and the others stuck here in Artimé, not knowing what to do for you."

"I totally agree!" said Thisbe passionately. She rolled to her knees and began gesturing as she continued. "There's got to be a better way to communicate. It would be great if the seek spell could work with a universal spell component, so we don't have to carry all the things from everybody in our pockets. I'm not very good at that, obviously. Plus it takes up space that we need for the other spell components."

"This idea has been high on my list as well," said Florence. "I'll bring it up at Advanced Warrior Training and see if we can get some people creating something more efficient." She paused. "What else do we need? We might not have the Revinir figured out, but we can at least improve what we've got. Who knows—maybe we'll come up with something new in the creative process."

Thisbe's mind began to churn out ideas based on all the needs she and Rohan had run into while in captivity. "Automatic lunch," she said, remembering their severe lack of food in the catacombs. "And water—that's even more important."

Florence nodded.

"Something like a magic ladder would be cool," said Ibrahim.

"I think we could do that," said Florence. "Though we have the magic flying carpets—that can usually do the job of a ladder."

"Not if the space is really narrow," Clementi pointed out. "Or if we need to go straight up or down—the magic carpets

67 « Dragon Curse

LISA McMANN

don't work like that. They can ascend and descend but need to move forward or backward at the same time."

"Good point," Florence said. "I'm very glad to get your fresh thoughts on this." Sensing the young mages were just beginning, she began writing things down.

Thisbe and the other two started brainstorming more and more ideas, some of them a little extreme. But by the end of their session, Florence had a long list of things to work on with her most skilled component creators. "Just remember," she said before she dismissed her pupils, "you only have so much room in your component vests. Too many spells might make it even harder for you to have the best mix in your arsenal. We need the exact right combination. And the number one thing that we need to figure out is how to stop the Revinir."

The young mages still didn't have the first clue how to do that. And despite the progress they'd made, it seemed more and more like the Revinir was unbeatable.

Finding Her Groove

Almost everyone in Artimé was planning to dress up in lavish costumes for the ball—far more than just wearing masks, like they'd done in past years. To Fifer's great consternation, Thisbe hadn't put an ounce of thought into hers. Finally, after much prodding on the morning of the party, Thisbe went to the theater to look for something to wear. There she found Samheed sitting in the auditorium reading an old book under one of the stage spotlights.

"What are you reading?" Thisbe asked him.

Samheed looked up and closed the book. Like many volumes

LISA McMANN

in Artimé, its pages were thick and wavy and yellowed from water damage, because most books arrived by washing ashore from some unknown place—likely coming to them through the Dragon's Triangle like Kaylee and the grandfather scientists had.

"I just finished it," Samheed said, holding up the tome. Absently he wiped a tear from one eye. "It's a book of plays I found in the Museum of Large library some time ago. I'd been meaning to read it."

"Is it sad?"

"The one I just finished is sad, but that's not why I'm crying."

"Then why?"

"The writing reminds me of Mr. Appleblossom, my old instructor."

"Oh," said Thisbe solemnly. She didn't remember him, but everyone knew that Mr. Appleblossom had died fighting for Artimé. "How does it remind you of him?"

"Mr. Appleblossom used to speak in iambic pentameter rhyme." He opened the book to the last page and gazed at it. "This play is written in blank verse—which is unrhymed iambic pentameter. But the rhythm is similar enough to hear his voice in my head."

"I'm sorry you're sad."

"I miss him." Samheed shrugged and smiled. "I miss a lot of people. What can I do for you?"

"Oh—I just need a costume."

"For tonight?"

"Yeah. I'll just get a cape or something."

Samheed frowned. "I thought you of all people would have been planning something very special."

"Yeah," said Thisbe with a sigh. "That's what Fifer thought too." She was starting to regret that she hadn't prepared for this. "But I've had a lot of other things to do. I'm getting ready to go back to the land of the dragons."

Samheed nodded solemnly. "Florence told me. She's worried about you. Aaron knows you're planning this, right?"

"Well . . . I mean, I'm not keeping it a secret or anything."

"Fair enough. You're thirteen now."

Thisbe nodded. All of a sudden she felt older.

"So, tonight," Samheed prompted. "If you had all the time in the world, what would you go as?"

Thisbe explained that she didn't even really want to go, but she felt like she had to—it was her birthday celebration, after all. And absolutely everyone would be there, with gifts and cake and Fox and Kitten leading the lounge band. So as tempting as it was to stay in her room, she knew she couldn't get away with it. "I don't have anything in mind at all." She peered at the book. "What's the sad part?"

"You mean in this?" Samheed held it up.

"Yes. Is there a girl in there like me? I'm sad."

"Are you?" asked Samheed, peering at her with concern. Then his expression softened. "Yes, I imagine you are. You have several things to be sad about." He didn't press her on what exactly she meant at that moment, and he didn't share his own sadness for fear of diminishing hers. Instead, he went on to tell her that the play was a tragic love story about two young lovers named Romeo and Juliet. "Their families are fighting," he said. "And they aren't allowed to be together."

Even though the situation wasn't the same, Thisbe's thoughts turned immediately to Rohan and how they weren't able to be together either. Then she blushed furiously. "Is that the sad part?"

"It's one of them. But the tragic bit is that Juliet fakes her death by taking sleeping medicine. Romeo finds her and thinks she's dead, so he takes poison and *actually* dies."

"That's terrible!" said Thisbe.

"Yes. But it. Gets. *Worse.*"

"Tell me!" Thisbe begged. This kind of play was right up her alley.

"Juliet wakes up, finds Romeo dead, and then takes his dagger and—"

"No!" cried Thisbe, clutching her shirt. Her eyes were wild. "Does she—?" She mimicked thrusting a dagger into her chest.

"Yes!" said Samheed, delighted that Thisbe was so enthralled by the story.

"That's sooo gory," murmured Thisbe. "I love it!"

Samheed regarded her for a long moment, tapping his lips. "Then I think I know exactly which character you should dress up as, in order to express your reluctance to celebrate in this terrible time, but also show the people of Artimé that you are a true actor."

Thisbe nodded. She knew too. In the echoing auditorium, the two spoke solemnly in one voice. "Dead Juliet."

LISA McMANN

A Wistful Moment

S amheed and Thisbe worked up a simple costume: mask, dress, dagger, fake blood. Then Thisbe borrowed the book and hid out in a tree on the lawn to read the Romeo and Juliet play. The tree had a small reclining bough that was somehow magically soft to curl up in. It felt strange to be sitting in such comfort and not having to be constantly doing something, like collecting firewood or fishing for her next meal. Or saving people from burning castles. Or fighting with Fifer. It was nice, Thisbe supposed. For a while.

But she couldn't help thinking about Rohan and Maiven Taveer and the work they were probably trying to do . . . alone.

LISA McMANN

It made her more determined than ever to get back and help them. And Thisbe knew that she alone couldn't possibly be enough.

It was great that Ibrahim and Clementi were willing to help—they'd be priceless to have around. But Thisbe needed . . . and wanted . . . her sister's help. And Seth's, too. And whoever else would come with her. Maybe after this stupid ball was over, Fifer and Seth would come to their senses and help her prepare. She had so much to do it was almost overwhelming. The biggest obstacle to overcome was creating spells that would be strong enough to work against the Revinir and her army of dragons. Thisbe still had no idea what would work. Maybe a dagger spell—Florence had mentioned briefly that there already was one of these, but nobody seemed to use it or have the component for it anymore. She'd have to ask Florence about it again, and any other old spells that they didn't think were as important as others.

Thisbe finished reading the play, finding it strangely satisfying in its tragic ending, because it left hope for reconciliation among those who remained alive. These same themes matched her mood today. She sat for a moment longer in her hiding

LISA McMANN

place and then realized with a start that the sun was going down and the lounge band was beginning to set up their stage on the lawn. Fifer would probably be frantically looking for Thisbe, wondering why she wasn't getting ready. It was almost like this party belonged solely to Fifer or something.

Thisbe slipped into her room as Fifer was flouncing about in front of Desdemona, their room's blackboard. Fifer wore a long crimson gown and a tall but delicate jeweled crown, like a princess. She held a long stick that had a mask attached to it, so she could put it against her face without worrying about a string getting stuck or tangled in her crown.

"There you are!" exclaimed Fifer, swatting her sister with the mask. "You'd better not ruin this for me."

"You look amazing," Thisbe said, ignoring the threat. And what she said was true. Fifer looked like a real princess. There were no real princesses anywhere in their world to compare Fifer to, but Kaylee had told them many stories about princesses in her world. And over the years they'd read as many books about princesses as they'd been able to find in the two libraries in Artimé. And they'd known Shanti, of course, who wasn't hard to improve upon.

"Thank you," said Fifer, thawing a bit. "That . . . means a lot." Then her expression grew concerned. "You're going, right? You've got something to wear?"

"Yes," Thisbe assured her. "I'm getting my costume on now."

"What is it?" Fifer asked. "Who are you going as?"

"You'll see. I'll meet you down there." Thisbe went into the bedroom and closed the door.

Fifer seemed torn between wanting to make sure Thisbe wasn't being sneaky and wanting to make her grand entrance right when the ball was beginning. She heard doors opening and closing in the hallway. Fifer opened their door a crack and peered out as a few others left their rooms in costume and headed to the exit. Fifer hesitated, then opened the door wide and went out into the hallway. "I have to meet Seth," she called to Thisbe. "I'll see you on the lawn. Soon?"

"Yes!" Thisbe shouted back. She opened the bedroom door a few inches and put her face in the opening. "And . . . happy birthday."

Fifer smiled warmly, and for a moment the two felt like friends again. "You too. I thought this day would never come."

"Same for me." Thisbe didn't add that she wished it would just end already so she could get back to the important stuff. She closed the bedroom door, and Fifer was off.

Thirty minutes later, Thisbe emerged to an empty hallway wearing the dead-Juliet costume: a medium-blue dress with a trick dagger attached to her chest, handle sticking outward so it appeared that she'd been stabbed. She'd spread a big stain of fake blood on her dress around the dagger, which had been quite satisfying to create, though it had left a garish mess that she'd have to clean up later in the bathroom. She slipped a sparkling blue mask over her eyes as she clomped down the hallway in her usual work boots—because if she was going to be stuck wearing a dress, at least her feet would be comfortable.

"It's a protest," Thisbe reminded herself, lifting her chin. Though now that she was almost at the party, she was sort of looking forward to it. She had a cool costume. And a break for one day wasn't the worst thing in the world. She tried not to think of Maiven and Rohan and Dev and all the other black-eyed slaves and innocent dragons under the Revinir's spell, being treated horribly. But guilt leaked in. "It's just a few hours," she told herself firmly. She descended the staircase to the main floor of the mansion, where Florence, Talon, and Simber stood near the main entrance. As in previous years, Florence wore a Simber mask, and Simber wore a Florence mask. Talon was dressed as a bronze giant, as usual. Music drifted in through the open door.

"Which of you is which?" Thisbe asked Florence and Simber, which was a tired old joke, but it had to be said.

Simber growled playfully, but Florence lifted her mask in alarm to study the girl. After a moment, she smiled. "Brilliant costume," she said. "It looks real. Are you supposed to be someone in particular?"

"Thank you," said Thisbe. "Yes. I'm dead Juliet." She quickly explained the play. "I'm protesting the idea of the ball. This is my way to make a statement without ruining it for everybody."

"Interesting tactic," said Florence, a smile playing at her lips.

"I'm going out therrre with you," Simber said with a rare rumble of laughter. "I want to see Fiferrr when she gets a glimpse of this."

"I'm quite excited to see her reaction myself," Thisbe said with a grin. "Shall we, Florence? I mean Simber?"

The cat rolled his eyes beneath his Florence mask. "We shall."

The two exited the mansion while Florence and Talon went to the window to watch from there. A moment later, Fifer let out a bloodcurdling scream. And then all of the windows in the mansion exploded, sending broken glass raining down, inside and out.

Masquerade Emergency

L ook out!" Aaron cried from behind the lounge band's stage on Artimé's lawn. Instinctively, upon hearing his sister's scream, he knew it would cause problems. And Aaron didn't need any more problems in Artimé right now.

By the time Fifer clapped her hands over her mouth, it was far too late to stop the windows from shattering. Thisbe's eyes went wild behind her mask as she and Seth dove for cover. Shards of glass rained down on the crowd of partiers, striking the ones closest to the mansion and sparing the rest.

Screams and shouts went up. Henry and Carina threw off

LISA McMANN

their masks and, when the glass stopped flying, ran to help those who'd been struck and were bleeding from cuts. Aaron yelled for everyone to stay calm, but his voice was lost in the din.

Inside the mansion pieces of glass slammed into Florence and Talon, who'd been standing at the window. Stunned and scratched but unhurt, Florence jumped through the opening to the lawn to help, her stone feet crunching on glass. She began lifting the ones who were most injured through the window and handing them to Talon, who ran to put them on a bed in the hospital ward. Soon others were flooding into the mansion through the door, blood flowing from their wounds, making the tile floor slick. Henry and Carina and the nurses brought more patients into the ward and began assessing them.

Back outside, Fifer ran over to Thisbe and Seth. "Are you hurt?" she cried. Then she looked around at all the people who were cut and bleeding. "Oh, crud. I'm so sorry, everyone! It was an accident!" As Thisbe and Seth got up and insisted they were fine, Fifer's flock of birds flew in from the treetops, responding to the unintentional call and causing even more chaos with the Artiméans. The brand-new class of Unwanteds, recently sent to Artimé by their uncreative parents in Quill—a tradition that had changed slightly over the years but refused to die—weren't used to seeing the birds either. Thisbe cringed right along with the others and covered her head. She still didn't like them.

"Why didn't you warn me you were going to be dressed like that?" Fifer said angrily to Thisbe. Her princess crown was tipping to one side, and she had a small cut on one arm. "Look what you made me do."

"I thought you would have learned how to control your shrieks by now," Thisbe said, immediately becoming just as angry for the rash accusation. "What else were you doing during the time I was a *slave* in the *catacombs*?" Spit flew from her mouth when she emphasized the last phrase. "I worked sixteen hours a day and still found time to learn to control my destructive abilities." She hesitated. "Though I'm feeling an urge to let them fly at you right about now."

"Stop." Seth stepped between the girls. "That won't solve anything. Just . . . both of you, knock it off."

Thisbe and Fifer looked at Seth in surprise. It wasn't like him to be so assertive.

Seth's face was grim as he stared beyond them to the streams of people heading into the mansion. "Look past yourselves for once," he muttered.

Behind the bleeding masses was another all-too-familiar group descending on Aaron, hollering about how he should have prevented this. There were worse things happening than whatever the twins were arguing about.

Samheed and Lani were nearby, unhurt. They rushed over to Aaron and Kaylee to find out what the dissenters were yelling about. Thisbe, Fifer, and Seth moved to the outskirts of the gathering to listen in. They'd seen smaller altercations, but this was the first time they'd witnessed such a large group coming at Aaron. It was alarming.

Frieda Stubbs got in Aaron's face. "A good head mage would at least try to control his dangerous sisters, like Alex would have done!"

"Yikes," muttered Thisbe.

"Oh no," moaned Fifer.

Kaylee stepped in angrily and went after Frieda. "Alex wasn't able to control them either," she retorted. "Amazingly, they are not controlled by anyone but themselves—imagine that. Besides, it was an accident that not even Alex could have prevented."

Frieda sneered at Kaylee, then continued to yell at Aaron. "At least Alex took after your father—he was a good man. And you tried to have him killed! You and your sisters are exactly like your horrible pirate mother. You might not look like her, as your sisters do, but your heart is cold and evil like hers."

"What nonsense is this?" Kaylee elbowed forward, and Frieda immediately threw a punch at her. Kaylee dodged it.

"Hey!" shouted Lani, getting between them as Aaron, carrying Daniel, stepped back to shield the boy. Samheed stared from one party to the other as if he wasn't sure what to do. Then he went to stand and protect Aaron as other dissenters edged toward the mage.

Fifer and Thisbe looked at each other. "*What?*" whispered Fifer.

Thisbe shrugged, wide-eyed. Something felt very strange about what Frieda had said.

"Frieda," said Aaron, trying to be patient, "what are you saying? What do you think you know about my parents?"

But Frieda clamped her mouth shut and circled Kaylee and Aaron, fists raised.

The twins didn't know what to think. They'd never heard

LISA McMANN

85 « Dragon Curse

anyone beside their brothers speak of their parents as if they knew them. Abruptly Fifer started toward the shouting match. "I'm going to find out what she's talking about."

Thisbe grabbed her arm. "Fifer, no! Have you lost your mind? Everyone's mad at you right now! And Frieda's looking for a fight!"

"These people are more mad at Aaron than me," Fifer told her. "They hate him because of all the stuff he did before we were born. They can't get over it, and they think Aaron shouldn't be head mage."

Seth nodded. "We missed a lot of the drama while we were gone, but Sean filled in me and Fifer the other day when you were training."

"Aaron told me some of it," said Thisbe. "But what was all that bluster about our parents? Our *pirate mother*? That's . . . that's just crazy." She frowned. "Isn't it?"

"She's probably just making stuff up to get Aaron mad. You can let go of me." Fifer yanked her arm from Thisbe's grasp.

Thisbe raised her hands in defense. "All right. Sorry. Do what you want. I'm . . . I'm going inside to help Henry." Troubled, she turned away.

Just then Crow came running up. "Thisbe, are you okay?" He seemed confused by the fake blood on her dress and the fact that a dagger stuck out from her chest. He hadn't seen anything other than glass fall from the windows. "You're covered in blood!"

"This is my costume," Thisbe said. "I'm not hurt."

"Oh," said Crow, relieved. "That's good." Scarlet came up behind him with a cut on her cheek and a small splotch of blood staining her white-blond hair. The two appeared otherwise unharmed. "Henry is desperate for help inside. Are you coming?"

"Yes, I was just on my way there." Thisbe started toward the door.

Fifer glanced over her shoulder at Kaylee and Aaron and the group of angry dissenters. Then she looked at Seth. "Maybe I'll stay and help Aaron. It seems like he needs it."

Seth shrugged. "Kaylee can handle Frieda Stubbs. And it's not the worst idea for you to be seen helping the injured— after all, you caused this."

Fifer cringed. She didn't need that reminder. "Right. Let's go help Henry." They followed Crow and Scarlet into the

LISA McMANN

mansion and went to the chaotic hospital ward. The place was overflowing.

"Does anybody know how to make this room bigger?" Henry called out as they went in. "Alex always used to do it."

"I'll get Lani," shouted someone near the door. "She'll probably know how."

Soon Lani was there to cast the spell that made the hospital ward much larger. Beds fell from the walls and supply stations dropped from the ceilings. Talon, who seemed uncharacteristically winded, helped the waiting injured go inside. Carina began to direct the worst of them to the new beds.

The mansion was a mess, but at least the injured people were all being cared for. Thisbe and the others did what they could to stop the bleeding while Henry and the nurses came around with their magic-infused herbs and medicines and applied them to the cuts.

After an hour, Talon limped out of the hospital ward to help Florence and Lani clean up the entryway. As the bronze giant came toward them, Lani glanced at his feet and did a double take. "Talon! Are you . . . ?" She halted, then stared again, like she couldn't believe her eyes. "You're . . . bleeding."

Dance Party

Talon stopped cold. "What? Where?"

"Your ankle," said Lani, pointing.

"He can't be," said Florence. "He's made of *bronze*. He probably just got someone else's blood on him."

Talon's face was troubled, and he quickly turned to look at his ankle. Sure enough, blood was flowing from it and dripping onto the floor. "Oh no," he muttered. "I'm bleeding. No wonder I feel so poorly."

"What?" said Florence. "How can that be?"

Talon didn't act surprised to discover he could bleed, but

LISA McMANN

he seemed more than a little concerned about what appeared to be a small cut. He whirled around and limped toward the hospital ward. "Henry?" he bellowed. Then more urgently: "Henry!"

Henry, looking disheveled but in control, came running as Lani and Florence followed Talon.

"What's going on?" Florence muttered. "I don't understand it."

Talon gave Florence an apologetic glance, then explained. "I'm made of bronze, but I have blood inside me. A single vein runs through my body from my heel to my head. It's virtually impossible to access it. But if you ever remember me vaguely implying that I have some slight human characteristics, this is what I meant." He looked at Henry, then lifted his leg for the healer to examine. "Do you have anything that will stop the bleeding somehow and seal the bronze to protect the vein? If we can't . . . I'll bleed to death."

"Talon!" said Florence, clearly shocked by everything that was happening. "I thought you were immortal!"

"Well, almost," said Talon, sounding anxious. "I just have

this one vulnerability. My ankle has a weak spot. It's always been so. But in all these years I've never injured it."

"Come with me," said Henry in a low voice. "Hurry." He helped Talon inside the hospital ward and onto a bed and began rummaging through his many medicines. Then he looked up sharply. "Somebody get Thisbe."

Florence went to get her from a different part of the hospital ward and brought her back.

"What can I do?" asked Thisbe, eyeing the rivulet of blood flowing from Talon's ankle.

Henry looked up. "Can you melt metal with your eye sparks?"

Thisbe was taken aback. "I don't know. I've never done it, but I can try."

"Here," he said, taking an old piece of a thornament necklace from a seldom-opened drawer. "See if you can melt this gold." He placed it in a stone bowl and handed it to her, then turned toward Talon.

As Henry began to work on the bronze man using an herb mixture to try to stop him from bleeding to death, Thisbe

LISA McMANN

took the bowl to an unoccupied corner of the ward and stared at the gold thorn in the bowl. She concentrated, remembering the horrible things that the Revinir had done to her, until she became furious. Then she narrowed her eyes and sent fiery sparks flying from them. They hit the gold thorn. Clouds of smoke billowed up. When the air cleared, Thisbe could see that a tiny drop of gold had melted.

"It's working," she reported. She went through the process again and again until she held a scorching bowl of liquid gold in her hands. She grabbed a towel and, using it like an oven mitt, brought the steaming bowl over to Henry.

Talon lay quietly, looking ill. Florence held his hand.

"Hang in there with me, Talon," said Henry. "Do you feel pain?"

"Not really. It doesn't matter. Do what you must."

Henry went to work. Talon winced, making the others wonder if he was just trying to be brave.

After a moment, Henry lifted his instruments and looked up. "The vein is closed," he announced. He picked up the bowl of melted gold. "Now, brace yourself. This might burn a little." Henry held the giant's leg steady with one hand and poured the steaming liquid into the slice in his bronze ankle. Steam rose up, and Talon squelched a scream. The gold cooled quickly and solidified, filling the space.

Henry checked it all over, then breathed a sigh of relief. "Your leg is sealed up again. I think it should be okay, but let me know if you feel strange or light-headed."

Talon opened his eyes, relieved. "It feels better already," he said.

Once the Talon emergency had passed and he was sitting up, and many of the other injured had been patched up and discharged, the remaining Artiméans realized the band had started playing once more outside. Fifer looked up. "Is the party continuing?" she asked, incredulous.

"I don't see why not," said Henry. "People are back out there already. I just need to check a few others before I'll be going out there myself."

Talon slid to the edge of the bed and set his feet on the floor, testing his ankle. Then he stood up. "It seems like I'm back to normal," he said. "Let's not let a good costume party go to waste." Looking decidedly more healthy, he took Florence's hand. "If you're finished with us, Henry, we'll be going out to show these youngsters how to dance."

Henry dismissed them, laughing. "Don't start the dance competition without me and Thatcher," he warned.

With a grin, and almost forgetting about how she'd caused all of this in the first place, Fifer led the others out of the mansion and onto the decorated lawn to continue the party.

A Twinge of Something

Sky had planned to avoid the celebration and stay in her room. It was too painful to imagine celebrating in Artimé without Alex. But the epic glass-breaking incident and the chaos that followed had forced her out to see what was going on. She found herself helping others clear away the broken glass and actually feeling hopeful about the camaraderie that always prevailed in Artimé during challenging times. People here were mostly good, and they always stepped up to help. It was an important reminder for Sky . . . and for all of those in Artimé. The magical world united in tough times. It was so reassuring to live in a place like that.

LISA McMANN

Unfortunately, there were Frieda Stubbs and the dissenters. When the twins and Seth went back outside, they found Sky on the lawn near the dance floor talking earnestly with Aaron and Kaylee. Aaron carried Daniel in the baby carrier, and he bounced gently in place to soothe the boy. Kaylee was beside them. She had a black eye.

Thisbe ran over to Sky to give her a hug and saw the deepening bruise on Kaylee's face. "What in the world? Kaylee, what happened? Or wait—did Frieda . . . ?"

"You shoulda seen the other guy," Kaylee quipped.

"What does that mean?" asked Fifer.

"Frieda landed a pretty good left hook. It's fine." Kaylee smiled, but her expression was strained. "Is it time to start dancing?"

Seth, Fifer, and Thisbe stared at her. "She actually punched you?" asked Thisbe, incredulous. "And you punched her back? Like, *here* in Artimé?" For some strange reason this type of brawl seemed impossible to imagine, though they could picture Kaylee valiantly fighting just about anywhere else. But with a sword, not with her fists. And not against a fellow Artiméan.

Kaylee shrugged, then said primly, "I don't condone fist

fighting, children." Aaron kept his lips pressed tightly together as Kaylee continued. "I only punched her after she landed this one. And, well, she's gone now, isn't she?"

Sky looked away and squelched a grin as the band struck up a slow tune. "So, dancing?" she prompted, sensing Kaylee's discomfort. "Want me to hold Daniel?"

"Don't you want to dance too?" Aaron asked her.

Sky's expression froze, then turned pained. She glanced at Thisbe, who stared back at her.

"I'll dance with you," Thisbe whispered. She wasn't sure what else to say. Alex's glaring absence had struck them all without warning.

"Oh, Sky. I'm sorry," Aaron said quietly, touching her shoulder. "I—I said that without thinking. It's been quite a night so far."

"It's okay." Sky recovered quickly, or at least appeared to. She went on, a decisive tone of voice. "I'd like to hold Daniel while you two dance. You—it seems like you could use . . . some time . . . together." Her voice cracked, but she smiled bravely and held out her hands to take the child.

Kaylee nodded. "Of course." She unhooked Daniel from

the carrier and handed him to Sky. Aaron took off the carrier and set it on the ground so Sky could use it if she wanted to. Before Aaron could accidentally say something else insensitive, Kaylee grabbed his hand and pulled him to the dance area.

Nearby, Florence and Talon were dancing and gazing into each other's eyes. Talon seemed good as new.

Sky held Alex's young nephew close, her eyes shining. She began to sway, dancing with the baby as he pointed to the decorative lights. "S'at?" he asked. "S'at?"

"That's called a light," Sky answered.

"S'at?" asked the boy, pointing to another.

"That is also a light," said Sky. She gave Thisbe a side-eye glance, and the two shared a tearful laugh.

Seth and Fifer looked at each other. Then Fifer pointed with her mask stick to the dance area. "Come on," she said, and started toward it. Seth followed, while Thisbe stayed with Sky and Daniel.

On the dance floor, Seth turned to face Fifer. The slow music made things feel weird. He glanced around at the other dancers. Hesitantly he put his hands on Fifer's shoulders like many of the other people were doing with their dance partners.

Fifer froze, arms stiff and straight at her sides. "What are you doing?" she said with a look of disgust. "This isn't dance class."

"Sorry," said Seth, hastily removing his hands, and then, unsure what to do with them, he balled them and stuck them into his pockets. That made it really hard to dance, but he was committed.

Fifer frowned and crossed her arms in front of her. The two swayed side by side, a foot apart, to the music. Not looking at each other. There was nothing more awkward in all the land that day.

Fifer was desperate for the feeling of mortification in the air to dissipate. To help it along, she asked, "So, did you hear what that Frieda woman said about my mother? That she was a pirate?" It couldn't be true, of course. The woman had also said some pretty horrible things about Aaron and the girls that weren't true.

"I heard," said Seth, relaxing a bit. "I hope Kaylee really pounded her."

Fifer laughed uneasily. "Me too."

"Don't tell my mom I said that."

"I won't."

The slow song ended, and they both looked relieved to hear an upbeat one beginning. Seth took his hands out of his pockets and seemed more comfortable. Aaron and Kaylee stayed together, talking earnestly and quietly as if the slow song were still playing. Florence and Talon started dancing faster, doing some swing-type moves that Fifer knew from Claire Morning's teaching sessions. But there was no way she was going to do those moves with Seth if it wasn't required for the class. She glanced at Thisbe to see if her sister would be interested in being her partner, but Thisbe was busy with Sky and Daniel, dancing and laughing with them.

It was good to see Sky laughing again. And Thisbe, for that matter. With a start, Fifer realized Thisbe had hardly laughed since they'd found her. Again she noted how much Thisbe had changed during her captivity and as a fugitive. Fifer felt like she barely knew her anymore. A sharp pain speared through Fifer's chest as she realized that Thisbe had become like a stranger. It was troubling, and the distance between them was growing, not lessening. It felt like an emergency that nobody else could see— as if Fifer alone had to fix it, but she had no idea how to do it.

That Thisbe didn't seem to think there was any problem at all was probably what hurt the worst. Fifer didn't like any of it, but she didn't know what to do about it. She and her identical twin, who used to be practically the same person, didn't think the same way anymore. She teared up unexpectedly and turned away.

Fifer also felt unsettled about what had just happened with Seth, who had sort of taken Thisbe's place in her life. He'd just been easier to be around lately. And now that they were home and safe, she could actually care about him again instead of worrying every second that he was going to die. But not if he was going to think she wanted to dance with him like *that*.

The whole dancing thing made Fifer wonder if she was *supposed* to like anybody enough to touch their shoulders now that she was thirteen. She definitely hadn't ever thought about it and didn't want to. But Thisbe had seemed very close to Rohan. Fifer had caught them gazing into each other's eyes seriously back before they parted ways, and they'd held hands, too. Fifer didn't feel that way for anybody in Artimé, least of all Seth. After thinking about it, she concluded that she didn't have to, either. It was perfectly fine for her to like herself most of all.

LISA McMANN

Fifer managed a small smile at the thought.

"What are you grinning about?" asked Seth, who was growing bored. After all the planning Fifer had made him help with, this party wasn't very exciting.

Fifer glanced at him, then turned back to watch Florence and Talon looking deeply in love with each other. "I'm smiling about my own awesomeness," Fifer said confidently, though she struggled to feel it.

"Oh, great," Seth said, and rolled his eyes. "Of course you are." He looked around the lawn and spotted Ibrahim and Clementi. They were both gifted dancers and had studied for the past year with Ms. Morning and Samheed, learning ballet as well as a variety of other styles of dance for theater so far. They were really shaking things up and laughing and enjoying the party. And they weren't afraid to touch each other, Seth thought wryly. Of course, they were fourteen now, like him.

"See ya." Seth turned sharply away from Fifer and made his way through the crowd toward Ibrahim and Clementi, leaving Fifer standing alone. The smile faded quickly from her face.

Bittersweet

The night grew late before Henry and Thatcher finished patching up the remaining injured and joined the extravaganza. Many Artiméans had turned in by then, but several couples remained, and the band music turned romantic.

Horribly so, as far as Fifer was concerned. She didn't understand what was so great about being all lovey-dovey like Aaron and Kaylee. And Thatcher and Henry, and Florence and Talon, and the other couples who were all sweaty and hanging on each other. Whenever Fifer got sweaty, she didn't like anybody touching her. That just made her more uncomfortable.

LISA McMANN

She watched Seth dance with Ibrahim and Clementi—or at least he tried to dance, but he wasn't an actual dance student like Fifer and them, so he wasn't very good. Despite that, he seemed to be really enjoying himself, and Fifer knew deep down that that was what really mattered. She frowned. Seth didn't seem like he was planning to return. Maybe she should go over there. She looked around, feeling lost and lonely and tired of her crown falling off on what was supposed to be a very special night. It hadn't gone anything like she'd planned, and it was hard to come to terms with the disappointment when every time she turned around, somebody with a bandaged head was nearby, reminding her that their injury was her fault.

Thisbe and Sky had grown tired of dancing, and Daniel had fallen asleep, so the three of them rested on the lawn to watch the others. They weren't laughing now. Instead, with heads bowed together, Thisbe and Sky talked quietly about missing Alex, and about Rohan and Maiven Taveer, and they cried a little too.

"Every time I think I'm getting used to Alex being gone forever," Sky said, "something happens to remind me of him. It's like I experience that awful realization of his death all over again. Remember it?"

Thisbe nodded. "It was awful." Stumbling across Alex's grave had been a horrible way to discover it.

Fifer wanted to join them, but their intimacy made her hesitate. She knew Thisbe and Sky had grown much closer during their time together. It made Fifer feel a bit left out of that relationship. She turned back toward the band and saw that Fox and Kitten were taking a break from playing in the band and were dancing together, Fox standing upright on his hind legs and Kitten sitting on his front paw, which was outstretched so he could see her clearly.

"Mewmewmew?" Kitten would ask with a sly double blink. Fox would go into a long explanation of something that was likely unrelated to whatever Kitten said. But she purred anyway. Words didn't matter with them. Fifer thought it was ridiculous yet charming. Love was weird.

In the shadows, Sean and Carina were swaying together and kissing, to Seth's obvious dismay, and Samheed and Lani were kissing too. Henry rested his head on Thatcher's chest as Thatcher held him close, and Crow and Scarlet slipped away and started walking along the shore holding hands.

"Everything is so dumb," Fifer said, dropping her mask to

her side in frustration. Her vision for the evening, realistic or not, had showcased her as the center of attention—after all, she'd been the one leading the rescue team home to safety after Alex had died. She'd hoped by this point *someone* would have thought to honor her for her leadership, temporary as it was. And acknowledge that she was growing up and showing strong skills. She'd even thought people would be congregating around her and showering her with birthday gifts and praise for doing such a good job under horrible circumstances.

But, in reality, she'd been getting looks all night from people who hadn't appreciated getting glass shards rained on them. To them, Fifer was still an uncontrollably dangerous kid. To top off the evening, now that mostly just friends remained to close down the party, everyone seemed so focused on the special person they were with. Fifer felt awkward approaching any of the couples and small groups. Romantic or not, no one seemed to want to have a deep conversation with Fifer now that she wasn't leading things anymore. No one was paying any attention to her, especially her soul-mate sister. She searched the lawn one last time, hopping up and down a little to get Seth to notice her. But his back was to her as Clementi showed him how to dip her.

Fifer stopped jumping. Her shoulders slumped. "This entire night is a disgrace," she muttered. With a sigh, she went into the mansion to see if Simber was around—maybe he'd give her the approval and attention she was so desperately seeking tonight. But he'd disappeared once things settled down. Perhaps he'd gone to the jungle to visit Panther as he sometimes did. They were probably being all kissy too.

As Fifer meandered toward the stairs feeling very sorry for herself, her feet crunched down on some broken glass on the floor, apparently having been missed in the cleanup efforts. Fifer checked her costume pockets to see if she had anything that would help with the mess. Finding no magic broom components, she went to the kitchen to get an actual broom. Maybe one of the cooks would want to chat while Fifer had a bedtime snack.

But the kitchen was dark and empty—a rare sight. Light from the moon streamed in through a broken window.

Fifer stood in the moonlight for a moment, then got a broom and dustpan and went back to clean up whatever glass she could find. She returned the items and fixed herself a fig jam sandwich and an orange cream drink. Feeling despondent,

LISA McMANN

she didn't bother going all the way to the tubes by the dining room, and instead she stepped into the room service tube in the corner and sent herself up to her room. She was beginning to worry about what age thirteen would bring. If tonight was any indication of how it would go, she wasn't very eager to find out. She arrived in their room to Thisbe's big mess of fake blood all over their bathroom. Disgusted, Fifer cleaned it up.

By the time Thisbe came into their bedroom and slipped into her bed, Fifer startled awake. "Finally," she said angrily.

Thisbe's eyes widened in the dark room. "What is that supposed to mean?"

"Nothing," Fifer said grumpily. "Just be quiet so I can sleep."

"I *am* being quiet." Thisbe wrinkled her nose at her sister. Things were definitely getting unbearable between them. They used to agree without exception and do everything together, but now they couldn't be further apart on their thinking. They each wanted the other to see things her way. It was terribly unsettling. And it was starting to suffocate them both, stuck in this room together. Unfortunately, neither of them knew how to stop their relationship from changing and spiraling out of control.

Changing Times

I suppose I should get my own room," Thisbe said a few days later at breakfast. She was already mentally preparing for her training with Florence for the day, but the thought had crossed her mind several times since the night of the party. Having her own room might be nice—she could practice her magic and go to bed whenever she wanted without disturbing Fifer.

Fifer looked up, her hand poised to take a spoonful of boysenberry oatmeal. "What?"

"Now that we're thirteen, I mean," Thisbe said, wiping her mouth and tossing her napkin on her plate. She pushed back

LISA McMANN

her chair. "Everyone else has their own room. And last year Alex said we could split up if we wanted to once we were thirteen, remember?"

Fifer set her spoon on the table. "Well, sure, I remember, but I thought we said we weren't going to."

Thisbe looked down and said carefully, "Yes, but we were pretty young then. Now, after everything we've been through . . . I mean, I love being your roommate, but there's extra space in the mansion, so why not split up? We've never tried that before." Her gaze flitted up to her twin's face. "And it seems like maybe it's time."

Fifer's expression was unreadable. "What about when the Revinir roars and you get paralyzed? Don't you need me to help you?"

"I'll manage," Thisbe said. "She doesn't do it very often anymore—I think all the dragons must be there by now. Maybe she's forgotten about Drock and me." She noticed Fifer's eyes glistening and tilted her head, confused. "Are you upset?"

"I'm fine," Fifer said, her voice pitching slightly upward. "Yeah, whatever you want to do is . . . fine." She hurriedly glanced around, as if she wanted Thisbe to stop looking at her, and pretended to spot someone. "I should go. Let's talk about it later."

Thisbe shrugged. "We don't have to do it," she said. "It was just a thought." She could tell Fifer was angry, but she seemed more upset than Thisbe would have imagined over getting some privacy and extra space to spread out. Plus, Fifer had seemed so annoyed to be awakened the other night, so Thisbe had thought Fifer would like the idea. "Maybe there's a way Aaron could extend the hallway and slip a room in right next door, so we wouldn't be far apart?"

Fifer's eyes shone, and she got up quickly; then she made her tray of mostly uneaten oatmeal disappear. "Maybe," she said lightly. She pushed her chair in and grabbed her rucksack. "Bye."

"Wait!" Thisbe said. "Do you want to help come up with new spell components today to fight the Revinir? Clementi and Ibra—" She stopped abruptly as Fifer fled the room.

Thisbe didn't know what to think. Fifer was very upset, and Thisbe wasn't exactly sure why. Was it what she'd said, or the way she'd said it? She went outside to meet Florence, replaying the scene in her mind and realizing with regret that she hadn't been sensitive about suggesting the split to Fifer. After all, they hadn't discussed it in a long time, so maybe it felt like the idea had come out of nowhere. Clearly, they weren't thinking along the same lines like they used to.

Fifer had been acting distant lately—ever since they'd gotten home. They'd both noticed that the other had changed, even if they didn't exactly talk about it in so many words. They used to understand each other so well without having to talk things through, though, so after the other night, Thisbe naturally assumed that Fifer was thinking about the two of them splitting up into separate rooms too. Apparently not.

Thisbe didn't have time to dwell on it further—she had a lot on her mind, and not knowing anything about the status of Grimere with the Revinir in charge, she felt a lot of pressure to hurry up and go back. With or without her sister. Just as soon as she had the right weapons.

Unsurprisingly, Fifer didn't show up for their spell brainstorming session, and Seth wasn't there either. But Aaron was there with Thatcher, Samheed and Lani, and Ibrahim and Clementi. Thisbe soon forgot all about Fifer.

"Let's start with revising the seek spell," Florence said. "Does anyone have ideas for how to improve it?"

Aaron spoke up. "Kaylee told me how people communicate over distances in her world. They each carry a device—Kaylee showed me hers, though it stopped working around the same time she arrived in the seven islands. She said people push buttons to create words on the device. You can type whatever words you want to say, like writing a letter. Then they can send the message to anyone, anywhere. The person they send the message to gets it almost immediately."

"I thought Kaylee said her world wasn't magical," Thisbe said.

"She seems to think it's done by some other means," said Aaron. "But whatever the case, do you think that's something to explore?"

Samheed scratched his stubbly beard, then pulled out the small notepad he kept in his pocket and opened it to a blank page. He ripped the page out and held it up, studying it. "Maybe we make the paper a component," he murmured. "There'd have to be a writing tool to go with it, of course, which could be bulky. But something that can send itself with a short command from the mage. Perhaps it travels somehow like a magic carpet?"

"Or like an origami fire-breathing dragon," said Lani, seemingly understanding Samheed's cryptic musings. "Where we command the location it needs to go to—or, rather, specify the person it needs to go to. But I think we can apply the faster trajectory that already exists for the seek spell instead of the magic carpet speed."

"I imagine that wouldn't be too hard to instill," said Thatcher.

Ibrahim and Clementi exchanged a glance, clearly marveling over this opportunity to be so involved in the planning side of spells with some of the people who'd been responsible for designing so many great ones already.

"I like where you're going with this," said Florence. "Do you two want to run with that idea and come up with a prototype?"

"It's going to take several steps," Lani said. "But yes, of course. I think we're onto something."

"Great," said Florence. "Off you go." Samheed and Lani got up and went inside to get supplies and start planning out how the spell would work.

"Now," said Florence, turning to Aaron and Thatcher and

the three young mages, "what about fighting the Revinir? Have you come up with anything?"

"I've been thinking about it, but haven't really gotten anywhere," Thisbe admitted. "I've mostly been focusing on learning existing spells so I can, you know . . ." She flushed. "Actually earn my component vest. Which . . . I'm still . . . waiting . . . for."

Florence looked at Thisbe, as if seeing her clearly for the first time in a while. "Why haven't I given you yours yet?" she wondered aloud.

"I don't know," said Thisbe. "I assumed I still wasn't trustworthy. I mean . . . I've terrorized the people of Artimé my whole life. I get why you wouldn't want me handling components. Especially with Frieda Stubbs and her gang spouting off about how terrible Aaron and Fifer and I are."

"Don't listen to her," Aaron said, clipping his words. "If she or any of her friends come near you, find me immediately."

Thisbe saw the anger in his face. She wanted to ask him what Frieda had meant about their mother, but now didn't seem to be a good time for such a private discussion. Instead she nodded. "I will."

"Oh, my dear Thisbe," said Florence. "I'm sorry you've had this burden on your shoulders—you don't deserve it. I think it's time to show everyone that *I* trust you. And I'm in charge of the vests." She stood up. "Come with me. Clementi, Ibrahim, keep brainstorming new spells with Thatcher and Aaron to combat the Revinir's power. We'll be back in a bit."

Thisbe jumped to her feet and followed, jogging to keep up with Florence's long strides. They entered the mansion, then climbed the stairs and went down the mostly secret hallway, which both of them were able to see, unlike many mages. Florence's pace slowed as they went past two unmarked doors, behind which were rooms nobody'd been inside before—at least nobody alive today.

"Are you okay with going into Alex's apartment?" Florence asked gently. "That's where I put your vest after I gave Fifer hers. I . . . I figured Alex would want to be the one to give it to you after he . . . after he brought you home."

"Oh. Ahh . . ." Thisbe swallowed hard. She thought about what it might look like inside. How would Alex have left it? Reminders of how awful their relationship had been began pounding incessantly in Thisbe's head. After a moment she

LISA McMANN

cringed and nodded. "Yeah, I'm okay with it." Maybe it would be nice to see something so closely related to Alex again. Maybe it would help her.

Florence stopped at the door to the head mage's quarters and rested her hand on the knob. She looked at Thisbe. "Ready?"

Thisbe nodded again. "Let's do this," she whispered.

Florence uttered a magical phrase under her breath, and the handle turned. She pushed the door open and went in, then moved out of the way.

Thisbe stepped inside. Sunshine flooded through the windows, and dust particles hung in the light. The room smelled stale, having been closed up for a long time. The bed was neatly made, and there was a single robe hanging on a hook on the wall. The closet stood ajar, as if, in a hurry to get going, Alex had swung it closed, but it hadn't clicked shut.

There was a pile of books collecting dust on his desk, and a sweater was slung over the chair back. Thisbe blinked and looked around, expecting a blackboard to greet them, but she didn't see it. "Where's Cromwell?" Cromwell was Alex's blackboard—the one who'd replaced Clive after Clive had died in the final battle in Artimé. Alex and Cromwell had never hit it off quite like Alex and Clive had.

"I reassigned him to a new Unwanted once we knew Alex was gone. It was torturous for poor Cromwell, being stuck in here knowing his person would never return."

"That was really thoughtful of you," Thisbe murmured. It would have never occurred to her. She pressed her lips together, then lifted Alex's sweater and held it tightly in her hands, feeling the silky fabric. She brought it to her nose and breathed in. She closed her eyes tightly and grimaced, feeling a startling pain inside her ribs. "It smells like him."

"I would imagine it does," said Florence, trying to read the girl's expression. "Is that comforting to you? Or . . . perhaps just the opposite."

"It's . . . okay," Thisbe said. "It's weird, I guess. I mean . . ." Thisbe could only think about the last time she'd seen Alex, before she and Fifer had run away with Hux. He'd been angry with them, as usual. The last in-person memory Thisbe had in relation to Alex was his angry, disappointed face. Something she'd seen time after time.

Since that moment, Fifer had been given a chance to work

things out with Alex. And to see him change and become more like his old self—at least that's what everyone said had happened. Thisbe found it hard to believe, but she felt terrible for thinking that way. Tears sprang to her eyes. Her feelings about Alex's death were so complicated. She wouldn't dare say it out loud, but the truth was that she didn't actually like him very much, and never had. But how could she express that now that he was dead and everyone was saying such nice things about him? She tried to remember the good bits of their relationship, but there hadn't been all that many. Guilt pounded through her veins. This wasn't how grief was supposed to feel. Was it?

Florence gave Thisbe a sympathetic smile. "I'll get the vest."

"Thanks." Feeling numb, Thisbe put the sweater down and smoothed the wrinkles. "I'll come back another time, I think. Maybe when Sky is ready—she hasn't been up here yet. Or Aaron."

"Yes. And perhaps Fifer would want to come too?"

"Right. Fifer too. Of course."

Thisbe turned sharply and let out a ragged breath before her conflicted feelings could build up and overwhelm her.

LISA McMANN

Suddenly, getting her component vest didn't seem very exciting anymore. "I'm going to wait outside."

"I'll be right there," said Florence. She ducked through the doorway to Alex's closet and grabbed the vest she'd hung there shortly after she'd given Fifer hers. Then she followed Thisbe out and closed the door. She handed the vest to her. "Are you okay?"

Thisbe wasn't sure how to answer. If Sky had asked her that question, Thisbe would say no. And Sky would understand, because she wasn't okay either. But anyone else?

"Yeah, of course," said Thisbe with a weak smile, taking the vest and slipping it on. "I'm good."

Frieda Stubbs Strikes Again

Florence and Thisbe returned to the lawn to find Aaron, Thatcher, Ibrahim, and Clementi in deep conversation about various spells that could potentially stop the Revinir in her tracks. Thatcher was the only one of the smaller group who'd actually fought the dragon-woman, so the others had given him the final say on whether he thought the ideas would work until Thisbe and Samheed and Lani returned.

"Have you gotten anywhere?" Florence asked as she and Thisbe took their seats.

"Not really." Aaron flashed Thisbe an impressed grin and

121 « Dragon Curse

LISA McMANN

nodded at her vest. "The challenge is immense. We talked about a spell to remove dragon scales so that our spells might penetrate better, but we only have Drock to practice on. And, well, you know Drock."

Thisbe flushed and smiled back. "You could try it out on me," she said, holding out her arms. "Though I quite like my scales. I feel wiser and more intuitive with them. I wouldn't want to lose that extra sense—they seem to stand up when something awful is about to happen." She gazed at the flat scales on her arm, twisting it to catch the light and thinking about the proposed spell. "The Revinir's whole body is different now," she mused. "Much larger. Removing her scales might help, but we'd still have to have something lethal that would work on someone several times larger than our typical enemy."

They batted other ideas back and forth a while longer, but Thatcher and Thisbe kept shaking their heads at every suggestion. The Revinir's size, strength, and firepower seemed to make her impossible to beat.

At one point during the session Thisbe grew quiet, deep in thought. Every kind of magical weapon they were coming up with was physical, but the dragon-woman was physically indestructible. Was there some other way to get to her? Thisbe contemplated the time she'd spent with the woman. Was there anything she could remember that seemed like a weakness? Any other way to beat her?

But Thisbe couldn't put a finger on anything in particular, at least not at the moment. Eventually the group members parted one by one, each having some other commitment to work on, until only Thisbe and Aaron remained.

Unlike Alex, Aaron and Thisbe had always gotten along pretty well. "How are you doing?" Thisbe asked him. They hadn't talked about Alex's death very much lately.

Aaron's expression softened. "It hurts," he said. "Pretty badly sometimes."

Thisbe's eyes welled up. She felt more for Aaron's pain than for her own grief over Alex's death. That seemed wrong too, but she couldn't change it.

They talked a little more, and then Aaron turned the conversation back to the Revinir. "I'm not sure what you're thinking about as far as attacking the Revinir," he said seriously. "I know you believe you need to go back there. And I respect that you feel that way. But I'm also very scared for you. I don't want to lose another sibling."

Thisbe looked up at her brother's tender words, but she felt threatened by them too—was he about to forbid her to go? Thisbe had been dreading this conversation, but she was going to be very firm with him. "You won't lose me," she said quietly. "Not to death, anyway. There's no way she'll outsmart me. I'm already planning." She hesitated. "But I just want you to know that if you try to keep me from going, you might never see me again." She surprised herself with the ultimatum.

Aaron took in a sharp breath. "Wow. That's harsh," he said, but then a pained half smile curled up his lips, and he squeezed her hand. "Besides, I wasn't planning to forbid you. You're old enough to make your own decisions now."

Thisbe gave him a puzzled look. "So why are you so scared?"

Aaron looked at her long and hard, then turned his gaze to the sea. "No one is invincible," he said lightly, though he didn't sound like he believed it. "If Alex could be taken by surprise, anyone can. Even you."

Still puzzled, Thisbe shifted uncertainly on the lawn. But she felt a surge of hope now that Aaron said he wouldn't try to stop her. Before she could answer, she felt a tiny ripple over her skin and looked up to see what danger lurked. This time it was the dissenters, and they'd spotted her and Aaron. "Oh no," Thisbe muttered. "Look who's coming."

Aaron looked, then sighed deeply. "Here we go again. If they threaten you, I give you permission to fight back any way you see fit. You've got your vest now—just try not to kill anyone."

Thisbe thought greedily about taking out the whole lot of them in one explosion and was shocked by her own thoughts. It reminded her that the Revinir had called her evil. Thisbe believed it could be true, and she felt guilty again. But there was something else on her mind that pushed aside the guilt and the urge to fight. As Frieda Stubbs approached and the two Stowes stood up, Thisbe blurted out, "How did you know my mother?"

Frieda Stubbs was taken aback. Then she snarled and said, "She moved in next door to me when she got thrown off her pirate ship. It was right as Justine was repairing part of the wall around Quill that had been damaged. She snuck inside before the workers closed it, and my neighbors took her in."

LISA McMANN

Aaron and Thisbe stared. "You lie," said Thisbe. "My mother was not a pirate."

"When was this?" Aaron demanded. "As adults?"

"No. It was a year before I was purged. She was my age." Frieda snorted angrily. "And *I* ended up being the Unwanted. Can you believe that?"

The other dissenters chuckled uneasily. Just before Thisbe was about to ask Frieda why she seemed so angry about being declared Unwanted when it led to being in Artimé, her head was filled with a wild roar. Her eyesight was taken over by blinding scenes of dragons and castles and fighting. She fell to the ground, quivering on the grass, until she lay still.

"Look at that evil girl!" cried Frieda in alarm, stepping back and pointing. "She is possessed! All of you remaining Stowes are filled with the evil of your mother. And Alex is no longer here to control you."

Pushing Forward

The Revinir's roar brought Drock to the shore of Artimé looking for support. He came on land as Thisbe was sitting up. Luckily her episode had scared off the dissenters for now.

"She knows we're out here," said Drock, more agitated than Thisbe had ever seen him since they'd been back. "She's after you, Thisbe. And me. I knew this would happen." Drock swung his head around, his eyes wild.

"What makes you say that?" asked Aaron with alarm. He knew dragons had special senses, and he wasn't about to discount Drock's words and actions as hysterics.

LISA McMANN

"I can feel it," said Drock, beginning to pace the shore. His tail curled and unfurled. "I told you before—it's the dragon curse. It's like a great foreboding weight in my bones. It's our flaw. Our weakness. She found it, and we can't resist."

Thisbe rubbed her aching head. "What are you talking about?" she asked weakly. "You're not making sense."

"She's exploiting it. It's finally coming together," said Drock. He couldn't stop his neck from fidgeting or his head from bobbing and constantly turning to look to the west. "We dragons are not all-powerful. Not like anyone thought."

"I'm not sure I follow you, Drock," said Aaron. "We know that you were captured—that you could be kept against your will. So we already knew you weren't all-powerful."

"But at least we had hold of our minds back then!" Drock roared, causing the mansion's new windows to rattle. "This is different! The Revinir has discovered the dragon curse! She's rendered us useless except to do her bidding. Where she failed before, allowing my siblings and me to escape, she has now rectified—she stole our minds, Aaron.

"Worst of all," Drock went on, "she knows she doesn't have us all. She's going to keep at it until you and I go to her,

Thisbe—she won't stop until we succumb to her call. I believe we're the only ones left. The only . . . ones." He cringed and squeezed his eyes shut, as if the pounding in his ears was growing worse. His words began to slur. "If we don't go there, she'll come after us. Yes, I'm certain she will."

Thisbe and Aaron exchanged an alarmed glance. This wasn't news to Thisbe, but it seemed like nobody in Artimé had taken it seriously whenever she'd tried to explain it to them. "But why does she want us so badly when she has all the other dragons?" Thisbe asked.

Drock opened his eyes and gave her a pained look. "Because we can help her . . . but we can also still beat her. You, Thisbe. She knows you can beat her."

"I wish I knew how." Thisbe felt sick to her stomach, and for a moment she desperately wanted to doubt everything Drock was saying. "Why can't she be happy with what she has? Why can't she leave us alone?"

"What makes her strongest is also her downfall," Drock muttered. "This curse will come back to haunt her. It must!"

Though some things were becoming clearer, Thisbe and Aaron were still puzzled. Drock was acting delirious and not always making sense. And Thisbe was struggling more than usual to get her strength back after the most recent roar. "Stay strong, Drock," Thisbe urged him. "Do you hear the roar still?"

"It's not the roar of the Revinir that continues to haunt me," Drock said as he turned to go. "It's the deafening silence of no other dragon minds fighting back." He hesitated, then looked over his shoulder at Thisbe. "We two are the last to battle the curse with our minds intact. I'm not sure how much longer I can withstand it. If we are to go, we must go soon."

"Soon?" Thisbe whispered, clutching her chest. Was she ready?

Drock shoved off into the water. "I'll be back." He propelled himself to the west. Thisbe's head ached. She turned to her brother. "What do you make of that?" she asked, feeling breathless.

Aaron stared after the beast. "I think we're in for a long brainstorming session, little sister," he said. "You and me. If what Drock said is true, that the Revinir is not going to stop until she has you two, we need to cut off her ability to control the dragons. Who knows what she's capable of? If she comes here, or even if she sends dragons to collect you, all of Artimé and the seven islands will be in danger. We don't have the ability to fight an enemy like that."

Thisbe stepped into Aaron's space and said accusingly, "I've been saying this for weeks! Finally someone believes me." She shook her head. "Finally. Thank you, Aaron."

"I'm sorry I didn't give this my full attention before," said Aaron. "With everything going on, it's been . . . difficult. Hard to focus on this. But you have me now. We must prepare for the inevitable." He was quiet for a long moment, then glanced around worriedly for the dissenters. He lowered his voice. "Even if we can fight off the Revinir somehow and miraculously sustain no injuries, the dissenters will blame me for her showing up, of course. And I don't know how much more blame I can take before they grow strong enough to oust me for good."

"That would be a huge mistake," said Thisbe.

"Or a huge relief," Aaron said under his breath. He lifted his hand to shield his eyes from the afternoon sun and stared toward Warbler. "Hmm," he said.

"What?" Thisbe turned to look.

"Drock is coming back."

The scales on Thisbe's arms and legs shifted, and Thisbe felt a looming sense of dread. She stood up and stared at Drock, speeding toward them. "Something's not right," she said.

Aaron stood up too, and they waited until Drock made a splash landing in front of them.

"What is it?" Thisbe asked the dragon, feeling her heart leap to her throat.

Drock was out of breath. "It's happening," he said, panting. "They're coming. The Revinir is coming."

Underprepared

Thisbe felt like her head was underwater. She heard what Drock was saying, but his words were muted because her heart was pounding so loudly. "Oh, Aaron," she said with a groan, "she's coming for me." There was no question in Thisbe's mind. She knew it by the way her scales rose. She was part dragon, and with it came certain instincts, some of which she was still figuring out. But this was definitely one of them.

She also knew the dragon-woman had sent soldiers out looking for her and Rohan after their escape. But why did she want Thisbe back so badly when she had everyone else?

LISA McMANN

One more black-eyed slave seemed inconsequential when the Revinir had all the dragons from everywhere and beyond. Was there something to what Drock had said about Thisbe being able to beat her? If so, she certainly didn't believe it. Or was it more about being able to help her with her awful plans? And what did it mean that the Revinir was coming now? So soon? If she was venturing way out here, did that mean she'd already captured Rohan and Maiven? Or didn't she care about them anymore, because they hadn't drunk the dragon-bone broth?

"Are you sure?" Aaron demanded of Drock. "The Revinir herself is coming?"

"She and a few other dragons have crossed the gorge. At the rate they're flying, and if they don't stop, they'll be here in a day and a half."

"A day and a half?" Thisbe cried. "What are we going to do? We're not ready." She took a few paces up the shore, absently trying to brush her scales flat, then turned sharply and walked back toward Aaron, a most fearful look on her face. "We can't fight them. We're not equipped! We're not strong enough! And we don't have the right weapons. They'll destroy us all."

Aaron was standing in shocked silence. Then he shouted at the top of his lungs, "Florence! Simber!"

Seconds later the door to the mansion flew open, and the two came running.

Thisbe grabbed her brother's sleeve and choked back a sob. "You have to give me up. She'll destroy everything! Everyone! The only human she wants is me. You've got to let me go to her!"

"Don't be ridiculous. I will never give you up."

"What's going on?" Simber growled as he and Florence arrived.

Aaron explained everything as quickly as he could, while Drock muttered and grumbled at the shoreline.

"A day and a half?" Florence said, incredulous. "There's no way we'll be ready."

"You have to let me go," Thisbe pleaded again. "It's the only way to save Artimé."

"Absolutely not!" said Simber. "Stop that kind of talk. Let's all take a few minutes to think this thrrrough."

Drock, Aaron, Thisbe, Simber, and Florence all went silent as they tried to collect their thoughts and figure out a plan.

But Thisbe already knew what had to happen, and she wasn't deterred. She was way more familiar with the Revinir's tactics than any of them. And once the dragon-woman decided she wanted something, she wouldn't stop until she had it.

Before the group could discuss anything, the Revinir's roar pierced into Thisbe's ears again, knocking her flat and blinding her with the same old images for several minutes. By the time her senses returned and she opened her eyes, she found that Sky had joined them and was sitting near Thisbe's head waiting for her to wake up. A few others had gathered as well and were talking gravely through the options.

"Aaron, please listen to me," Thisbe said, though her voice and her whole body was still weak from the Revinir's call. "I told you what needs to happen. I can solve this and make it all go away."

"Thisbe, I told you already. The answer is no," said Aaron sharply. "That's not how Artimé does things."

"He's right," said Florence. "And who really believes that the Revinir will go away peacefully once she has you? I don't trust her for a minute to just leave quietly. She's greedy, and she has a lot of anger toward all of us after what we did to her years ago."

Florence had a point.

Thisbe lay quietly, eyes closed, gathering her strength and hoping the dragon-woman wouldn't roar again. The way the roar permeated right into Thisbe's mind was frightening. That the Revinir had such control of the deadly dragons and black-eyed children was shocking. Everything was so mental with her—and the people of Artimé had no way to fight something like that.

Thisbe's eyes popped open. She stared at the blue sky, where a single fluffy cloud floated. The scales on her arms and legs began to tingle, and she sat up swiftly. "Could that be it?" she said softly. They'd been so focused on designing a physical spell to beat dragons and the Revinir. And that was definitely important. But what if the Revinir really was impossible to beat in a physical way? They had to come up with something else, or she'd have control of all of these dragons and people forever. Thisbe touched Florence's arm to get her attention. "Florence, I know what we need to do."

Florence stopped talking and turned to Thisbe. "What?"

"We need a different kind of magic."

LISA McMANN

Another Direction

Yes. A different kind of magic," Thisbe repeated as her thoughts came together. "Not just physical, like components that we throw to cause injury. We need mental components. Something that will affect the Revinir's mind."

Everyone looked at Thisbe with varying levels of confusion. "Okaaay," said Florence after a moment. "I see where you're going. But we don't really do that kind of magic here."

"Nobody did *my* kind of magic before I came along," Thisbe argued. "Or Fifer's."

"True," said Florence, still looking skeptical. "But you were

LISA McMANN

born with that. You weren't taught it. We didn't create it."

Thisbe wrinkled her forehead. "Good point." She slumped for a moment.

"I think Thisbe is onto something," Samheed said. "Obviously, different kinds of magic exist even if we don't use them. Remember Gondoleery Rattrapp? Hers was element based. Fire, rain, ice, wind. And the Revinir definitely has a different sort of magic from us. When she was Queen Eagala on Warbler, she placed that silence spell over the island. And now she's using two types of bone broth as her components."

"Not everything we do requires a physical component," Thisbe added, sitting up again. "Like the glass spell. We use our minds to send that. So why can't we try to . . . I don't know . . . develop *that* kind of magic some more?"

"Therrre's a big differrrence between conjurrring up a piece of glass and stopping a drrragon-woman frrrom mentally commanding hundrrreds of drrragons," said Simber. "We'd have a lot of experrrimenting to do."

"And no time to do it," said Aaron. "There's no way we can develop anything of that sort in months, much less by tomorrow."

LISA McMANN

"We can try, at least," said Thisbe. "Maybe it's easy. You don't know."

"I wouldn't know where to start," Aaron admitted. "I don't even understand how her whole roar thing works."

"I do," said Thisbe.

"As do I," said Drock from the water, surprising the others. They hadn't expected the dragon to contribute to this part of the conversation, but perhaps he had some insight the rest of them didn't have.

"Great," said Florence. "Thisbe and Drock, you two see what you can come up with while the rest of us speed up the work on Alex's old obliterate spells. I cringe to imagine what would happen if anyone makes a mistake with one of them, but that's the only thing we have going for us in this short amount of time. I think our backs are against the wall. I wish there was a way to hold them off—even a week would give me enough time to properly put together the obliterate spell. Then at least we wouldn't be caught flat-footed."

"Do what you can," said Aaron. "Even if you can only put together one component before they get here, it'll be much better than none. I'll go alert the blackboards and get the word out about the threat." He seemed to deflate a bit as he imagined the reaction to the news. "This isn't going to be easy."

Sky gave him a sympathetic smile. "It never was for Alex, either. But at least he didn't have the gang of dissenters to deal with. He'd be so furious about that."

"Yes, he would be," said Aaron, catching Sky's eye with a hint of a smile. "I'm afraid to see what they'll do when they hear this. I guess we'll soon find out." His smile faded and was replaced by a look of determination as he strode toward the mansion.

Thisbe turned to the dragon. A desperate feeling rose in her throat. "Where do we start, Drock?" she asked.

"I don't quite know," said Drock. "Perhaps pooling information based on our experiences will help us gain more understanding of the way she works. Then we can try to figure out how to stop her."

"Can I help?" Sky asked them. "I'm not much use in the component-building department. But I grew up with her—she was Queen Eagala back then. She was my leader on Warbler until Crow and I escaped."

"Oh, yes, that's a great idea," said Thisbe. "You probably

have a lot of insight about the way she was when she had Warbler under her thumb." But would it help them actually accomplish anything in time? Thisbe doubted it.

Knowing the Revinir was less than a day-and-a-half's distance away was overwhelming, and it made Thisbe want to give up—there was no chance that they'd figure out a solution to this plan in so little time. But it was their only hope. The three sat together on the lawn and talked about their experiences with the Revinir, hoping for a breakthrough.

Sky explained what it was like when the Revinir was Queen Eagala. "You might not know that Eagala was the younger sister of Marcus Today and the High Priest Justine. She was quite a bit younger, and when Justine and Marcus left Warbler as teenagers to begin Quill, they left Eagala behind. Some say that Eagala never got over that. She desperately wanted to go with them. When they wouldn't allow it, she hated them."

"Wow," said Thisbe. "So decades later, she took it out on her own world to prove how powerful she'd become? And she attacked anyone who came from Quill—right? Like Samheed and Lani. Was that all because of her grudge against her siblings?"

"That's what most Warblerans believe."

Drock snorted angrily, making Sky and Thisbe dodge a blast of smoke.

Sky continued. "She took over the rulership of Warbler when her parents died, and completely changed everything. Even her name—she began to call herself Eagala and demanded everyone use names related to earth and nature. Thus my name and my brother's: Sky and Crow. And Copper. And Phoenix, and Scarlet, and Thatcher . . . You get the picture."

Thisbe thought this through. "It's interesting. I'm not sure how it can help us, but maybe there's something more to the story of how she felt spurned by her brother and sister."

Sky shrugged. "I'm not sure either, but it seems important to her motivations, I guess." She shared a few other stories about Eagala's penchant for having a throne room to keep her secret writings and possessions in. Thisbe shared that the Revinir had done the same thing in the catacombs.

Then Sky told the other two about how Eagala had eventually put a silent spell over the entire island so she could more easily detect strangers coming ashore.

"Why?" asked Drock. "Was she afraid of strangers?"

"She was very possessive of her people. She didn't want

LISA McMANN

anyone leaving. She believed people would come and steal us away."

"That rings true," said Thisbe. "That must be why she's coming all the way out here. She can't stand it that Drock and I escaped. She told me once that she had big plans for me—she kept trying to get me to be her special assistant."

"So she's greedy, she's possessive, she's power hungry, and she's angry about her siblings not including her," said Sky, summing things up so far.

"What was her reason for the thorn necklaces and the orange eyes?" Thisbe asked.

"That was part of her controlling process," said Sky, touching the scars at her throat. "The orange eyes were like a brand—like what she did to the back of your neck, Thisbe. It's her symbol that she owns you. She came looking for Crow and me back in those early days too, after we escaped and landed here, because she said we belonged to her." Sky paused thoughtfully. "The thornaments came about after she realized that her silence spell over the island didn't stop humans from being able to speak. She wanted to control us and keep us from communicating."

Drock looked up. "That was part of the reason for the muzzles on my siblings and me. Mostly to stop us from breathing fire or attacking her with our teeth, of course. But she didn't like us communicating."

"And now she controls minds in order to stop ordinary communication between slaves," said Thisbe. She turned to Drock. "Tell us more. How did she manage to capture you in the first place?"

Drock frowned. He didn't like to talk about it. But after a moment he gave in and shared about his time in captivity and how the Revinir had first captured the dragons. "We'd just arrived across the gorge, and we were hungry and innocent and looking for water so we could fish. We knew that was supposed to be our land, and I suppose we expected the people there to be good. We should have noticed there were no other dragons around—we thought we just hadn't gone far enough yet to find them. We shouldn't have trusted the first person we happened upon. But she gave us food, and we told her our story. Then she . . ." Drock cringed, then continued. "She told us there was special lodging in the castle for guest dragons. She went to arrange it."

LISA McMANN

"Oh, Drock," said Thisbe, pivoting between incredulousness and pity as the story unfolded.

"I know. We were naive. But her offer of special lodging in the castle—it sounded like a dream come true. After ten years of running and hiding from the pirates and giant eels in this world, we wanted desperately to believe that the land of the dragons was everything our mother remembered it to be. Finally we felt we were being treated properly! That's what we thought, anyway. We didn't know the dragons had all been driven out by the current rulers." He grimaced, and a line of smoke rose from his nostrils. "We found out later that the Revinir had negotiated with the king to take us captive. And that together they would use us as their slaves."

"That's the saddest story I've ever heard," said Sky. "I can understand how you were taken in because of your expectations."

"After we were muzzled and chained in those dungeon stalls, they only used one of us at a time and threatened to kill the remaining four if the one being worked tried to escape." He hesitated. "Captivity was horrible. After a while I . . . stopped speaking."

"You've taken it up again, though," said Thisbe encouragingly, "which has been very helpful. We're going to find a way to fight this and make you all free again." But even as she said it, her heart sank, because there was no possible solution to this imminent problem.

Sky spoke up. "How are you able to withstand the Revinir's call, Drock?"

Drock looked out to sea and was quiet for a moment. "I'm not like other dragons," he said finally. "That's all I know. My lack of focus and inability to concentrate is saving me, I suppose. I hear and feel the roar, though. And its pull is getting stronger. I fear . . . I fear one day . . ." He didn't finish.

Thisbe nodded solemnly. She knew his fear all too well. That someday they might succumb to it like everyone else had.

Drock turned to Thisbe. "How are *you* managing to resist the roars?"

"I drank a vial of the ancestor broth, in addition to the dragon-bone broth. She forced me to test it. We didn't know if it held power—in fact, the Revinir still doesn't know that it does anything at all. She tried it, and it doesn't affect her. I lied to her—told her it did nothing to me. But it's as powerful as

LISA McMANN

the roar. Its effects fight against her call, leaving me paralyzed and blinded by images of that troubled land's history."

"Did you take in equal amounts of both broths?" asked Drock.

"I guess so," said Thisbe.

Drock shifted and looked intensely at Thisbe. "Where does she keep the broths?"

"In the throne room inside the catacombs," Thisbe told him.

"Oh." Drock seemed to deflate. "It's a shame we can't get more of it to dilute the dragon-bone broth's effects on your system," mused Drock. "It might tip things in the right direction for us."

Thisbe's eyes widened. "But, Drock," she said slowly. "I *do* have some more." She jumped to her feet. "Wait here. I'll be right back."

Splitting Up

Thisbe ran into the mansion and up the staircase, then down the girls' hallway to her room, shouting at her magical door to let her in so she wouldn't waste time. She smashed her shoulder into it, for it unexpectedly didn't open. Grabbing the handle, she rattled it hard. "It's Thisbe!" she said. "Let me in, stupid door!"

But the door remained locked. "What is happening?" Thisbe muttered. And at such a hectic time! Had Aaron's announcement put the mansion on lockdown or something? "Hello!" she shouted.

LISA McMANN

The door opened, and Fifer's face peered out. "Hi," she said stonily.

"I'm in a hurry." Thisbe pushed the door impatiently, but Fifer's foot blocked it from being able to open wide enough. "Fifer, what are you doing?"

"I—I moved your stuff out," Fifer said. Her eyes were red rimmed. "Just like you wanted. There was an empty room down the hall—I piled everything outside. You can't miss it."

Thisbe stared. "Fife," she said, and brought her hands to her forehead in dismay. "What the— Why? Are you serious?"

"You said you wanted your own room. I figured I'd help." Fifer crossed her arms and blinked furiously to keep the tears back.

Thisbe let out a frustrated noise, then backed out of the doorway, defeated. She looked all the way down to the end of the hallway. Sure enough, there sat a messy pile of her things. "You picked a terrible time to be awful," Thisbe said in disgust. "Check your blackboard." She turned and ran down the hallway.

Fifer frowned and closed the door.

As Thisbe approached her new room, the door swung open,

sensing her presence. But she didn't go inside. Instead she rummaged through her stuff, searching frantically for the ancestor broth that she'd swiped. She'd given one bottle to Rohan and kept the other one for herself. But where was it? She checked all of her pockets and treasure boxes and dresser drawers. Finally she uncovered it from the mess and held it up. The liquid glistened inside. "There," she whispered. "Thank goodness."

Leaving everything strewn about the hallway and the door to her room standing open, Thisbe took the vial of broth and ran back the way she had come, past her old room, where Fifer skulked inside, no doubt feeling terrible once she learned about the Revinir's approach.

Thisbe felt a twinge, but she hardened to it. Fifer had been mean. Sure, she was probably hurting. But she hadn't needed to retaliate in this ridiculous way like a child. And now Fifer was probably regretting it, for she certainly couldn't have known that the Revinir was coming for Thisbe.

"She'll be sorry soon enough," Thisbe muttered. "But right now she's not my problem." Breathing hard, Thisbe reached Drock on the lawn and held up the vial. "Here it is. Do you really think it will help drown out the roar?"

LISA McMANN

"It seems logical," said Drock. "And maybe it'll give you even more insight into the history of our land."

Thisbe bit her lip, feeling her stomach churn. The memory of the time she'd drunk it before was a difficult one. And the stuff had tasted pretty awful. In order not to gag, she had to get past dwelling on what was actually in that vial and just drink it down. She took the top off and sniffed it tentatively, then made a horrible face. "No doubt it tastes better steaming hot than lukewarm," she remarked. Before she could allow herself any more thoughts about it, she plugged her nose, then threw the broth into the back of her throat and swallowed. She gagged reflexively, but held the liquid down.

A second later, a new series of images flashed before her eyes. But she could hardly pay attention to them, because at that moment, a huge group of people burst out of the mansion. They were yelling harshly, demanding Aaron's immediate removal from the office of head mage.

Alone in her room, Fifer woke up her blackboard, Desdemona, and read the announcement that Aaron had posted to all the blackboards in Artimé.

Attention, everyone! I regret to inform you that Drock the dark purple dragon has spotted the Revinir (formerly known as Queen Eagala) coming this way with a fleet of dragons. They will arrive sometime tomorrow. If you are a trained mage, please load up your component vests and meet Florence on the lawn tonight after dinner for more details and training exercises. If you can use traditional weapons, gear up and join the mages, for we need you most of all. We believe the Revinir is seeking to capture Thisbe Stowe and will attack Artimé ruthlessly to get to her. Unfortunately, our magic is not strong enough to fend off her or the dragons she controls. We are working on a solution now. Stay tuned for further details and instructions.

Fifer stared at the words, hardly comprehending them. Then she looked around the room, now void of everything belonging to Thisbe, and groaned. "I'm a terrible person." She ran to the window and looked out, spotting Thisbe on the lawn with Sky and Drock. Aaron and Florence and a few others were nearby. And streaming out of the mansion was a huge group of dissenters—way more than Fifer had ever seen before. They were heading straight for Fifer's family. And they were spitting mad.

The Chaos before the Storm

By the time Fifer found Seth and the two wormed their way through the crowds to the lawn, the number of dissenters had increased even more. Cleary, Frieda Stubbs had been recruiting followers in her quest to stop Aaron from being their leader. And the recent news that the Revinir was coming to attack had convinced a whole lot more people that maybe Frieda was right.

Florence tried to quiet them all down, but she made no progress. They began chanting "Fire the mage! Save our land!" over and over again in unison.

"Like that'll help," muttered Seth to Fifer. "Let's all stand around shouting while the Revinir closes in with a bunch of enemy dragons."

"These dissenter people have no idea what they're talking about," said Fifer. "They weren't there. They didn't see what the Revinir has become." She squinted, then pointed toward the jungle. "Come on. I see Thiz hiding over there behind Drock."

"Thank goodness he's here, or this might be a hundred times worse."

"It's already bad enough. Besides, I need to apologize to Thisbe. I screwed up."

"What did you do?"

Fifer told him.

Seth snorted and shook his head. "That was kind of ridiculous, don't you think? Why would you do that?"

Fifer frowned. "I don't know," she mumbled. "I've just been feeling really bad lately about . . . stuff. But it's not all my fault. She said she wanted separate rooms." Everything was a mess. And it wasn't just Fifer's relationship with Thisbe that had gone wonky. Seth had been annoying at the party, and though she'd forgiven him by now for walking off without her, their relationship was strained. And there was also Simber—she'd grown so close to him after Alex died. But since they discovered Aaron was the new leader, Simber had all but abandoned her. It felt like Fifer had lost everyone, and none of those people seemed to care. Why weren't their hearts breaking for her like hers was for them?

She couldn't wallow in her sorrows now, though. Her twin was in danger. And whenever Thisbe was in danger, Fifer stepped up. There was no other way to be twins, in her mind. No matter what arguments remained unsolved between them.

"Thisbe!" Fifer called out over the dissenters. She waved, then pushed through to Thisbe's side. "I was thoughtless and selfish. I'm sorry. I'll . . . I'll bring all your stuff back to our room."

Thisbe stared icily at Fifer for a long moment. "Do you think I care about any of that right now? Did you even read the blackboard?"

"Yes!" said Fifer. "Of course! That's why I said I was sorry. And . . . because of moving your stuff out too, but mostly I care about the Revinir coming after you."

Thisbe just shook her head and turned away. "Drock, can

we go somewhere away from this noise so we can figure out how to survive an attack by the Revinir? You know, since you and I are both in a lot of imminent danger?"

Fifer wasn't sure if the noise Thisbe referred to meant her or the dissenters. Her face fell. Before she could sort out whether she should try apologizing again, or do something else, Drock threaded his tail around Thisbe and put her onto his back. Then he lumbered to the water and pushed out to sea, leaving Fifer and Seth watching them go.

"Maybe we'd better try helping Aaron instead," said Seth dryly.

"She'll come around," said Fifer with determination. "I know my sister. At least . . . I used to."

"She'll come around? The Revinir is coming to abduct her! She's got a lot on her mind right now besides you." Seth just shook his head at Fifer. "Not everything is about you all the time. You know that, Fifer?"

Fifer stared at him, unable to think of a comeback. Why couldn't she get anything right? After a moment, Seth left. He pushed through the crowd to where Florence was standing, acting as a bodyguard for Aaron, and asked if there was anything he could do to help. Fifer frowned after him, not sure what to do.

Fifer's sadness turned to indignation as she mentally reviewed what had just happened. She knew very well that not everything was about her. It made her mad that Seth would say such a thing. Fifer also knew that this situation was really serious—why else would she step up and apologize to get back on Thisbe's good side when the whole "getting a new room" thing wasn't even totally Fifer's fault? She was just trying to quickly clear up that little altercation so they could work on the real problem, which was obviously the Revinir. But they had at least a little time before the dragon-woman would be here. Fifer had figured a few minutes patching things up wouldn't make a difference.

But Thisbe hadn't appreciated the gesture, much less understood it for what it was: an effort to get them on the same page so Fifer could help stop the Revinir. So now what? After a moment, Fifer plowed after Seth to Aaron's side, determined to get something right. Because everything she did lately seemed like a big mistake.

"Hey!" Fifer shouted, heading for the protesters. "Everybody just stop it! Stop acting like a bunch of babies! Do you seriously think now is a good time to get rid of the head mage? With the Revinir on her way here? Let me tell you what she's like, in case you haven't heard."

But the dissenters didn't want to listen. Especially Frieda Stubbs, who turned to Fifer and got right up into her face. "Your family is the reason the Revinir is coming here!"

Fifer felt her face get hot. "We're trying to fix this!"

"You caused it," said Frieda, "and the only way to fix it is if you go away. So I say you should *all* leave!"

Fifer gasped. Frieda's people started to chant: "Leave! Leave! Leave!"

Frieda smirked at her. "See? The people have spoken. You must leave! Or else we'll hand you over to the Revinir when she gets here."

Threats and More Threats

Move back!" Florence warned Frieda and the other dissenters. "Please! Allow us to figure out our plan so we can stop the Revinir from coming! We need silence! Your treasonous threats aren't helping anything."

"We need a new mage!" shouted someone from the group. It was met with raucous agreement. "Sacrifice the Stowes to save our land!" hollered someone else.

Fifer's eyes widened, and she hung back behind her brother. She'd faced a lot of things in her life, but never betrayal by people who were supposed to be on her team. It was greatly unsettling. Even Seth looked frightened on her behalf, which was a relief. Samheed and Lani arrived to see what was happening. Samheed eyed Aaron suspiciously—he seemed to be the cause of all of Artimé's problems lately.

Simber returned and forced his way between the dissenters and the ones trying to stop the Revinir. He let out a huge roar, which was effective in getting some of the protesters to back up a bit, if not scare them away completely.

Sky pushed her way through the crowd behind him and came up to Fifer. "What's going on? Where's Thisbe?"

"She's off with Drock," Fifer said, flipping her hand toward the water. "Everybody's lost their minds. They're blaming us for the Revinir coming."

Sky regarded the girl thoughtfully. "Well, they have a point. She wouldn't be heading this way if it weren't for Thisbe and Drock escaping."

"Sky!" said Fifer, appalled.

"I'm just trying to understand where they're coming from!"

Fifer frowned. "That's impossible, and it won't do any good. They're not making sense."

"Well, it doesn't hurt to try to reason with them. But I need to

LISA McMANN

understand them first if we're going to make any progress there."

Fifer rolled her eyes. "We don't have time for that! Simber, can you please get Frieda's people out of our faces so we can figure this thing out?"

Simber didn't oblige and instead looked at Aaron.

"Leave them be," said Aaron. "They have a right to be here."

Fifer crossed her arms over her chest in frustration. She could feel her face burn.

Seth sighed, exasperated. Samheed and Lani looked uneasily at each other.

Florence shook her head and went to Aaron. "Then let's go to Karkinos for a little while, where it's quiet. We don't have time for this fight right now."

After a moment, Aaron agreed. He climbed on Simber's back, then helped Fifer and Sky up too, and they flew to the nearby Island of Legends, where they could hopefully talk in peace. Samheed watched Aaron fly off, the troubled look on his face remaining. Then he and Lani pushed the crowd away from the mansion door so people could get in and out and went back inside to load up their component vests.

» » « «

LISA McMANN

Thisbe and Drock joined the group on the shore of the giant crab island. A bit later, Ibrahim and Clementi learned of the gathering and came with Scarlet in her skiff. Back in Artimé, Florence got Seth and Carina and a few others working on the obliterate spell. Once the chaos was somewhat controlled, she walked along the sea bottom to Karkinos to help the ones there.

After a couple of anxious hours, they still had no quick solutions other than the obliterate spell. Every now and then Aaron rose to look anxiously toward Artimé. "The crowd along the shore seems bigger."

They could faintly hear the chanting from the dissenters.

Simber paced the shore. "Theirrr numberrrs have been incrrreasing everrry hourrr," he growled.

"I don't care," said Aaron recklessly. "Let them shout until their voices are gone. We've got more important things to worry about right now." He scratched his head and turned to gaze at the group with him. "We might want to hide Thisbe."

"What about Drock?" said Thisbe. "He's in just as much danger."

"He can defend himself," said Aaron.

"So can I," Thisbe argued.

Simber, who had stationed himself on the edge of the crab island to watch Artimé, shook his head. "We shouldn't have left."

Florence looked up sharply. "What? Why not?"

"They'll say they've drrriven us off."

"That's ridiculous," said Thisbe. "They haven't done any such thing."

"Well," said Fifer, going to stand next to Simber, "they sort of did, I guess. Look at us."

Sky nodded. "It does seem that way," she said. "Does it matter?"

"Of courrrse it does," said Simber. "They werrre trrrying to drrrive the Stowes away, and they've succeeded."

"Not technically," said Thisbe. "We're just at our friends' island." But no one seemed to think that mattered.

Florence got up too and joined Aaron, Simber, and Fifer, looking out at Artimé. "Hmm," she said, growing increasingly troubled. "You may be right, Sim. I wish I'd thought of that before suggesting we come here."

Aaron frowned, and his face retained a troubled expression. "I'm honestly not sure what to do. Should we go back and try to deal with this? We need our people prepared for this attack.

But if I get caught up in the shouting match, we waste even more planning time." He hung his head, exasperated. "I wish they would just try to understand that and give us some time to take care of this immediate problem before it's too late for everyone. It's so frustrating!"

"How many of them are there, Simber?" Fifer asked.

"Overrr a hundrrred now, and grrrowing. This is a rrreal issue, Aarrron."

Thisbe looked up but remained with the other young mages and Drock to try to come up with a new spell that would stop the Revinir.

"Samheed and Lani came out of the mansion a while ago and werrre trrrying to calm them down," said Simber. "They gave up and went back inside." He growled under his breath. "This is out of contrrrol."

"But what should we do?" said Aaron, raising his voice in frustration. "I don't know what you want me to do, Simber. You seem to have thoughts—why not just say them?"

Simber glanced at Aaron. "I'm not the head mage of Arrrtimé."

"I'm asking you for advice!" Aaron said.

"Fine. Then I think you should go back and take charrrge of the situation. Don't stop until you have the people underrr contrrrol."

Aaron worked his jaw. He had no idea what he could possibly say to stop the people from protesting him and his sisters.

"And," Simber continued, "Florrrence and I should go with you forrr prrrotection and intimidation purrrposes."

"But what about the Revinir?" Aaron spat out.

Florence stepped in. "If you don't take control of this situation and get everyone prepared as much as you can, there will be mass casualties." She paused to let the words sink in. "We have to expect the worst, and we need to communicate that clearly. We must get these people settled down and ready to fight for their lives."

Aaron felt his face grow hot with anger. There was no time for this. He had never asked for this job, and he hated that he was forced to do it, especially under such stressful times. But he wanted to go back to Artimé for a different reason—to tell Kaylee to take Daniel back to the Island of Shipwrecks for a while. For their safety.

"I'll go with you, Aaron," said Fifer.

Thisbe shot her sister a frustrated glance. She needed more help than Aaron did. But it just proved even more solidly to Thisbe that Fifer no longer cared about the land of the dragons or their people. And there was nothing that could happen that would change that—Fifer had to want it. Thisbe couldn't want it for her. But clearly Fifer had a much stronger connection to Artimé than to the black-eyed rulers of Grimere.

"I think you'd better stay with Thisbe," Aaron told Fifer. He turned sharply to face the others. "I need all of you to work harder than you've ever worked while I'm gone."

Fifer sighed. She was no longer calling any shots—not just in leadership, but even when her own life choices were involved. Her time as group leader was deader than dead. She glanced at Simber, who wasn't paying any attention to her, then threw her hands up and went back to the small group of mages.

As precious time ticked away, more and more people of Artimé joined the dissenters in condemning the head mage and demanding his resignation. Florence quickly started walking toward Artimé, and Simber and Aaron prepared to fly back to settle things there once and for all.

LISA McMANN

Everything Is Awful

With the Revinir gaining ground, Simber and Aaron approached Artimé from the sky, and Florence emerged from the sea. Aaron could hear the chants loud and clear. "Down with the Stowes! Fire the mage!" Samheed and Lani had returned outside with Carina this time to try to control the protest. But they weren't having any luck.

Aaron felt terrible that the people had not only turned on him, but on Thisbe and Fifer, too. It was so strange that Frieda had implicated their mother as her reason to despise them—he'd never heard anyone speak like that about her before. Aaron had only known his mother to be a quiet, obedient, selfless person. Sure, she hadn't tried to stop Alex from being sent to his death, but no parent would've survived after standing against that practice back then. And she had died protecting her daughters. Perhaps that was her way of making up for past regrets. They'd never know.

But who had she been? Had she really been a pirate, as Frieda seemed so sure about? Where had she come from? The Island of Fire? And how had she gotten to Quill?

None of it mattered now. Simber flew over the people's heads and found a clear spot on the lawn to land. The protesters turned around and moved toward them, making a circle around the group. Florence reached the shore and ran to the crowd, shouting for the people to be quiet for a moment so they could communicate.

Aaron wasn't sure what he was going to say. He had no idea what kind of response could work with such rabidly angry people. Was there anything he could convey that would calm them? It didn't seem likely. Their minds were made up. If only Alex were here to fix all of this. . . .

Eager for something new to be angry about, the crowd quieted enough for Aaron to speak. He slid off Simber's back but stayed close. Sweat beaded on his forehead as he looked into the eyes of the people who hated him. "People of Artimé," he said, "I understand your anger. I know why you hate me."

A murmur went through the group.

"I believe you have a right to speak your mind, even if what you say hurts me. That's what Alex would've said too."

"He'd still be here if you hadn't killed him!" shouted one man, and a few others echoed their agreement with the statement.

"I did NOT kill Alex!" Aaron said sharply, and several dissenters began to argue. It was the worst accusation of all of them, and the way they so falsely and blatantly threw it out there hurt more than all the others combined.

"You had him killed, then!" said Frieda Stubbs.

"That is *preposterous!*" said Aaron, spit flying. Rage grew, and he felt himself losing all sense of decorum. "I loved him more than I can express!"

Simber emitted a low growl, perhaps trying to get Aaron back on track. But Aaron was tired and hurt and absolutely furious. His heart had been broken by his brother's death, and these people had spread such horrible rumors, not caring how much their words hurt him. This wasn't what Artimé was about at all. When had this happened to these good people?

Aaron tried to breathe, tried to control his tone while struggling to be heard against the voices around him, which were rising again. "Listen, everyone. I'm asking for you to delay your protest for a few days so that we can focus on stopping the Revinir from attacking all of us. I want you to prepare to fight and protect yourselves. Please! I'm begging you!"

"You're planning to have us all killed now by this Revinir dragon-person. Is that right?" said Frieda with a sneer. "Is that your answer to everything? If somebody bothers you, you just kill them. You know what you need to do to fix this, Aaron, but you're too cowardly to do it."

Aaron focused on the woman who had started Artimé's descent into madness and felt suddenly very weary. "I am trying to prevent you all from being killed," he said, his voice ragged, "while also protecting the Revinir's targets. Just as Alex would have done."

"You lie!" cried Frieda. "Alex would have gone immediately and destroyed that monster and saved all of us. You're just standing here, drawing her to us, when you could sacrifice yourself and your evil sisters, and we'd be safe!"

The chants began again. "Fire the mage! Sacrifice the Stowes!"

Aaron felt like he was about to explode. "You have no idea

LISA McMANN

how leadership works! And I didn't even want this job!" he yelled. "If anybody else would like to be head mage and can save Artimé from this attack, just say the word, because I have had it with all of this!"

There was a split second of silence in which everyone digested the mage's words.

"Aarrron!" roared Simber. But it was too late for Aaron to take the words back.

Samheed looked aghast. Lani's jaw dropped. She'd once wanted the job a long time ago, but not now. Not like this.

"Where's Claire?" Samheed whispered to Lani. "Claire!" he shouted. "Are you here?" But the woman was not present.

Frieda Stubbs stepped forward. "I'll do it."

Aaron stared at her. Everyone gasped. And then slowly Aaron took off the robe.

"Aaron, stop!" said Florence.

The head mage handed the robe to Frieda Stubbs.

"No, Aarrron!" said Simber. "This is disastrrrous!"

"I don't need a robe to try to save Artimé," said Aaron quietly. "It's better for everyone that this distraction ends now. Good luck, Frieda. You're going to need it."

Frieda grabbed the robe and held it up triumphantly, and the people on the lawn erupted in cheers and shouts and expressions of disbelief and horror. People began to panic. "But she's not even very magical," said one. "How is such an untalented person going to be in charge of all of us?" shrieked another. "This is crazy!"

"Aarrron!" Simber said once more, his voice awash in desperation and pleading.

Aaron turned to the winged cheetah. In that instant his face fell as he realized what he'd just done to the beast. His face flooded with regret. And then the regret cleared and turned to resolve. "You heard me, Simber. It's done. I'm . . . I'm done." He swallowed hard as the cheetah's face betrayed his feelings.

"Why?" said Simber softly. "Why did you do this?"

Aaron's face broke, and he covered his mouth with trembling fingers. Then he dropped his hand and turned sharply. "Go, Simber. Frieda is your new mage. I hope you'll help her like you've helped every mage of this land." He paused. "Please know I'll be fighting for Artimé more than ever. Believe it or not. We just couldn't go on like . . . that."

Florence was speechless. One hand went to her hip and

LISA McMANN

the other to her forehead, and she watched in shock as Aaron turned away. Then her eyes widened as chaos continued all around them. "Get him out of here!"

Before the protesters could descend on Aaron in a frenzy, Lani, Carina, and Samheed pressed through the crowd and grabbed Aaron by the elbows. They dragged him toward the water—it was his only means of escape. Lani stayed at the shoreline to help Florence hold the crowds at bay as Samheed and Carina swam out with Aaron to protect him.

"You really did it this time," Samheed muttered.

"Give him a break," Carina snapped at him.

Samheed frowned but was quiet, and Aaron didn't say anything either.

Once they'd swum halfway to Karkinos, Aaron stopped them and treaded water, breathing hard. "I can make it the rest of the way," he said. "Go back to Artimé and stay with Simber. And please . . . please find Kaylee and tell her to go to the grandfathers as soon as possible. She and Daniel aren't safe here. Tell her . . . tell her I love her. And I'll see them when all of this mess is over."

Time Ticks Away

Reluctantly Carina and Samheed let Aaron continue to Karkinos alone. Once they returned to Artimé's shore, Carina went to the mansion to help Simber and Florence in whatever way she could during such a disruptive time. But Samheed broke through the crowds of protesters and kept walking into Quill to find someone who could go in search of Claire Morning.

On his way, he had a lot of soul-searching to do. He felt angry at Aaron for messing this up without regard for anyone else, just like he always used to do. But Carina's reprimand had jerked him back to reality, and now he felt a little bit

LISA McMANN

guilty for acting so mean after all Aaron had been through. It was obvious Samheed hadn't wanted Aaron as head mage—the guy had brought a lot of baggage and complications to that position. But Samheed also hadn't wanted anything like *this* to happen. It was frightening to watch strong Artimé unraveling.

And as much as he'd preferred the idea of Claire as the head mage, Samheed wasn't going in search of her now to defy Aaron in any way—he would have never done this if Aaron hadn't resigned. He was doing it for the sake of Artimé's existence, because under Frieda Stubbs, it was only a matter of time before the magical world became a complete disaster. Sooner rather than later if they didn't stop the Revinir.

Knowing that many of the dissenters thought fondly of Claire and preferred her to Aaron, Samheed felt there was a good chance for Claire to smooth everything over between the Frieda supporters and the Aaron supporters. And with any luck, she could step in and take charge before the Revinir destroyed them all.

When Samheed reached the outskirts of Quill's neighborhood quadrants, he found a Necessary to go in search of Claire

Morning and ask her to come to Artimé as soon as possible. Then he turned back and went to help Florence try to control the crowd and get everyone settled down.

By that time, Aaron was approaching the Island of Legends. Karkinos reached out his coral-reef claw to assist him, lifting the sodden former head mage and placing him gently on the shore near the others. Once he'd caught his breath, he faced the ones there: Fifer, Thisbe, Sky, Ibrahim, and Clementi. They, with Drock's help, had kept an eye on the whole interaction and could tell bad things were going on, but they couldn't hear well enough to understand everything.

Thisbe and Fifer came up to embrace Aaron. "What happened?" Thisbe asked, alarmed. "Why did you give up your robe?"

Aaron, still a bit dazed, explained what had transpired. "There was no chance of getting them to listen," he said. "I'm a distraction. Way too big of one at such a crucial moment. I had to do it. I . . . I wanted to. I can't go on like this. Being head mage was never something I desired, anyway. Not . . . not now."

Fifer stared over the water, trying to make out the activity. "What about Seth? Did you see him?"

LISA McMANN

"No," said Aaron. "I saw Carina, though. They'll be fine. The dissenters don't have a problem with our friends. Just us. We're not safe there anymore."

Thisbe stared. What in the world was happening? This was unbelievable. All three of them, hated by this noisy group in Artimé. Banished, or so it seemed. After all their brother Alex had done for that world, his death had left the other three tossed out to sea. "At least we're together," said Thisbe, her eyes filling. And then she broke into a sob.

Fifer started crying too. "All our stuff in the mansion . . . We don't even have canteens or anything."

"Who cares about that?" said Thisbe sharply, swiping at her tears. "Sheesh, Fifer. You drive me crazy sometimes."

"You're mad that I care about having water?" said Fifer. "After what we went through in the land of the dragons? Did you forget that already?"

Thisbe stared. "Oh, yeah," she said sheepishly. "Right. Well, luckily we have water here."

Fifer nodded stiffly. There was still so much hurt between them, but she tamped down her urge to keep arguing. Sky placed a comforting hand on each girl's shoulder.

Aaron turned to Ibrahim and Clementi. "You two should go back to Artimé. Henry and Thatcher will be worried. The conflict there will settle down now. I hope so, anyway."

Ibrahim and Clementi nodded. They gathered up their rucksacks and took a few reluctant steps toward the water, still intimidated by Aaron even though he no longer wore the robe of the head mage. But then they stopped and whispered to each other. Clementi turned to Aaron. "We want to stay and help you if you'll let us. I think Henry and Thatcher would know that. We've been very vocal about our support for Thisbe and her quest to return to the land of the dragons. So I think they'll expect that we want to help you both now."

"Clementi's right," said Ibrahim. "I think they'll know. And if they want to make sure, one of them can come here to check on us. They'll understand."

Aaron considered their argument for a moment, then wearily agreed. "We could certainly use your creative minds," he said.

"Let's get back to work, then," said Thisbe. "We've got no time to waste." Thisbe ran over to where Drock was floating in the space between the great crab's coral-reef claws. "Drock!" she called. "Where is the Revinir now?"

Drock flapped his mighty wings and rose high into the air, showering everyone with water. He held steady overhead, eyes fixed to the west, then circled and rose higher and stared again. He seemed shocked. He muttered something under his breath and landed. "She's passing over the Island of Fire. Making incredible time. Much faster than I anticipated. She's moving as quickly as a regular full dragon can fly."

Thisbe's legs quaked, and her scales quivered. The report took her breath away. "So what's her estimated time of arrival?"

Drock gave the girl a pained look. "If they don't stop to rest? Not long after daybreak."

"Then," said Thisbe bravely, "we've got no time to lose. Let's figure this monster out once and for all."

Night fell. Drop bears appeared, weaving anxiously in and out of the trees, as if they could feel danger approaching. Talon and Lhasa, the snow leopard, emerged from the woods and stopped by the group to offer them food and drink.

As they gratefully ate, Aaron told the two what had happened. Talon offered to check on Florence and find out if everything was settling down and to let Henry and Thatcher know that Ibrahim and Clementi were choosing to stay with Aaron and the twins. He set off, and the group of mages continued to throw out ideas as they finished their hurried meal. But everything they could think of would likely be repelled by the Revinir's scales.

"What about a potion that affects the Revinir's sight?" asked Clementi. "Eyes are vulnerable."

"That would be something, at least," said Thisbe. "It won't break her control over the dragons, but it might buy us some time."

Clementi and Ibrahim began brainstorming but soon realized Karkinos didn't have the right kinds of herbs they'd need to make a potion, and there was no easy way to get them from Artimé. So they had to abandon the idea for now and try something else.

After a while, Talon returned. "It's still chaotic," he said. "A whole new group of protesters has formed—the ones who want you back as head mage, Aaron."

Aaron closed his eyes briefly as mixed emotions flowed through him. He wished they'd put their efforts into practicing their fighting skills, but he was grateful to have some support.

Yet . . . he didn't regret leaving the toxic situation. Though he still felt terribly guilty for what he'd done to Simber. "How is Florence?" he asked.

"She's more sympathetic to you than Simber is," Talon said carefully. "She held the training session, but it wasn't easy with all the activity and arguing. She has an awful lot to do to try to prepare the mansion for an attack, and she wasn't getting much cooperation."

"And . . . Simber?" asked Aaron, not looking up.

"Simber isn't speaking to anyone at the moment. Frieda has him busy doing meaningless chores for her. It's . . . not a good scenario."

"What about the obliterate spell?" asked Thisbe. "Is there one ready yet?"

"Not yet," said Talon. "Carina got pulled away to help with crowd control. She's back working on it again, but it's very slow going, she said."

Aaron sighed deeply. "I hope I didn't destroy everything."

Talon gave him a look of sympathy. "I think everyone knows how important it is to stop the Revinir. This will blow over."

"If we all survive to see that happen, it'll be a miracle,"

muttered Aaron. "We're going to have to leave your island soon—we certainly don't want to draw the Revinir to your shores. Perhaps Karkinos should swim out of the area for a while."

"But where will *we* go?" asked Fifer. "If Artimé isn't safe for us and we don't want to draw the enemies to Karkinos, will we go to the grandfathers? If so, we'll have to take a ship, since there's no way we can access the tubes. And we can't go to Warbler—the Revinir will see us."

"I don't think Warbler is a safe place to hide, anyway," said Sky. "She knows that island better than anyone."

Aaron sighed. "I haven't figured anything out quite yet."

But Thisbe had. She watched and listened to the conversations through the cover of darkness, taking it all in. She glanced at Drock, who looked back solemnly at her, and a strange new feeling of understanding passed between them that surprised her. She'd forgotten about the additional ancestor broth she'd taken earlier, before all this craziness broke loose. But maybe it was having an effect on her and her ability to communicate with dragons. Whatever the case, she and Drock seemed to be the only ones to fully understand what needed to happen here.

LISA McMANN

And the closer they got to daybreak, the more serious they had to become about doing it.

The group brainstormed long into the night until exhaustion overcame them. All agreed to get a few hours of sleep before they had to make a move. What move would it be? Only two of them knew for sure.

A Sacrifice

T hisbe had slipped away on the back of a dragon in the middle of the night once before. It felt strange to be doing so again after what had happened last time. When the others were asleep, she grabbed one of the canteens that Talon had provided them, silently thanking Fifer for the reminder, and tiptoed out to where Drock napped. As she did so, the roar of the Revinir blasted inside her head. Thisbe dropped to her hands and knees, prepared for the inevitable paralysis and the pounding of the images. But strangely, this time she merely had to fight through a misty haze. She rose to her feet and, after a moment to steady herself, continued to Drock.

LISA McMANN

Drock had been startled awake by the call, and he splashed, highly agitated, in the water as Thisbe drew near.

"She's getting close," Drock said. He flopped and dove underwater, disappearing for a long moment and leaving Thisbe wondering if he was ever going to surface. When he did, he rose with a loud splash.

Thisbe shushed him and looked over her shoulder at the others. She couldn't tell if they'd woken up or not. "I know it's hard, but try to be calm," she whispered. "Let's hurry." The images flashed at the edges of her brain, more like memories this time rather than the visions that blinded her. The extra vial of ancestor broth seemed to have done great things for her problem. She wished she'd taken it much sooner. The pull of the Revinir's call still made her feel like going toward it, sort of like how the pull of a late-night snack might make her want to get out of her toasty warm bed. It usually wasn't strong enough to get her to actually do it, but she definitely thought about it.

However, Drock was having a lot of trouble resisting the call this time, perhaps because the Revinir was getting so near to them. Thisbe became agitated too, just watching him and worrying that he was going to wake up Aaron or Fifer. If they found out what she was about to do, they'd probably stop her.

"Too bad," Thisbe murmured to herself, imagining the conversation with Aaron. "I'm going, no matter what you say." She heard a footfall in the sand behind her.

"Thisbe," said Aaron, too close for comfort.

Thisbe jumped. "Yes?" she hissed. All of her determination bled out of her.

"What are you doing?"

Thisbe pressed her lips together. "I'm going with Drock." She could see his outline next to her now.

"Going where?"

"Come on, Aaron. You know. There's no other way to stop this."

Aaron sighed deeply.

"We tried," said Thisbe. "We had ideas, but we didn't have enough time. You can keep thinking of ways to stop her if you want, but this will actually save Artimé, I think. She wants me back with her. She's furious that I escaped, and she'll be relentless until she has me back. And she wants Drock, too—she wants all the dragons. Every last one of them. She's greedy.

LISA McMANN

Perhaps . . . perhaps that's her weakness." Thisbe stopped and thought about that for a moment. "Yes, maybe that's it. Keep thinking about that while I'm gone, Aaron. And I will too. Ask Sky about what else might get to her. Maybe there's something left at Warbler that can help give us a clue."

"You think I can just let you go and turn yourself in to the Revinir? I can't, Thisbe. You know that."

"She won't kill me. I promise. I know her. I'll be okay. I'm a well-trained actor, remember? I know what to do."

Aaron was quiet.

"And I took the extra ancestor broth. It's helping me be stronger against her roar. She just sent out a roar a few minutes ago, and look at me—I'm fine. Pretty good, anyway. Just a little fuzzy."

"Thisbe."

"I'm dead serious, Aaron."

"Then I shall come with you."

This time Thisbe was quiet as she contemplated it. Her heart longed for his company. She didn't relish being alone with the Revinir again. Would she ever see her friends and family again? At least she knew how to get back through the

LISA McMANN

volcano system now. But how could she ask Aaron to come along? Why put his life in danger when it didn't need to be? He had Kaylee and Daniel and Fifer here. She frowned. And if he did go with her, what would the Revinir think? She wasn't calling to him—his presence might make her suspicious.

Aaron saw her hesitation. "Seriously, Thiz. My schedule is pretty open now that I'm not the head mage anymore."

Thisbe smiled ruefully. "Well, there is that." She thought a bit more, then shook her head. "I don't feel good about it. It seems like it'll complicate things and make the Revinir suspicious. I want you to stay and make sure Artimé is safe. I know how to get back here. And I'm actually relatively safe with Drock. As long as he can keep resisting the call, we can go along with the Revinir and maybe fake her out a little. You know? Pretend that we are actually heeding the call, and infiltrate that way. Then, once I figure out what I need to do in Grimere, I'll send a single seek spell to Florence to let her know to send a team to help me. Okay?"

Thisbe stopped abruptly, realizing that this plan might actually work and feeling her heart lift. "Yes," she said more confidently now. "That's exactly what we'll do. We'll play along. I doubt she wants to fight our people for the sake of fighting—not yet anyway. I'm confident she doesn't have full control over the land of the dragons and what lies beyond it yet. She won't tackle our world until she's sure she can beat all of us."

Aaron listened. After a minute he nodded slowly. "As much as I want to protect you, I think you're right—my presence would cause suspicion since she knows I haven't taken any dragon-bone broth. Your plan to infiltrate and pretend to be under her spell is a good one. While you're gone, we'll continue working on more complex spells to help you—and I'll talk to Sky like you asked. Just . . . just stay safe. Stay alive." Aaron looked carefully into Thisbe's eyes to read her expression.

Thisbe smiled. The plan felt good to her. And it was nice to have Aaron trust her. After all, Thisbe was the resident expert on the Revinir. "Thanks, Aaron. This is the right plan. I can feel it. I love you. And tell . . . the others . . . tell Fifer . . . that I love them all too. I'll be okay if I just play along. And just come when I call. Hopefully by that time Florence will have the new seek spell and the obliterate components finished. And with any luck you'll come up with some other solutions by then. Not just to help me with the Revinir, but also to fix things here with this mess."

Aaron nodded solemnly. "Don't worry about this—it'll all clear up in a day or two. We'll be ready and waiting for your seek spell." He bent down and kissed Thisbe's forehead, then embraced her. "Are your pockets loaded with components?" he asked.

Thisbe nodded and squeezed his arm. "Oh! I almost forgot," she said, then quickly unbuttoned the vest and stuffed all of the components into her pants pockets. "I don't want the Revinir to see that I have one of these—she'd recognize it and might search me for components." She handed the vest to Aaron. "Take care of it for me." She smiled reassuringly, then turned and ran lightly through the sand to Drock. She climbed up his tail and took her place in the hollow between his shoulder blades. As they moved away from the island, Thisbe began to tell the dragon about her plan. Knowing Drock's rebellious nature, she only hoped he'd go along with it.

LISA McMANN

Chaos Rules

The protests in Artimé continued long into the night. Lani helped Kaylee and Daniel get into the mostly secret hallway through a 3-D door that she kept hidden in her room for just such emergencies. The two escaped safely via the tube to the Island of Shipwrecks. Then Lani called an emergency meeting with some of the others who considered the Stowes to be friends. They also met in the mostly secret hallway to avoid as many dissenters as possible—including Frieda Stubbs, who wasn't able to see the entrance because she, like most of Artimé's residents, wasn't quite magical enough.

Florence was there, and Simber snuck in once Frieda went to bed. Samheed, Scarlet, Henry and Thatcher, and Sean and Carina and Seth were all there too—Seth having triumphantly discovered upon his return to Artimé that he could see the magical hallway now. This was his first meeting in that wing, and he felt rather important to be the youngest in attendance, despite being bleary-eyed with exhaustion and worry.

He knew better than to sit near Simber, who was still very angry about what Aaron had done. There was no way Simber would forgive the former head mage as long as Frieda Stubbs was in charge—that much was obvious. Once everyone had arrived, Lani updated them with all that she knew.

"Aaron, Thisbe, Fifer, and Sky are safe on the Island of Legends," she said.

"Ibrahim and Clementi are there too," Henry added for those who hadn't heard yet.

Seth frowned. He was the only one stuck here.

"Florence," said Lani. "Has there been any progress on a plan to defeat the Revinir? Do we know when she'll get here? Where are the updates?"

"Frieda's in charge of the updates now," said Florence, not

trying to hide her sarcasm. "And she's choosing to pretend that nothing is happening."

"Great," said Seth, sitting up in alarm. "We're all going to die."

Nobody jumped to contradict him, which was even more frightening.

"We've got a team working on the obliterate spell," said Florence, pointing to Carina and Seth. "It's our only hope on such short notice. I'm authorizing a limited number of them and assigning who they'll go to."

"Yikes," said Samheed. He'd seen firsthand what it could do. "Alex never wanted to produce that one again."

"I know." Florence's voice was terse. "But Alex . . . well. You know."

Samheed nodded. "I know—he's not here." He thought for a moment. "I could imagine him changing his mind under these circumstances. We're up against a wall." He frowned, hoping Claire was on her way.

"How are we supposed to, like, *do* this?" asked Seth. "Do we just sit around on the lawn waiting to be attacked?" He'd never fought a battle at home before. There was so much more to think about. They had an actual mansion to protect, and so many people here, some of whom were defenseless.

"I'll have details on your blackboards before dawn," said Florence. "Simber, how long before she gets here?"

"I rrreally have no idea," said Simber. "The Stubb has been keeping me busy with otherrr things."

It was the second scariest thing Seth had heard so far. How could Simber not know?

"Will you please go look?" asked Florence. "For me?"

Simber growled. "If I leave this hallway, she might find me."

"Go out through the head mage's quarters, then," said Florence. "Out the balcony. You can fit through those doors, right?"

Simber grunted and got up.

Once he left the room, Lani leaned toward Florence. "He's in a bad way," she whispered.

"I can hearrr you," Simber called from the hallway.

Several of the older contingent shook their heads and had a brief laugh, despite the serious problems that plagued them.

"Yes," said Florence in her normal voice. "He's not taking this well at all."

"Well, he might not have to for much longer if we all die," said Seth.

"We're not— Stop that talk," said Carina. "We're going to be okay. Right, Florence?"

"That's the plan. I can't count on anyone but this group, so please turn your blackboards on full volume so I can get ahold of you even if you're sleeping."

"Wait," said Sean. "You're counting on our little group . . . to do what?"

"To stand at the shore and launch obliterate spells at the Revinir."

"What about the dragons with her?" asked Sean.

"Not at them. If we succeed in destroying the Revinir," said Florence, "with any luck the spell will be broken, and the dragons won't follow through on her orders."

Lani stared. "With any luck?"

Florence sighed impatiently and got up off her special sofa that Mr. Today had made for her many years before. "If you have a better plan . . . ," she began.

"I know," Lani muttered. "I know. I'm sorry. It's just that—"

"It's just that everything has gone completely bonkers, and

we don't have any other way to do this!" Florence said, her voiced raised and scaring everybody. "We aren't equipped to fight enemies like this!"

The room was quiet. They could hear Simber's footsteps in the hall, and seconds later he appeared.

"I estimate the Rrrevinirrr will be herrre at dawn," he said.

Nobody said anything for a long moment. "That's very soon," said Lani softly.

Then Florence spoke again, quieter this time. "Go to bed, all of you. Get a little rest. I'll have more news in a couple of hours."

They Meet Again

Thisbe and Drock took off speeding over the water. As the two went toward the Revinir, Thisbe told the dragon what she'd talked about with Aaron. When she finished, she said tentatively, "So, what do you think?"

"That's what I've been thinking too," said Drock. "The Revinir's most recent call gave me the idea. We should go with her and play it as though we are under her mind control. Then we'll see what we can do to break the connection between her and the others and get my family and your black-eyed friends to safety. And restore our land."

"Do you think you can . . . you know . . . kill her?" Thisbe cringed. In spite of everything, she still hated talking like that because of how much evil the Revinir had told her she possessed.

"If I can get close enough without other dragons around, I might be able to," said Drock. "She's smaller than me. Hopefully she hasn't gotten any stronger than when we saw her last."

"I'm afraid to find out," said Thisbe grimly. "She's probably continued guzzling the dragon-bone broth."

Drock was silent. He seemed to focus for a moment on a spot in the distance, and he sampled the air. His neck stiffened, and his scales shifted. "She knows we're coming," he said over his shoulder. "They're slowing down."

Thisbe swallowed hard. She couldn't see them in the dark, but her scales had been raised for quite some time. The only things she could see were pinpricks of burning lava coming from the Island of Fire, way off in the distance. "How far away?"

"Not far now." The dragon shivered and shook for a moment, then calmed down.

They talked through their plans to infiltrate the Revinir's operation. And how they'd each go for it if they had a chance

LISA McMANN

to take her out of commission. They discussed how to behave the right way so that the Revinir would be convinced they were under her spell. Even if that meant doing things they didn't want to do. Thisbe knew Drock would have a hard time with that, but he promised to do his best. However, that was the least of Thisbe's worries. She feared he wouldn't be able to withstand the Revinir's roar for much longer. Especially if he was right next to her. Maybe she'd stop roaring once Thisbe and Drock were with her—Thisbe could only hope.

After a time, flying over the sea, Drock began to slow down. Thisbe could see the shadows of dragons against the sky ahead. It made her feel very small and completely useless, and she crouched on Drock's back, hugging her knees and peering over his shoulder. She wondered seriously if they were making a huge mistake.

Drock landed on the sea and glided to a stop. With his head down, he floated on the water, waiting as the Revinir and her team of dragons circled overhead, observing them. Thisbe pinched a fold of Drock's skin in her hands, feeling like she was going to throw up. "Let's get this right," she whispered, going into character.

Drock's skin quivered, but he held steady.

The Revinir shouted in a terrible voice, "Who are you? Why have you come to meet me?"

Thisbe's insides screamed. The Revinir knew full well who they were. She was testing them to see if they were under her spell. She stayed silent and let Drock speak first.

"We've come to answer your call, Revinir," said Drock.

Thisbe slid to one side of Drock's back so the moonlight would strike her face. "We have come to work with you," she said.

The Revinir took in a sharp breath, and then she smiled evilly. "It's about time," she said. "You've wasted precious days for me." She eyed Thisbe with a look that turned the girl's stomach.

Thisbe tried her best to fix her gaze to be lifeless and appear like the other black-eyed slaves she'd seen. Complacent and obedient. Glassy-eyed. Monotone when speaking. Even as she did so, she attempted to see who was with the dragon-woman, but the moonlight was behind them, and all she could detect were a few shadows of small humans on the Revinir's back. There were three or four more on the backs of unidentified

LISA McMANN

dragons that were with her. If Drock could smell one of his siblings or his mother among them, he didn't let on.

"You will join me on my back now, Thisbe," ordered the Revinir. "We won't be going through this rigmarole again. There's no escaping."

"Yes, Revinir," said Thisbe, though everything inside her screamed to run away.

"Help her, Drock," the Revinir commanded. Obediently Drock unfurled his great purple wing and held it up for Thisbe to climb out on. The Revinir swooped low and hovered nearby, close enough for Thisbe to take a running jump. Despite her fears, Thisbe leaped and landed on the Revinir's back, her legs and arms splaying in all directions as a pair of hands reached out to help her stand. Thisbe, trying hard to maintain her glazed-eyed appearance, didn't get a good look at any of her new companions, here or on the accompanying dragons. She realized with a sinking heart that they weren't the old blue-uniformed soldiers that guarded the catacombs. They were probably the black-eyed slaves that Thisbe had once worked with. She faced forward, as they did, and then she couldn't see them at all.

The Revinir ordered Drock to take flight and join the other

dragons that circled, and Drock obeyed again, to Thisbe's relief. But what next? Would the Revinir be satisfied now that she had the two rogue ones? Would she turn back to Grimere? Or did she want to fight Artimé anyway?

The dragon-woman seemed to be thinking about that exact thing. As she and the dragons circled above the sea, and the black-eyed slaves sat as still as possible on their backs, Thisbe squeezed her eyes shut tight and prayed to whoever might listen. *Take us away from Artimé. Go back to Grimere.*

After the Revinir gazed long and hard toward Artimé, which was a visible little lump now that the sky was growing lighter, she turned her head to look closely at Thisbe, a suspicious expression on her face. Thisbe stared straight ahead, continuing to make her eyes as glassy as she could.

"What made you finally heed my call?" the Revinir asked accusingly. "Why didn't you come before?"

Thisbe stared, her mind whirring. What should she say? What would appease the woman? Did she suspect that Thisbe and Drock were playing her? Thisbe's heart pounded. Her hands grew clammy, and her throat became dry. Her mind was blank. Her answer would likely determine what the Revinir would do next, so it had to be a good one. She knew the Revinir. Knew that the woman was not only greedy, but she loved herself more than anything or anyone.

Thisbe cleared her throat. Then she said in a voice that sounded strange in her ears, "You finally became strong enough. I can no longer resist. And . . . I no longer want to. I am one with you."

The Revinir regarded the girl for a long moment, a smile creeping along one half of her dragonlike face. "You are my lucky one," the woman murmured. "You're my secret weapon. And you're worth ten times more than any other of these that stand with you. Together, Thisbe, we will conquer the world."

"Yes, Revinir," said Thisbe.

"But there is one more black-eyed child I must have. I'm sure you understand. And you will help me, won't you?"

Thisbe's lungs froze. She knew the Revinir must be talking about Rohan, though he, like her, hardly seemed like a child anymore, after everything they'd been through. Her throat felt like it had a big, sticky lump in it. "Yes," she said, as firmly and as loudly as she could.

"Good. We must have your sister with us. Where is she?"

Thisbe's muscles went weak. *Fifer?* She'd thought the Revinir had forgotten about her sister by now. Was she going to go to Artimé after all and ruin Thisbe's great sacrifice for her homeland? And . . . why didn't the Revinir say Rohan? Thisbe knew she valued him—according to her he was mostly good and worked very hard. It made more sense for her to want him than Fifer. Or had she already done something to him? The thought made her waver and her eyesight grow dim.

She fought through it, trying to breathe normally, and managed to squeak out a suspicious-sounding story, but it was the best she could come up with. "Fifer left yesterday for the Island of Fire. She used the volcano network to get back to your land. She . . ." Thisbe hesitated, then continued blindly, hoping she wasn't making a big mistake. "She's planning to fight and conquer you to return the land to the old rulers." She paused. When the Revinir didn't speak, she added, "We'll have to capture her there."

The Revinir seemed to believe Thisbe. And why wouldn't she? All the other black-eyed slaves told the dragon-woman painfully honest truths while they were under her control. Thisbe would never come willingly—nor would that

LISA McMANN

troublesome dragon, Drock, if their minds weren't being fully affected by her.

Thisbe blinked and continued with her dead stare, feeling cold sweat break out, like she might faint. The Revinir spent a painstaking moment studying her, then faced forward and ordered the fleet of dragons to abandon the mission of attack. "Return to Grimere!" she roared. "If we come across Fifer Stowe, capture her and bring her to me."

Thisbe stood steady, but her insides were collapsing. Everything had just gotten a thousand times more horrible. But at least they were turning away from Artimé. That was the main goal. Now . . . if only there were a way to tell Fifer to stay clear of Grimere forever.

As the party flew to the west and the sun rose behind them, Thisbe started to feel a little calmer. She'd gotten through the moment and had accomplished what she'd intended. And hopefully Simber or Spike or someone from Warbler would notice and be able to tell the people of Artimé and Quill that the Revinir was retreating. She'd bought them more time. She and Drock had succeeded. And Artimé would be functioning normally again in no time.

Thisbe relaxed her stance a little, and her faint feeling subsided. Exhaustion was hitting her hard now that the immediate stress had lessened and Artimé was safe. The people around her knelt on the Revinir's back to help keep their balance, so Thisbe knelt too, holding on to one of the many spikes that now adorned the Revinir's spine between her wings. Clearly the woman was continuing to take dragon-bone broth. Was she intending to fully become a dragon? Would she ever decide she was dragon enough?

With the Revinir focused ahead and the sunrise providing light, Thisbe slowly sat back. Carefully she glanced over her shoulder and confirmed that the people around her were black-eyed slaves. She recognized the glazed look of one fellow worker on the left—it was Prindi, the girl Thisbe had tried to talk to on her first day in the catacombs. Prindi didn't return her gaze. Thisbe faced forward again to make sure the Revinir was still focused on steering everyone toward Grimere, then turned to glance over her other shoulder. Her eyes widened. She took in a sharp breath and nearly clutched her throat but stopped herself from reacting just in time.

It was Rohan.

A Momentary Relief

They'rrre turrrning arrround!" Simber growled from the air above the mansion. He circled and flew down to Florence on the lawn. "They'rrre turrrning arrround! Something must have happened to stop them."

"Did you see anything? Anyone?" Florence asked anxiously.

"They'rrre too farrr away. I can only detect that they'rrre moving west now."

Florence's expression was steel-like, as if she wasn't quite ready to believe him. "Can you look again? I want to be completely sure."

Simber didn't argue—he almost couldn't believe his eyes

either. He took a running leap and flew up and around, going farther out to sea this time and hovering for a good long moment, eyes trained on the spot of movement heading back toward Warbler and the volcano island. The sky was brightening, which helped. He stared so long his eyes began to water. When he was certain beyond all doubt, he returned to the lawn. "They arrre definitely heading west," he said. "I'd bet my life on it."

Florence brought her hands to her forehead, her expression awash in relief. "I'm shocked," she said. "I really can't believe it. We're saved." She hesitated, then dropped her hands and said, "Do you want to alert the head mage? Or do you want me to do it?"

Simber's face turned pained. He didn't like asking anyone for favors. But he considered the task, finding such a simple thing exhausting. Frieda Stubbs was sucking the life out of him. "Will you do it forrr me?" he asked meekly.

"Of course. I'll do anything to help you. You know that."

"And I, you. Thank you, Florrrence. I . . . I rrreally apprrreciate it."

Florence flashed a sympathetic smile. "Any time." She

gave the cheetah's shoulder a reassuring pat, then went inside the mansion, where bleary-eyed mages were just starting to emerge, thinking they would soon be fighting.

"You can go back to your rooms," Florence announced. "We'll have an update soon." She went up the stairs and entered the family hallway to Frieda's room, feeling a tiny bit smug that Frieda wasn't magical enough to move her residence to the mostly secret hallway, and therefore wouldn't sully Alex's old place with her horribleness.

She rapped hard on the woman's door, putting a small dent in the wood.

There was a flurry of noise inside, and then the woman threw open the door. Her light brown hair was standing up in all directions, and she had bags under her eyes. She wore the head mage's robe.

Florence tried not to cringe at the sight of her.

"What is it?" said Frieda, as if she was annoyed to see her. "What do you want?"

"I have good news," said Florence evenly. "The Revinir and her party of dragons have turned back. We are no longer under threat of attack. We'll continue to monitor the situation, and I will keep you informed if anything changes."

Frieda's expression first registered relief, and then her eyes widened and a smile grew. "They must have found out that I'm the head mage now."

Florence frowned. "I . . . don't think that's the reason."

"Sure it is." Frieda's face brightened even more. "They discovered that I overthrew Aaron, and they grew scared. Why else would they turn back?"

Florence could think of a few explanations, but she could hardly stand being in Frieda's presence, so she didn't begin to list them. "I'll keep you informed," she said again, and turned to go. "You should put out a statement on the blackboards letting everyone know that they can relax. Do you need me to help you write it?"

"Of course not," said Frieda. "I'm not a baby." She closed the door.

Florence sighed in disgust. She went back down to the main floor of the mansion and outside to let Simber know that the job was done.

When she returned inside, a small group of dissenters had gathered by the dining room blackboard and were reading the statement from the head mage. Florence stopped to read it as well.

Attention, people of Artimé! This is your head mage, Frieda Stubbs. I have defeated the Revinir, and she will not be returning to our shores ever again, as long as the Stowes are banished and I am head mage. I accept your thanks for taking charge of the situation and keeping everyone safe. If Aaron Stowe had been in power, this most certainly wouldn't have happened! Now we have peace! And no one trying to turn us into a bad place anymore! I will hold a celebratory reception for myself and my supporters on the lawn this afternoon. If you still like Aaron, don't come. He is gone forever too, by the way.

—Frieda Stubbs, Head Mage of Artimé

Florence closed her eyes as a wave of defeat and depression washed over her. This was going to be a long road. And she wasn't sure she was up for the challenge.

Feeling Lost

S ky sat at the fire on the shore of the Island of Legends with Aaron, Fifer, Ibrahim, and Clementi. Lhasa lounged behind them silently, inches above the ground, wanting to be supportive and respectful of their problems. Soon Talon flew down from his lookout on the top of the tallest tree in the middle of the forest, near Vido the golden rooster, to give them an update.

"The Revinir has turned back," Talon said.

Aaron, who'd told everyone by now what Thisbe and Drock had done, looked up with a mixture of fear and relief on his face. "Really? Are you sure? The plan succeeded?"

LISA McMANN

"Yes. Thisbe and Drock met them. They stayed still for a while. Then the entire group turned around and began heading back toward the gorge."

"Amazing." Aaron dropped his head heavily into his hands. "I hope Thisbe's okay. I fear . . ." He still wasn't convinced that this was the best thing to do. They'd lost Thisbe once—had they just lost her again? Time would tell if the sacrifice had been worth it. "At least Artimé is safe for now."

Fifer was glad the Revinir had turned back, but she was also hurt. Thisbe had gone off without her while she'd been sleeping—she hadn't mentioned one word about it, or even woken her up to say good-bye. It seemed typical of late, but that didn't make it sting any less. The twins used to go everywhere together, and Fifer couldn't help but think about that. Obviously, Fifer, like everyone else, hoped Thisbe would be okay. But she couldn't push the hurt feelings away, especially when she found out that Aaron had learned about Thisbe's plan. Did Thisbe trust him over her now? Had he become her number one ally? Was Fifer's importance in the family dwindling too?

"I don't think the Revinir will hurt Thisbe," said Clementi.

"That wouldn't make sense. Thisbe wasn't being a threat to her, and why would she come all the way out here just to put an end to someone who wasn't bothering her? I think Thisbe's plan is genius. I wish I'd thought of it."

Fifer wrinkled her nose.

"It was definitely smart," Ibrahim said to Clementi. "But dangerous. The Revinir wants to use her to further her purposes in Grimere. I just hope Thisbe doesn't have to do anything too horrible before she sees a way for us to come and help."

"I also hope Drock is okay," Aaron said. "Let's not forget he made a big sacrifice too."

Everyone nodded. It was easier to think Drock could hold his own against a dragon-woman than Thisbe could, so they weren't quite as worried about him.

"Thisbe is very powerful," Sky reminded everyone, including herself. "Especially now that she has Artimé's magic components and has been trained—it'll be an entirely different situation for her than before. She'll fight back if and when she needs to. I was shocked to hear what she did, but after thinking about it, I believe it was the smartest and most generous thing any of us could have done. She saved us."

Fifer remained silent and frowning. She glanced back at Artimé and could make out Simber flying over the sea, no doubt realizing that the Revinir was retreating. All thanks to Thisbe. "I miss Simber," she said with a sigh. "I hope Frieda Stubbs isn't being too horrible to him."

"He'll be fine," said Aaron gruffly. He still wasn't sure he'd done the right thing. But at least here on Karkinos, Aaron had fewer distractions and more time to develop magic that would be potent against the Revinir while they waited for Thisbe to summon them. "Let's hope that now that some of the pressure's off, we'll be able to create some effective magic. This is far from over."

"I'm worried about Thisbe," Ibrahim said. "I wish we'd known what she was doing so we could have loaded her up with extra components."

"Her pockets were full," Aaron told them. "She left her vest here, though, because she knew the Revinir would recognize what it was and confiscate it."

"That was smart," Fifer admitted. At least Thisbe was making good decisions.

"Wouldn't it be great if Thisbe could actually figure out

how to break the Revinir's spell?" said Sky. "I wonder if she can somehow reach your other black-eyed friend—what's his name again?"

"Dev," said Fifer. "I doubt it. He wouldn't listen to me."

"But those two worked so closely in the catacombs," said Sky. "Maybe he'll recognize her and listen."

"I worked closely with him too," said Fifer, a bit stiffly.

Sky glanced at Fifer. "Oh, that's right," she said apologetically. "I forgot that part of your story. So much has happened."

Fifer softened. "It's okay. I hope Thisbe can do something to snap Dev out of it too. I just . . . I doubt it." She sniffed, wanting desperately to stop talking about how amazing Thisbe was and feeling bad at the same time for it. "By the way, how are we supposed to go help Thisbe when she gets around to calling for us? We don't have any dragons left to fly us."

Aaron looked up. "I assumed we'd take Spike and Simber and your birds to the Island of Fire and travel through the volcanos."

"Oh," said Fifer. "That makes sense, I guess." She hesitated, feeling weird about everything. "Well, let's get back to work, then. Are we, uh . . . What are we doing, exactly? Should we go back to Artimé now that the threat is gone?"

Aaron and Sky exchanged a glance, then looked at Talon, who'd been there most recently. "What do you think?" Aaron asked him.

"From the mood of the mansion last night," said Talon, "none of the Stowes are safe there anymore. The line has been drawn. As for the others, by coming here and declaring your loyalty to the Stowes, I'm afraid you are on the wrong side of that line."

A Blank Stare

Thisbe's heart sank at the sight of Rohan. His face was expressionless, and his eyes were dead and completely void of the mirth and compassion that used to be there. Clearly he was under the Revinir's control. But how had this happened? How had the Revinir gotten to him? The last thing Thisbe knew was that Rohan and Maiven Taveer had found her family's abandoned house in Grimere and were going to use it as their secret headquarters to figure out how to fight the Revinir. Apparently some part of their plan had gone terribly wrong.

Had the Revinir forced Rohan to drink the dragon-bone

broth? She must have, or he wouldn't be acting like this. Thisbe didn't dare risk another cursory glance at the other dragons around them to see if Maiven was one of those riders, but when the group of dragons shifted leader positions, Thisbe saw that the old woman wasn't anywhere among them.

Dev wasn't there either. Fear sliced through Thisbe—had he been one of the soldiers to fall to his death in the palace battle? What else could it mean that he wasn't here, when there were six or seven other black-eyed soldiers present? Didn't the Revinir keep them all close now, like she'd done in the castle back when it was on fire and the ghost dragons were circling? Thisbe ached to move, but she didn't do it. She had to stare forward like the others, or the Revinir might notice. Even if the dragon-woman couldn't see Thisbe, the girl was sure she could feel the slightest movement on her back that could give her away. But it was hard to remain like this when everything was so horrible. She hadn't expected to see Rohan anywhere near this operation. In fact, she'd thought that Maiven's house could be a good refuge for her when it came time to get away. Numbly she kept her position and continued acting like the others.

As they traveled, Thisbe barely registered the height to

which the Revinir rose above the water, so she forgot to be afraid of it. Instead her head spun with questions that might never be answered. Would she be able to communicate with the others when they were so deeply controlled? If she did try to talk to them, would they report that to the Revinir? Was there any way for her to talk to Rohan, and would he even know who she was? Would he remember their time together? Would he be the same as before in any way? The fear of Rohan not knowing her was making Thisbe feel sick to her stomach. She wasn't sure how she'd handle it.

And where was Dev? Where was Maiven? What had happened? All these unanswered questions were about to kill her.

As they flew over Warbler, the Revinir ordered three of her dragons to fly low and pepper her old island with a spray of fiery breath, lighting up trees and the shipyard and sending people running and diving for the underground tunnels there. Appalled by the cowardly act, Thisbe tried not to react, but again, it was hard. Sky's mother was the ruler there, and Thisbe knew others on that island too, like her friend Phoenix, who worked as Copper's assistant. They could be hurt! Thisbe hoped they were safe.

Thankfully, the Revinir urged everyone to continue on after that. Things went along more quietly in the hours before they passed by the Island of Fire. Thisbe thought she saw a big flash of white and blue in the sea and wondered if it was Spike Furious twisting in the water. It made her heart ache. She was leaving all of her friends and family behind again. But that wasn't even the hardest part. It was more the fact that the place she was headed was in such turmoil. And the people she was going back to—and with—were compromised.

Thisbe's heart kept sinking as she thought about what would come next. How was she supposed to break this blasted Revinir mind control spell and free her people? Especially without Rohan's assistance. He was the one who'd so nobly stayed back to help save his people. Thisbe wanted to carry through with that plan, but she hadn't expected to do it alone. Was it possible that she could find Maiven? That question led to another: Would Thisbe be free to roam in Grimere now that the Revinir was in charge and she was supposedly under her mind control? Or would she be confined to the castle or stationed as a soldier somewhere? She wondered how hard it would be to move around and do what she needed to do to find Maiven. Whatever

LISA McMANN

the situation was now, Thisbe knew that things would be different from last time . . . she just wasn't sure how.

Exhausted from being up all night, Thisbe kept nodding off, but she wasn't sure how to go about actually sleeping—did the others ever sleep? She hadn't thought about that part of things before. What if they no longer needed it for some reason? But that sounded absurd. They were still human. Even the Revinir slept sometimes—or at least Thisbe assumed so.

But she didn't dare lie down. Instead she hung on to the Revinir's spikes so she wouldn't accidentally tumble off, and focused on examining the rows and rows of the dragon-woman's thick scales to see if there was any sign of weakness. Or any sparse spot where Thisbe could send off sparks that would actually penetrate the skin.

Soon Thisbe's heavy lids closed, and she slumped over, unable to stay awake any longer.

When she woke many hours later, night was falling. All Thisbe could see was water. The gorge wasn't yet in sight. Once she remembered where she was and what she was doing, she fixed her expression and slowly sat up and faced forward. As she moved, she noticed that a couple of the black-eyed slaves on the other dragons were lying down, and she felt better about having taken a nap. It seemed normal after all. That was a relief—learning how to act was tiring and stressful.

Drock was flying off to Thisbe's right. Though Thisbe couldn't see him directly, he seemed to be doing all right and wasn't making any outbursts or defying the Revinir, so that was good. Thisbe didn't know any of these other dragons, and she wondered what would happen with them if Thisbe were able to break the Revinir's spell. They were complacent now, but would they turn on her and attack once they regained control of their minds? Pan and Arabis and the others from their world were safe enough, but these strangers were unpredictable and frightening. This wasn't just a quest to take the Revinir out of power. It was a quest to restore a world to its rightful ruling body. But what if the rightful ruling dragons no longer wanted to share the land with the black-eyed people? What if they just wanted to tear them to shreds or eat them for dinner?

Everything Thisbe was doing was such a big risk. And she was completely alone, except for Drock, in her attempt to stop a ruler who was more dragon than woman these days. How long could she last against those odds?

As bleak reality set in, Thisbe grew more and more anxious about her situation. She was still glad she'd done it—it had worked, and Artimé was saved. But now what?

More of the black-eyed soldiers lay down on their dragons to rest for the night. Though she wasn't tired anymore, Thisbe lay down too, placing her head so that she could see Rohan. Perhaps, if she watched him long enough, he'd look her way. Perhaps there would be some recognition in his eyes. Perhaps all of this was just a horrible nightmare, and her dearest, deepest friend wasn't really under the Revinir's spell after all. Perhaps.

Darkness consumed them. Thisbe kept her eye on Rohan, though she couldn't see him very well. When he shifted, she chanced to lift her head and peer at him through the darkness. But his eyes didn't connect with hers.

LISA McMANN

A Bad Situation

laire Morning arrived in Artimé, having come as soon as the Necessary asked her to. Along the way she'd learned from passersby that Artimé's head mage, Aaron, had handed over his robe to the chief dissenter, Frieda Stubbs. It was hard to believe.

Claire found Florence and Simber on the lawn, arguing in hushed voices. Frieda Stubbs was standing in the doorway of the mansion surrounded by her new fans. A semicircle of protestors calling for Aaron's return to power was around them.

"What's happening?" Claire demanded, coming up to Florence and Simber.

Florence turned and saw who it was. "Oh, Claire. Thank goodness you're here."

"Samheed sent for me. What's going on?"

"Frieda Stubbs has taken over as head mage, and everything is bedlam around here."

"So the rumors are true." Claire took a breath and blew it out. "And what about the Revinir?"

"She's retreated, thankfully."

"Frrrieda is taking crrredit forrr that," said Simber with disgust.

"She didn't do anything," Florence told Claire, and her voice turned worried. "I haven't had a chance to find out why the Revinir turned back, but I have my guesses." She didn't say what it was that she feared.

"Where's Aaron?" asked Claire.

"On Karrrkinos," said Simber. "The girrrls arrre therrre too."

"We think," muttered Florence, looking out to the west. There was nothing to see but waves and an outline of the island.

"You should have stopped this," Simber snapped.

Florence narrowed her eyes and stared down her lifelong friend. "There was nothing I could do, and you know it."

227 « Dragon Curse

LISA McMANN

Simber growled low and long, but he didn't argue further.

In all her years in Artimé, Claire had never seen Florence and Simber disagree so heatedly before. It was unsettling. "What can I do?"

Florence glanced over her shoulder at Frieda Stubbs in the doorway, then back at Claire. "The dissenters wanted you as head mage after Alex died. Perhaps . . . if you're willing . . . for a little while, at least . . ."

Claire understood. She nodded. "Of course. Temporarily, I mean. Until things get sorted out."

"It won't worrrk," Simber muttered.

"Simber, please," said Florence, exasperated. "We have to try. And I really don't need your negativity right now."

Simber glared at Florence. "My life has changed disastrr- rously," he said. "I'm sorrry you don't like how I'm rrreacting to that." He sniffed, then loped toward the back entrance of the mansion without another word.

Florence sighed. "He's having a terrible time with her."

Claire nodded. "I'm happy to do anything to cheer Simber up—if he's not happy, no one is."

Florence gave a sardonic laugh. "You've got that right."

She turned toward the spectacle at the entrance. "Let's go talk to them. Tell them you're interested in the job, just like they wanted. I believe they'll be for it."

Claire eyed the group, trying to assess the situation. "Do you think the Aaron supporters will object?"

"Not at all," said Florence. "They'd be very supportive of you too. They just want Stubbs out before she wrecks everything."

"I see." Claire straightened her shirt and smoothed her component vest, then let out a resigned sigh. "Okay, let's go."

They walked over to where Frieda Stubbs was speaking to her people. "Artimé is safe now," she was saying loudly. "The Revinir has been banished forever. What Aaron Stowe couldn't do, I did." Cheers erupted.

Frieda Stubbs smiled and bowed ever so slightly, as if she were feeling a little bit humbled by the praise, though everyone knew she was anything but humble and was probably doing it for show.

"She must've been an acting student," Claire whispered to Florence.

"Right on," Florence replied.

Frieda noticed them coming. She froze for a microsecond, then smiled demurely. "Look who it is!" she said. "Has Quill

LISA McMANN

heard about my success already?" She laughed and tried to appear modest. "Word spreads so fast."

Others turned and seemed pleased to see Claire. They knew her, had been taught by her, and trusted her—Mr. Today's daughter was the next best thing to the original mage himself. They parted, making a path to Frieda. The Aaron supporters stopped chanting for his return and watched what was happening, looking a bit hopeful to see the woman. Everyone loved Claire Morning. Perhaps she was the solution to all of the unrest in Artimé.

"Hello, everybody," said Claire. "It's so good to see you all again, though I'm sad about the circumstances. And I'm surprised and troubled by the way people have been acting around here. That doesn't seem quite like us, does it?"

A few of the dissenters looked down sheepishly. Others' faces hardened slightly, as if they didn't really need or want a lecture.

"I've banished the Revinir," said Frieda. "Did you hear?"

"I heard she retreated," said Claire. "That's wonderful news for our island."

"She must have learned of my takeover," said Frieda.

The protesters who supported Aaron's return murmured angrily.

Claire tilted her head and narrowed her eyes. "Really? You think *that's* what did it?"

Frieda's smile didn't crack. "I'm certain of it," she said coolly.

Florence stepped in. "I'm sure you are all delighted to see our wonderful Claire Morning back in Artimé. And we have some exciting news. Remember when you all wanted Claire to take over as head mage?"

Several people from both groups gasped excitedly in anticipation.

"Well," Florence continued, "Claire has agreed to step in and take over. Isn't that wonderful?"

More than half the people gathered outside cheered. Others talked excitedly. And others seemed hesitant but positive. Claire grinned and nodded. "It's true," she said.

Frieda's expression was far from positive.

"Is this what you all would like?" asked Florence in her most encouraging voice.

"Yes!" shouted a large contingent. "Claire Morning! Head

LISA McMANN

mage!" shouted one, and then others chimed in. The two opposing groups began to merge, unifying over what seemed like the perfect fit. The ones who loved Aaron were just as happy with Claire, and the ones who supported Frieda had been desperate to have Claire lead them from the time she was trying to restore the world after Alex's death. It was a perfect solution.

Claire put her hands in the air, laughing and trying to quiet them so she could speak. "Okay, okay," she said. "What has to happen here to make it official?"

Florence turned to Frieda, who still wasn't smiling or speaking. "It's a simple procedure," said Florence. "Frieda, just hand over the robe to Claire and declare her the new head mage, and the magic will transfer. And all will be good in the world again."

Frieda stood in stony silence. She surveyed the people gathered there. There were many who had been praising her just minutes ago. Only a few close friends had joined her in her silent protest. She looked from face to face in the crowd, and then came around to Claire again. "You said a few months ago that you didn't want to be head mage. That's why you gave it to that terrible person, Aaron Stowe."

Claire's warm smile stiffened. "I changed my mind," she said.

The crowd quieted and looked at one another uneasily. A few of them in the back started chanting, "We want Claire! We want Claire!"

Florence hushed them with a look, then turned back to Frieda. "Just hand her the robe," Florence said again. "And say something that implies she's the head mage now."

Frieda crossed her arms over her chest. "I don't trust people who change their minds," she said. "Besides, I'm the one who ended the threat from the Revinir, not her. I think it's pretty clear who the natural leader is here."

The crowd shifted uneasily. A few of the dissenters weighed their leader's words and came back to Frieda's side, now that they knew she wanted to stay.

"Frieda," said Claire, trying a new tactic, "we're all so grateful for the work you've done during this transition. Thank you. You definitely . . . played a part in . . . well, everything. But it's best if the head mage is someone with leadership experience. And has an understanding of the inner workings of Artimé. And . . . is an expert at our magic. I think . . . I think we are all glad that the Revinir retreated, whatever her reason for doing so, and your part in that. But now that things have calmed

LISA McMANN

down, it's best to go forward with someone more . . . suited . . . for the job." She stretched out her hand authoritatively, waiting for Frieda to give her Aaron's robe.

Frieda Stubbs stared back at Claire. Then she snorted and turned in the doorway. "No," she said, looking back at the crowd. "I won't do it. *I'm* the best suited. Artimé is mine now." She took a step inside, then shouted in a most annoying voice, "Simber!" She turned and retreated up the staircase to her room.

A few people followed her. The rest stood in stunned silence, staring after her through the open door. Seconds later the place erupted into bedlam again. Simber gave Florence a nasty look, then followed the head mage.

Claire dropped her arm to her side and looked at Florence. "What just happened?"

Florence stared back. "I'm not sure," she said, shaking her head slightly. "I think . . . I think we've just experienced a coup d'état."

A Touch and a Whisper

The Revinir and her grand party of mind-controlled dragons and slaves made it back to Grimere, arriving to much fanfare from those on the ground. Dragons of all species lined the road that led up the hill to the castle. They bowed to the Revinir as she and her group soared between them.

Hundreds of the former king's green-uniformed soldiers were hard at work on the castle and surrounding grounds, building a new drawbridge and repairing the entry and turrets, which had been partially destroyed by fire and dragons fighting. Thisbe resisted the urge to gawk at the ridiculousness of it all and instead played her part, acting like the others. The Revinir soared into the charred grand entrance to the castle, while the other dragons landed outside and let their passengers off to walk in. Thisbe didn't dare look back at Drock. She could only pray that he would behave according to their plan and manage to continue resisting the Revinir's call. She wasn't sure when she'd see him again.

As the Revinir landed in the huge entry room, Thisbe noticed that the gilded tigers, which had once belonged to Princess Shanti, were gone. In their place were a few soldiers in blue uniforms. Thisbe recognized them from the catacombs. She saw them point at her. Her cheeks burned at the pleased looks on their faces.

But Thisbe stayed seated like the others. She didn't move, though her body ached from the journey. She longed to get off the Revinir's back and look at Rohan. To talk to him. To try to wake him up and make him recognize her. But she knew she had to wait, especially now. She struggled not to give the soldiers nasty looks as they informed others nearby that the Revinir had captured her.

"It didn't take long to capture that one," said one soldier.

"My powers have grown," boasted the Revinir. "She and Drock came right to me once we grew close enough." She chuckled, though it sounded more like a deep rattle in her chest.

"What about the twin?"

"Have you seen her around?" asked the Revinir. "Apparently she's somewhere in our land, planning to attack me."

"No sign of her," said the soldier, looking alarmed.

"No doubt hiding in the forest as usual," said the Revinir. "I'll have Thisbe working up some broth again in no time so that when Fifer emerges, we'll be able to get her. Surely she'll accept anything Thisbe cooks for her." She turned her head slightly. "Everyone, disembark."

Thisbe's stomach churned, and she fought to keep her expression steady as she got down off the Revinir's back. As much as she and Fifer had been at odds lately, there was no way Thisbe would have any part in feeding her sister the dragon-bone broth. And the thought of being put back to work in the Revinir's kitchen made Thisbe want to run away screaming. She hadn't expected to continue that line of work now that the Revinir had taken over the castle! But clearly not everything

LISA McMANN

had changed with the Revinir's operations. Thisbe realized the dragon-woman would still be in need of broth to feed her own personal greed, as well as to control the people who reported to her.

That number appeared to be growing, too. Thisbe thought back to when she was first making the dragon-bone broth, and how Dev had spent a day selling it in Dragonsmarche. With a start, Thisbe realized that anyone who'd drunk it would also be affected by the Revinir's roar—it wasn't like the ancestor broth, which only affected the black-eyed people. The dragon-bone broth's magical properties worked on anyone. Was that why so many people seemed to be calmly working in the castle without anyone forcing them or overseeing their work? Had the Revinir made the king's green army drink the broth too?

"Go to your rooms, children," the Revinir said. "Back to work tomorrow."

Thisbe wasn't sure where to go. Did the black-eyed slave soldiers have rooms in the castle now? To her great dismay, Rohan and Prindi and the others turned obediently toward the ramp that led to the dungeon and filed down it. Were they being held down there now? How horrible! Thisbe went with them, uncertain if it would be unusual for her to ask the dragon-woman what she was supposed to be doing.

The Revinir offered no instruction and didn't accompany them down. When they reached the bottom, the soldiers stationed there saw who they were. Instead of ushering them to the cells, they opened the door that led to the catacombs. With a sinking heart, Thisbe filed past the empty dragon stalls and through the doorway, and followed the others into the underground maze, knowing that unless something had changed, they had an extremely long walk to their crypts, which would give them little opportunity to rest before morning. Why would the Revinir be so awful, making them walk when she could have had a dragon take them to the elevator entrance in far less time? It was a power game. The Revinir had all of it, and the black-eyed slaves were at her mercy. Thisbe was sure the dragon-woman enjoyed every moment, knowing the slaves had no choice but to obey.

"You might want to walk fast so you can get to your crypts before the workday begins," said one of the castle soldiers unhelpfully. Then he slammed the door shut behind them and turned the lock, leaving Thisbe and the six others seemingly alone in the catacombs.

They started jogging. There were no blue-uniformed soldiers in sight as far as Thisbe could see, which seemed strange compared to how it used to be. But if all the slaves were under the Revinir's mind control, it made sense that she didn't need as many soldiers controlling them. Thisbe's pulse quickened. Last in line, she glanced behind her, seeing the backs of the adult soldiers' heads through the small window in the door.

Now what? Thisbe wondered. Should she try to engage Rohan and the other slaves? Would they just stare blankly at her? Or would they report her for suspicious behavior? Thisbe didn't know enough about how the spell affected them, and she didn't dare risk blowing her cover until she had it figured out.

She had plenty of time to think about it on the long journey to their crypts. None of the others spoke. They jogged until they couldn't keep up the pace, then slowed to a speed walk. Now and then they passed a few soldiers stationed at the intersections. They didn't seem like they had anything to do now that the slaves were no longer an escape risk, and barely looked at them. That was the first encouraging sign Thisbe took from the experience. She'd be less scrutinized. That was never a bad thing.

Halfway through they took a break to rest. Thisbe was careful not to look at Rohan or any others too closely, even though she was dying to study them and ask a few questions. But she was deathly worried about the Revinir finding out—it would ruin everything if she were even the least bit suspicious. Thisbe had made it this far under scrutiny, and she still had her components. There were fewer soldiers down here than before, so that offered her some hope. She'd have to ride on those positives for a while until she had a better grasp on how to get information safely.

When they got up, Thisbe repositioned herself so she was behind Rohan. Seeing him offered her a slight bit of comfort. But along with it came an unidentifiable ache that was marginally akin to how she felt about Alex's death—grief and loss, mixed with tremendous guilt. Obviously Rohan wasn't dead, so that made the comparison weak. But if Rohan couldn't recognize her after all they'd been through, didn't that sort of make him dead to her, in a way? Could Thisbe have done something to prevent this? Was there anything she could do now to snap

LISA McMANN

241 « Dragon Curse

him and the others out of it? And she still wondered where Maiven was. Did she know Rohan was down here? Was she doing anything about it? Or had she been captured too and put back in her dungeon cell?

As they came upon the first hallway containing a slave crypt, one of their group peeled off from the others and went down it toward the open door. Not long after, Mangrel, the crypt keeper, rounded a corner and came upon them, apparently having received word of their arrival and preparing to lock them into their rooms until it was time to wake them up.

When Mangrel caught sight of Thisbe, his expression changed. "They got you, too," he murmured, and shook his head slightly.

Thisbe's eyes widened, but luckily Mangrel had turned and didn't see it. Had he seemed disappointed about Thisbe's recapture? As if he'd hoped Thisbe had actually escaped for good? It couldn't be. Though Mangrel was not one of the Revinir's soldiers, and perhaps had shown an ounce or two of kindness in the past, he'd always seemed to support the dragon-woman. Perhaps she'd finally gotten too horrible, and Mangrel had changed loyalties. Thisbe was determined to find out.

The man locked up the first slave, then returned and led the tired group to each crypt, securing them inside. Finally only Rohan and Thisbe remained. Thisbe sped up slightly so she could walk side by side with Rohan. And despite his vacant stare, her skin tingled being near him. She wanted desperately to take his hand, to look into his eyes and wake him up. To talk to him like they'd done so many times before. But even when she dared to steal a glance his way, he stared glassy-eyed at Mangrel's back. Thisbe knew that any sort of familiarity she expressed might only be met with confusion, so of course she didn't do those things. It was so sad and strange to have her best friend not know her.

Just as they came to Rohan's hallway, Thisbe stopped obediently like she and the others had done each time. As Mangrel and Rohan turned off to go to Rohan's crypt, Rohan's pinkie brushed Thisbe's. And she thought she heard something. She froze and looked up. Had he done that on purpose? And had his lips twitched the slightest bit just now? Had his eyes focused on her for a split second? Had he . . . Had he whispered something to her?

But no. Rohan didn't look back. Feeling delirious, Thisbe stayed still and waited as Mangrel locked Rohan inside. When

Mangrel returned, she followed him to the next passageway to her crypt, which backed up to Rohan's. With a surge of hope, she remembered the tunnel she'd created between their rooms.

But just as suddenly the hope faded, for she knew full well that the Revinir was aware of the tunnel. And she most certainly must have filled it in by now, unless she trusted the mind-controlled slaves so much that she didn't think any harm could come of them intermingling—after all, wouldn't they just go tell her everything truthfully? But Thisbe also knew that the Revinir didn't trust anyone so blindly. Her shoulders slumped. Thisbe walked into her old familiar space with its old familiar smells and memories and felt a sense of dread come over her. Before she turned to watch Mangrel close the door in her face, she glanced up the huge pile of dragon bones that led all the way to the back wall. The tunnel to Rohan's crypt, which she'd created by using her explosive magic, wasn't visible anymore. In fact, the entire back wall was now covered with a thick plate of gold. That would surely keep Thisbe from getting to Rohan again.

"Get some sleep," Mangrel said gruffly. He hesitated, then fished a piece of hard bread from his pocket and set it inside the door before closing it. It was almost endearing.

Thisbe picked up the bread and sat down, her feet aching. She stared at the new back wall and gnawed at the bread. A few minutes later she was surprised to hear her door opening again. Without a word, Mangrel's wrinkled face and wispy hair appeared low to the ground as he slid a pitcher of water inside. The door closed again.

Fighting sleep, Thisbe kept staring at the back wall, trying to remember exactly where the tunnel had been. Wondering if the hole was still there, behind the metal, or if it had been filled in.

As she contemplated, her eyes began to close. But her thirst was great. She moved heavily over to the pitcher and drank. Then she climbed up the bone mountain and grabbed a small bone at the top. She tapped lightly along the gold wall to see if she could hear a difference from one spot to another. Perhaps there would be a hollow sound if she found the spot she needed.

But everything sounded the same. After a few moments, Thisbe concluded that the tunnel must have been filled in, making her job even more impossible.

She set down the bone. As she prepared to slide down to her sleeping area, a familiar sound met her ears: three distinct knocks from the other side of the back wall.

Old Familiar

Thisbe turned with a start. It couldn't be Rohan tapping the wall like old times, could it? But what else could it be? Three taps—that was their signal. Though she'd never mentioned it to Rohan, in her heart his three taps stood for words. "How are you?" Or even "I miss you." She blushed furiously and picked up the dragon bone again. She tapped the gold wall four times in response. "Oh, Rohan," she whispered. "I miss you, too. Please come back to me."

Having her dearest friend so close yet unable to recognize her was already terribly difficult. Knowing who he'd been before he was under the Revinir's spell made it all the harder to see him like this. Like a shell that the real Rohan had abandoned. Had their bond somehow brought him back? For a moment, at least?

Thisbe strained to listen. Then two taps came, and this time Thisbe was certain beyond a doubt that somehow Rohan was doing it. She tapped twice in response. "Good night." And then she slumped, barely able to stand there. All sorts of emotions churned and poured out of her, leaving her body feeling utterly broken and exhausted.

She had to rest or she'd never be able to pull off her glassy-eyed ruse without messing up. Hopefully there would be time to figure out how to get through the back wall tomorrow. But for now . . . she waited.

There were no more knocks. Still, Thisbe stayed another minute before finally sliding down the bone pile. At the bottom she curled up with the thin blanket and tried not to think about how this very room had seen some other harsh action too, after she'd escaped. Alex had died here, not far from the spot where Thisbe lay. Trying to find and rescue *her*. There was perhaps nothing more horrible than imagining what Alex might have looked like, dead on the floor in this lonely, forsaken place.

Thisbe fell asleep with those pictures in her mind and woke up disoriented and still thinking of them a few hours later. The sound of the door lock turning brought her back immediately, and she sat up, then scrambled for her pitcher of water so she could drain the rest of it before Mangrel could take it away.

He stepped back in surprise.

Thisbe froze, then moved deliberately to sit down and fixed her vacant stare.

Mangrel studied her suspiciously, then set a tray of food on the floor at her feet. She took a slow bite of food, pretending that she hadn't just lunged for the pitcher of water. After a long moment, Mangrel stepped out. "I'll come back for the tray," he said, his voice measured. "The Revinir wants you to report to the kitchen to make dragon-bone broth. She said you'd know what to do."

Thisbe nodded slightly. "Yes, Mangrel," she said in a monotone voice, and put another spoonful of something disgusting into her mouth. It was better than nothing. Slightly.

Seemingly satisfied, Mangrel left. Thisbe sank against the wall in relief. Then she hurriedly choked down the rest of the food and water and set out into the hallway, heading to the kitchen. She slowed when she went past Rohan's hallway, but he wasn't anywhere around that she could see while still maintaining her low-key glassy-eyed stare.

She thought about last night. Had she imagined the knock exchange? She'd been delirious with exhaustion. And Rohan hadn't recognized her at all on the entire journey—even the accidental pinkie-brushing was hardly evidence of anything. How would he have known to do the knocking, especially when he was in a trance like everyone else? Maybe she'd just wished it so much that she'd only thought she'd heard it.

By the time she reached the passageway that led to the kitchen, Thisbe had concluded that she'd imagined the interaction with Rohan from the middle of the night and chalked it up to exhaustion and weird dreams about being back here. Once she entered the warm, smelly kitchen, she immediately forgot all about Rohan. Because standing with his back to her, stirring a cauldron of bone broth, was Dev.

Thisbe abandoned her role momentarily. "Dev!" she cried, then slapped her hand over her mouth and whirled around to make sure nobody was around, especially the Revinir. But the throne room off the kitchen was empty, and there was no one else about either.

Dev turned slowly.

"You're alive!" Thisbe said softly. Tears threatened to brim over. It was a great relief to see him.

Dev stared blankly. His eyes looked dead. Thisbe could see he was even more covered in scales than before.

"Oh, Dev," Thisbe whispered, walking toward him. It was a reckless move, trying to engage him—he could report her. But she couldn't help herself.

He turned away, continuing to stir. "The bones are there," he said, and pointed out the obvious pile of dragon bones behind him.

"Dev, please look at me," Thisbe whispered. She glanced over her shoulder anxiously, then reached out to him. "It's me. Thisbe. I'm your friend."

Dev was quiet, making Thisbe wonder if she was actually getting through to him or if the spell he was under was making him not know how to have a conversation. She feared the latter.

"The bones," said Dev again, though his voice faltered. He pointed a second time.

A couple of the Revinir's original soldiers came into the room. "Ha-ha! I heard she was back," one said with a sharp edge to his voice. He poked the other guy.

The other one was unimpressed—she'd gotten past him in her escape with Rohan, which had made him look bad. He sneered at Thisbe. "Don't try anything stupid."

Thisbe really wanted to practice her boom spell on him. But that would blow her cover and keep her from freeing Rohan and the others. She wasn't ready to make any hasty moves. She needed to learn a lot more about how things worked before going into attack mode, and figure out some way to get at least a couple of the other slaves to help her free the rest of them. In the meantime she needed to raise zero doubts in anybody's mind about her being under the Revinir's mind control. This wasn't going to be easy when she was regularly interrupted by people she couldn't stand.

Dev wasn't one of those people, though. How she wished she could talk to him! To get him to snap out of it! She wanted to know everything about what the Revinir had accomplished in the months since her escape. And what she was trying to do next. And at the back of her mind was the worry about

Fifer. How far would the dragon-woman go to track her down? Would she go all the way back to Artimé if Fifer didn't appear locally like Thisbe had said she would?

As Thisbe began constructing a dragon-bone broth on her fire, she sent out silent wishes to the universe: *Please let Aaron and Florence and the others figure out some new spells to take down the Revinir. Please let them be safe. Please make the Revinir forget about Fifer. Please.*

The soldiers moved on to continue their rounds, leaving Dev and Thisbe alone together like old times. But now it was awful. Thisbe tried talking to him again, but he just kept his back turned to her and ignored her. Soon Thisbe gave up, too worried about him reporting her.

It was sad. Dev wasn't anything close to the boy Thisbe had gotten to know so well in their time together down here. He no longer had any personality. And no emotions—that was the hardest part for Thisbe to get used to. The old Dev had been anything but dull. He'd been sullen, or angry, or generous, or torrentially sobbing in Thisbe's presence. There was always something going on with him. But now, like with Rohan, he was a cardboard cutout. An unfeeling puppet without a hand to guide it, who merely resembled Thisbe's old friend. It was so draining just being near someone like that. And it seemed hopeless to try to get through to him.

Thisbe didn't have power like that—the power to break this invisible spell. She wasn't even close to being strong enough to stop whatever it was that gave the Revinir so much hold over everyone. Much less take down the dragon-woman herself.

As the day drew on, Thisbe felt her resolve and her confidence slipping. What was she trying to do here? What could she possibly accomplish on her own? She'd managed to trick the dragon-woman into leaving Artimé alone—that was something. But now what? Whatever grand schemes she'd had of helping Rohan and Maiven save the universe seemed to be crumbling into dust. There didn't seem to be any way to defeat such a powerful monster. It was silly for Thisbe to think there was anything she could do. Until she could find the Revinir's weakness, Thisbe's presence here was futile. What had she gotten herself into? Stuck down in the catacombs again!

Hours later the soldiers returned, then left again. Dev didn't say much. The Revinir never appeared, perhaps too busy in her new castle. Or too big now to fit through the catacomb

LISA McMANN

passageways. Thisbe bottled her broth and prepared to go back to her crypt to spend a lonely night thinking about all the things she couldn't do.

Her mind turned to wondering how she could use her magic to break through the golden barrier in front of the tunnel. Was it worth the effort, even if Rohan was so zombielike? Perhaps it wouldn't be too hard to melt the metal, rather than try to break through it. After all, she'd melted the gold thorn for Henry so he could repair Talon's ankle. She'd definitely try that, though it could take quite a while to clear a big enough area. And Mangrel would certainly notice a large melted spot like that, unless she could hide it behind a bone pile as she'd done before. That would take time too.

Deep in thought alongside Dev, Thisbe ladled broth into the glass vials, then brought them into the throne room and stacked them with the supply of others. When she heard a clattering of bones, she went to the door to see who had delivered them.

Rohan was standing just outside the kitchen, staring straight at her. Bones that were distinctly not from dragons littered the floor around his feet. The corner of his mouth twitched into a sly half grin. "Hello, *pria*," he whispered.

A Team Effort

Thisbe's heart thudded in her chest, and she almost dropped the vial of broth she was holding. "Rohan?" she said softly, then strained to look behind him to make sure no guards were nearby. She checked Dev, too, and he was ignoring them. "Are you . . . ? I mean . . . are you, like, *yourself* right now?"

Rohan grinned. "Right now and always," he said, keeping his voice low too. He frowned at Dev's back. "Maybe we can talk tonight? Once you figure out how to be a beast, that is, and break through the wall again."

Thisbe stared. She couldn't believe it. Tears of joy and

relief popped to the surface and streamed down her cheeks.

Rohan's face melted. He went to her, and despite the risk, they embraced. Thisbe felt the sobs come, and she tried to do it quietly without getting any snot on Rohan's shirt, but she was having a hard time. He held her and whispered, "Shhh. I'll explain everything later."

Thisbe sucked in a breath and steadied herself. "It was so awful seeing you like that."

"I know. I felt the same way when I saw you and Drock coming. I thought the Revinir's mind control had gotten the best of you after all. It was only that night on her back when I saw you lift your head and look at me that I realized you were faking too. You're very talented."

Thisbe eked out a smile. "I know," she said, and the two laughed quietly.

Dev turned at the sound, and Thisbe and Rohan immediately went into their roles.

"Make broth," Rohan said in a monotone voice, indicating the bones he'd brought.

Thisbe stifled a giggle at how stiff he sounded. She could feel a tidal wave of laughter at her throat, threatening to spill.

Thankfully, Rohan kept it together, and soon footsteps in the hallway sobered them both up quickly.

"Hurry," Rohan whispered. "Get them into the pot before someone sees what they are."

Thisbe had been so preoccupied with everything else that she hadn't noticed what the bones were. She studied them, and with a sickening feeling, she realized soon enough. "Ancestor," said Thisbe, frowning. "I thought . . ."

Rohan put a finger to his lips and turned away, slipping out of the kitchen as the soldiers entered.

Thisbe's mind raced. She quickly gathered up the armload of bones and threw them into her cauldron, then poured a giant bucket of water over them. She stoked the fire and stood in front of the pot in such a way that Dev and the soldiers wouldn't be able to look into it without getting past her. All the while her mind whirled. The Revinir had given up making the ancestor broth because it hadn't worked for her. Thisbe had managed to steal a couple of bottles of it before the rest was destroyed. She was quite sure the Revinir didn't want any of the ancestor broth made. So why did Rohan bring these bones? It couldn't have been a directive from the Revinir.

LISA McMANN

As Thisbe stirred the water and bones, she realized exactly what was happening. And she felt foolish for not having thought of it herself. The ancestor broth had kept Thisbe from being pulled to the Revinir until now. Taking the second dose had given her even more control against the effects of the dragon-bone broth. And it had given her more clarity in the historic images that sat almost pleasantly in her memory now, rather than blinding her whenever the Revinir roared.

The ancestor broth was the answer to one big part of Thisbe's problem. It would combat the mind control, and it worked on people with black eyes. They'd just have to get the other slaves to drink it. And to stop taking the dragon-bone broth. It was brilliant!

But the more Thisbe thought about it, the more it seemed like a difficult task—there was no way Dev or the other black-eyed slaves would just obediently drink something Thisbe offered them. And would they tell the Revinir that Thisbe was trying to get them to drink it? She'd have to figure that part out. Maybe Rohan had an idea.

"Finish up," said one of the soldiers, poking his head into

the cooking area. "Time to go back to your crypts once your overnight batch of broth is cooking."

Thisbe startled but managed to keep her body steady. She watched out of the corner of her eye at how Dev responded— slowly and deliberately putting one last log on his fire. Thisbe did the same thing, then added a handful of herbs to her pot to provide some cover over what was inside. There was nothing more she could do.

Together they turned to go out. With a tiny bit of worry burning a hole in her stomach, Thisbe walked with Dev in silence, wondering if what she'd done with the herbs would be sufficient to hide the bones. Or if she'd be discovered and questioned in the morning.

But there was little time to think about that, for she had another huge task to accomplish before the broth would be ready.

Breaking Through

Thisbe backed up to her crypt door and faced the golden wall, trying to visualize precisely where the tunnel had been before. Chances were pretty good that someone had filled in the tunnel, because she hadn't heard any hollow spots. But the wall had already been compromised in that place once before, so perhaps it would be easier to break through it again. It helped that Thisbe's magic had improved. But it was too bad that Florence's team hadn't finished making obliterate spells before Thisbe had left—it seemed like they could be useful here. Though if Thisbe had possession of one of those, she might have to save it for the Revinir.

Staying far away for better aim, which is how Thisbe's natural magic worked best, she concentrated on the spot that seemed right. She raised her hand and pointed at it. Then she unleashed a long stream of fiery sparks. The impact was loud, making quite a metallic din. In the closed space, the spell produced a lot of smoke that had little place to go. Thisbe coughed and peered through the smoke, then went again with another round. When a river of gold trickled all the way down the bones, Thisbe stopped and climbed up through the smoky haze to see her progress.

To her delight, a huge section of gold had melted away in the right spot, exposing the tunnel that had been filled in with rocks and bones. Fueled by adrenaline and feeling powerful, Thisbe shook her head and laughed. "You'd think they'd understand who they're dealing with by now," she said. Going down the bone mountain halfway, Thisbe stood back and pointed, her sparks slamming into the hodgepodge of filler, sending gravel and sand and bone bits spilling out.

From the other side of the wall, Rohan pounded three times, which gave Thisbe assurance that all must be well over there. Thisbe sent off another round of sparks to break the tunnel contents loose. Climbing back up, she grabbed the end of a giant bone that was sticking out and tugged at it with all her might, working it back and forth. Finally it broke loose and sent her tumbling down the mountain with a bunch of silt flowing out after her. Once more she climbed to the tunnel, her muscles burning from all the exertion. Taking a short break to catch her breath, she stared into the tunnel to assess the remaining stuff plugging the hole.

A few minutes later she was back at it again, firing into the space. The explosion shook the walls and made the bones around her rattle. Fearful of being heard, Thisbe waited a while and tried to wave the smoke away, certain that someone would come to see what was making the racket. But no one did. Thisbe was determined to get through this thing. Tonight.

Piece by piece, Thisbe cleared out the rest of the debris. After dragging out the last bits, she climbed into the hole, coughing and choking on the smoke and dust. But there was no light at the end of the tunnel leading into Rohan's crypt. Crawling in to figure out why, Thisbe slammed into something solid where the other end of the tunnel should be.

"What is this now?" Thisbe said, exasperated. She started

feeling all around, finding a flat piece of something that spanned the diameter of the tunnel opening. "Rohan, are you in there? What's covering this?" She pounded on it.

"It's a sheet of gold," came Rohan's muffled reply from the other side.

"Oh." Thisbe paused to catch her breath. "Well, I suppose that makes sense. You'd better stand back. Like, way back."

"Aye, Captain," said Rohan. Thisbe could hear bones knocking together as he scrambled out of the way. "Ready when you are."

Wearily Thisbe backed out of the tunnel to get some distance. Then she pointed her less-tired-and-singed hand at the gold panel that separated her from Rohan. This time she aimed a narrow, laserlike line of fire at the gold plate that blocked her way, making a circle. Soon she could see hazy light appear as the sparks burned through and melted the precious metal. After she made it all the way around, the solid middle disk that remained fell out onto the bone pile in Rohan's crypt.

They both coughed and waved away the smoke. Eventually, when it was easier to breathe, Thisbe went inside the tunnel once more, dirt-covered and sweaty, and collapsed. When the

LISA McMANN

opening on Rohan's side was sufficiently cooled off and no longer smoking, he climbed up and peered into the tunnel at Thisbe. She patted the space beside her. Rohan stepped over the molten bits and slid into place. "Hi," he said.

"Hi." Thisbe's heart swelled.

"Just like old times," he said, beaming.

Thisbe grinned. Though she was exhausted, filthy, and triumphant, she never wanted the moment to end.

News from Underground

Tell me everything," said Thisbe. "Is Maiven okay? I've been anxious to ask ever since I saw you without her. I thought you must have been captured. I pictured Maiven in the dungeon again . . . It was so depressing."

"Maiven is—" Rohan stopped abruptly, as if thinking something through. Then he glanced at Thisbe's worried face. "Oh, she's fine. Wonderful, in fact." He flashed a smile. "I would have let you know what happened if I could have. But I thought you were compromised by the Revinir, just like you thought I was."

Thisbe grasped Rohan's hand. "Thank goodness we are both such good actors," she said with a laugh. "And you haven't had any training!"

"When your life depends on it, you don't need training," said Rohan. He peered out of the tunnel at his door. "And speaking of that, I'm surprised no one has come to check on the racket you've been making. Where's Mangrel? He's been acting different lately."

"I noticed that as well! Maybe he slept through the noise this time." Thisbe checked her door too and grew uneasy. "He'd have been here by now if he'd heard, though, right?"

"I imagine so. But with fewer guards around, maybe nobody heard or felt the explosions."

"Well, then," said Thisbe, feeling a little more at ease, "tell me whatever you can before it's time to go back to work."

"First, may I express how glad I am that you're alive? I was a little worried about the volcano network." He gazed earnestly at her.

"That's a story for later," said Thisbe. "We ended up in a very creepy place, but made it out all right."

"Did you find Sky?"

"Yes! She was in our world."

"Thank goodness." Rohan settled in. "After you and your friends left, I explained to Maiven everything I knew about the broths and what they did to you—how they affected you. She and I determined that the ancestor broth worked something like an antidote to the dragon-bone broth. And we knew from what you'd told me that the ancestor broth worked only on those with black eyes, like our fellow slaves. So once we got settled and Maiven started feeling better, she and I slowly hatched this madcap plan for me to fake being affected by the Revinir's roar so I could infiltrate the catacombs and try to get our fellow future rulers back to our side."

"That was very smart of you," said Thisbe. "But dangerous, too—what if she forced you to drink the dragon-bone broth?"

"I drank the vial of ancestor broth you gave me as a protectant right before I came."

"Ooh." Thisbe leaned forward. "So you see visions now too?"

"Oh . . . ," he said, seeming suddenly troubled. "Yes. I . . . We'll get to that later. I wonder if we're seeing different parts of the same events of the past . . . or if maybe we're getting slightly different points of view."

LISA McMANN

Thisbe was intrigued, but she had a million other questions to get to in such limited time. "How did you come to join this group, though? Didn't the Revinir suspect something when you didn't have scales?"

"Ah, but I do have them." He pulled up his sleeves and showed Thisbe. "Maiven and I stuck them on with a glue she made out of sap. They look real, don't they?" He pulled a small container of glue and a bag of scales from his pocket. "I have more in case I lose any."

Thisbe pulled a magical highlighter from her pocket and lit it so she could see better. "Wow!" she said. "That's amazing. How did you find actual dragon scales?"

"Maiven," said Rohan. "She had a whole wooden box full of them in her house. We found them when we were cleaning up, and that planted the first seeds that led to our little plan."

"Why would she have a box of dragon scales?" asked Thisbe, trying to imagine the answer.

"She said she and her siblings collected them when they were young, sort of like you and I might collect bird feathers or leaves from different kinds of trees today. It was very common back then, since the dragons were plentiful around here."

"They're plentiful again," said Thisbe wryly.

"Indeed they are. The circumstances are quite different now, though."

"Yes." Thisbe paused for a moment to check the door once more. "So you glued the scales onto your arms and legs and just knocked on the castle door? Or what?"

Rohan laughed. "I wasn't quite that bold. I hid near the castle and waited for her to roar, then showed up as if responding to the call." His smile faded. "She was calling for us—you and me. And she was delighted to see me, to say the least. She asked where I got the dragon-bone broth. I told her I'd stolen a bottle at the market after you and I split up, because I was so hungry. She's continued to sell it there, you know."

"Is that why so many people are just blindly doing what she wants?"

"Yes. She's given it to all the king's green-uniformed soldiers too. Just enough so they obey her."

"Oh no." That was hundreds, perhaps even thousands of people. "I guess I knew she had to be planning to do *something* with all of those vials. She's taken more herself. I can see the difference." Thisbe shook her head. "You told her you and I split up? We should get our stories straight."

"I . . . yes." Rohan looked pained. "I wasn't expecting the question. I should have been. I told her you were rescued—I couldn't think of anything else plausible that would cause us to separate. I should have said you were killed or something. I'm sorry. I'm afraid I inadvertently sent her in search of you and put you all in danger."

"Well, don't feel bad," said Thisbe. "She saw all of my fellow Artiméans fighting her, so she would have assumed they'd taken me with them when they left. She's known for a long time how to find us. You didn't ruin anything."

Rohan blew out a relieved breath. "So you must have seen us coming and heard the roar—is that what made you and Drock decide to infiltrate?"

"Mostly we left Artimé because we were afraid the Revinir would attack our people. I assumed the Revinir wouldn't have stopped until she found me."

"You're right," said Rohan. "She was prepared to attack anything in her way. And she would have sent us in to find you—that's why we were along for the ride. I was determined to get to you first and convince you to come. She's not going to kill us. She just wants our loyalty."

"We thought that too." Thisbe almost smiled. How cool it was that she and Rohan had been thinking so similarly while they were apart. But her thoughts returned to the Revinir. "She's greedy, and she won't stop until she has everything and everyone. Drock and I believed that if we gave ourselves up, she'd be satisfied and leave Artimé alone. And thank goodness she did, because we weren't prepared to fight dragons."

"You did the right thing."

"The problem is that I hadn't expected her to want Fifer, too, since she'd hardly seen her and never had her working for her before. But I should have known better. She and the pirate captain have had their eyes on us since we were toddlers."

"You were smart to tell her Fifer was here. That was quick thinking." Rohan looked admiringly at Thisbe.

Thisbe felt her face grow warm. "Thanks, but I'm worried for when she figures out I lied."

"The good thing is that as long as she believes you're under her mind control, she won't be expecting you to lie. So you

LISA McMANN

should be able to continue tricking her if you don't make a mistake." Rohan shifted. "And we'll just take things one day at a time. Keep sounding certain that Fifer is in this land somewhere. That's how we're going to get through this. Besides, didn't Fifer and your other friends hide out in the forest for a long time before this?"

"Yes."

"Then it'll probably be a while before the Revinir starts to become suspicious."

"I hope so." Thisbe suppressed a yawn. It had to be very late, but she didn't want to sleep. "How are we going to explain the tunnel to Mangrel?" She waved her hand at the opening in the wall.

"Same as last time. I think just piling up bones to cover the view of the hole is our best option. He won't be expecting it, since we are supposedly fully obedient while under the Revinir's spell."

"I'm starting to grasp that—and I think it can work in our favor." Thisbe nodded slowly. "Do you think Mangrel is . . . maybe . . . I don't know . . . sympathetic? A little bit?"

Rohan looked sidelong at Thisbe. "It's funny you noticed

that too. When I arrived, I think he was truly troubled to see me back here."

"That's exactly what I mean," said Thisbe, sitting up. "Me too."

"But he certainly isn't trying to help us escape," Rohan said bitterly. "Not him or the soldiers. They have the power to help us, but they have no inclination to do it. I wonder how they are human at all."

Thisbe slumped again. "I've wondered that many times."

"If they don't support what the Revinir is doing, they are too cowardly to stand up and speak out against it."

"Unfortunately, unlike them, we can't afford to be cowardly," said Thisbe. Her eyelids drooped, but one question remained unanswered. "How were you planning to get the other black-eyed slaves back on our team when you weren't able to make ancestor broth?"

Rohan lolled his head sleepily to one side to look at her. "I was still trying to figure out how to cook a secret batch when the Revinir called us to assist with the mission to capture you and Drock. So your timing, Miss Thisbe, was impeccable."

They dozed side by side, cradled by the curve of the circular tunnel walls. Before Mangrel could discover them in the

LISA McMANN

morning, Rohan snapped awake. He crawled carefully over Thisbe so as not to disturb her and built her bone pile to cover the view of the tunnel. Then he did his own before gently waking her and sending her down to the floor to await the crypt keeper's arrival. The ancestor broth, simmering in the kitchen, would be finished and ready to bottle.

But when Thisbe arrived in the kitchen, Dev was already there. And her cauldron of ancestor broth was empty.

One Vial at a Time

D ev!" hissed Thisbe. "What have you done?" She ran over to her cauldron and stared inside. It was clean and empty.

"You made a mistake," said Dev evenly. "The servant, Rohan, gave you the wrong bones. I had to dump it out."

"Oh," said Thisbe, crestfallen but trying to regain her composure. Inside she was throwing a fit. Outwardly she fought to control her frustration. "I am sorry for my mistake."

Dev didn't respond and turned to his station, starting his new batch for the day. Thisbe looked around helplessly. Where had he dumped it? Was it salvageable?

"I bottled and shelved several before I saw that the bones were wrong," Dev said. "You should remove them from the throne room. They're the ones on the far end."

Thisbe's pulse quickened. She moved deliberately to the throne room and looked at the long stretch of table that held stockpiles of dragon-bone broth. At the far end were a handful of bottles that had a slightly richer, golden-colored broth within. Shaking, Thisbe shoved a few ancestor broth vials into her already full pockets, and then slipped a few more into the waistband of her pants, pulling her shirt over to hide them. She took a handful of dragon-bone broth vials and ceremoniously uncorked them and dumped them down the drain so that Dev would notice and be able to report that she'd done it, if asked. She hurriedly rinsed the bottles and put them with the empties, then turned back to her station. With no more ancestor bones in sight, and with Dev there to stop her from making the same "mistake" again, Thisbe wasn't sure what else to do but begin a new batch of dragon-bone broth, which she reluctantly did.

Sometime later, two soldiers on their rounds stopped in to check on them. "The Revinir has ordered you slaves to take another dose today," one of them announced. The woman stood there waiting for Thisbe and Dev to act on the command. "Bring me enough for the others so I can distribute them."

"Yes, soldier." Thisbe kept her expression dull, but inside she was freaking out. "I'll go get them." She went into the throne room again, trying to come up with a plan on the fly. Was there a way to start slipping the ancestor broth to the others so that they didn't keep getting more and more embroiled in the Revinir's plan? Thisbe didn't have enough bottles in her pockets and waistband for everyone, but she had enough for most of them, at least.

She pulled all but one of them out, counted them, and grabbed a couple of the dragon-bone broth vials too. Returning to the kitchen, she handed one of the bottles from her pocket to Dev, hoping he wouldn't scrutinize it or notice its darker color, and kept one for herself. The rest she gave to the soldier. She uncorked hers and drank it obediently, trying not to make a face at the horrible taste. A rush of warmth rolled through her, and the familiar images posted like wallpaper around her mind, not impairing her vision at all but still distracting her with the sounds that accompanied the scenes. *Maiven Taveer! Maiven Taveer!* echoed in her ears. She set the glass container on the counter.

Dev uncorked his vial, barely looking at the contents of the bottle before chugging it down. He frowned after swallowing and wrinkled his nose. "Prindi and Reza must have made that batch," he said, and set his bottle into the sink. "They got fired from kitchen duty."

It was the most information Dev had given since Thisbe had been back. Thisbe rinsed the bottles, still feeling a bit dazed by the broth. The image of the girl being taken away by pirates loomed large.

Satisfied, the soldiers left.

Thisbe glanced at Dev, who stood with his back to Thisbe, hands pressing on the counter as if to steady himself. He didn't move for a long moment, and then he shook his head and made a noise.

Thisbe glanced over her shoulder at the doorway to make sure the soldiers were gone, then went over to him. "Are you okay?" she whispered.

"I think so," Dev whispered back, but he appeared unsteady.

"Let me help you sit down," said Thisbe, eyeing him care-fully. His face was flushed and covered in sweat. Thisbe took his arm and lowered him to a sitting position on the floor.

Dev pressed his palms against his eyes and let his head fall back against the cupboards. He didn't say anything, and Thisbe, though she wanted to pelt him with questions, knew to stay silent or risk being thought of as suspicious. Instead she took a moment to close her eyes and focus on turning off the volume in her ringing ears. To her great surprise and relief, she managed to quiet the screaming of Maiven's name.

After a moment, Thisbe returned to her station to light her fire and get her broth going. Dev got up and went back to work too, his once blank expression looking slightly puzzled now. Thisbe held her breath and watched him closely. Was he lucid? Had just one dose helped counter the effects? Should she say something to him?

"Feeling better?" Thisbe asked tentatively.

Dev startled. He turned toward her, still mildly puzzled, and studied her face. Then he looked away again without a word and carried on with his work.

Thisbe did too, all the while wishing there was a way to

LISA McMANN

tell Rohan she needed more ancestor bones today—she knew he wouldn't risk bringing more when he'd just done it, and he probably expected there to be plenty of ancestor broth to last several doses for each slave.

But even if Rohan did bring more, how was she going to make the broth with Dev's watchful eye on her?

As she worked her familiar tasks in the kitchen and puzzled over how to get to the next step in the plan, she let her focus stray to the images that had found a permanent place around the edges of her vision. In general she'd gotten so used to them that she hardly noticed them. But since taking the extra dose of ancestor broth just now, they were more prominently displayed in her mind. She focused on the girl and the pirate ship, which was the scene she saw far more often than any other.

When Thisbe studied it this time, she noticed the girl's face was much clearer than it had been in the past. With a start, she thought the girl looked a lot like Fifer and her. The memory of what Frieda Stubbs had said in Artimé came pounding back too, as well as the suspicion she'd felt but hadn't had time to linger on. Frieda had said that Thisbe's mother was a pirate who'd come to Quill as a girl around Frieda's same age, before their group had gone through the purge. That would have made them twelve or so. The girl in the image could totally pass for twelve.

What if Thisbe's mother hadn't actually been a pirate? But instead she'd been torn from *this* land before the worlds split and had somehow arrived in Quill by pirate ship? What if the girl in the image wasn't Maiven Taveer, whose name was being screamed by someone Thisbe couldn't see? What if the girl was . . . Thisbe's *mother*?

Willful Ignorance

Frieda Stubbs, head mage of Artimé, couldn't access the mostly secret hallway. So in order to get the grand living quarters she felt she deserved, she evicted the people in the apartments on either side of hers, busted down the walls between them with a magical sledgehammer, and turned the space into a giant suite for herself.

While her supporters and opponents clashed daily on the lawn outside the mansion, Frieda ignored them all and took to collecting as many weapons as she could find around the magical world, taking a great number of them from the theater auditorium, much to Samheed's chagrin. She decorated her extra-large space with them, happily making up stories about how she'd used each piece in a previous battle ... though she'd never actually participated in any battles. She counted the stories as real when she began retelling them to her faithful followers. Some of them believed her. Others didn't, but they let her tell them anyway.

Florence struggled to control the two factions fighting in Artimé, and Simber sank into a deep depression. The only thing keeping him sane was a lie he'd told Frieda—that he couldn't access the family hallway where she lived because he wasn't part of anyone's family. It was a weak excuse and totally untrue. Simber could go anywhere in Artimé as long as he could fit. But he almost never went down that hallway—not that anyone could remember, anyway—so his plan worked, at least for now. It kept him from having to spend so much time with the mage.

Simber was still upset with Aaron. But he cared about him too, as well as Fifer and the rest of them who were camped out on the Island of Legends. And now that Thisbe had so bravely gone with the Revinir, Simber had to spend some of his emotions worrying about her, which left less anger to express toward Aaron.

Karkinos had become something of a respite from the chaos growing on Artimé's shores, and a few others from the old rescue team occasionally snuck over for a day to get away from the noise and help with the brainstorming. But whenever Simber tried to sneak away to see how the banished ones were doing, Frieda always found out and called him back. He began visiting at night instead, when Frieda was asleep, but the problem then was that Aaron and Fifer were exhausted. They preferred to work on their plans in daylight to conserve their magical highlighter components.

And work they did, for as many hours a day as they could think straight. Knowing the new, improved seek spell would be the first thing they'd need when Thisbe finally contacted them, Florence commissioned Fifer, Thatcher, and Clementi to help Samheed come up with it. Samheed, still skeptical of Aaron, was glad not to be stuck working with him. His goal was to turn the seek spell into a broader communication device using Samheed's idea of a magical pencil and paper component. The problem for them was the size of it—the prototype of a notepad took up way too much space in the component vest, and so far they hadn't been able to figure out how to reduce the size while still leaving enough room to write a note.

"Plus we'd also want to be able to provide Thisbe with a way to respond if possible," said Clementi. "Like by including a pencil."

"I don't think there's a way to do that," said Fifer. She'd never heard of any spell that would be able to provide the recipient with a fresh component. "That would be an entirely new spell we'd have to create on top of this one. Like a delivery spell or something." She frowned, deep in thought. They kept working.

Aaron, Lani, and Ibrahim doggedly put their heads together to come up with a way to stop the dragon-woman who was covered in protective scales and able to use mind control to surround herself with more dragons. And, as before, they continued having a terrible time of it. "She's just too powerful," Ibrahim muttered now and then.

"There's got to be something," Lani said firmly. "We've never not been able to come up with something. We just need to think harder. Can't we at least cut off the mind control somehow? Then we'd only have to destroy the Revinir and hopefully not worry about the other dragons."

"There are risks there, too," said Aaron. "If the dragons aren't being controlled, will they turn on anyone who gets in their way? We're dealing with something so much bigger than anything we've ever faced before."

Frustration built as solutions remained elusive. And their worries grew for Thisbe. How was she holding up? Was she able to avoid being caught or fed the dragon-bone broth? And was Drock doing okay in that environment? They hoped he was handling obeying everything the Revinir asked him to do.

The shaky state of the unknown contributed to the stress of coming up with creative spells. Forcing creativity during a stressful time was hardly conducive to the process, and all of them at one point or another lashed out, especially Fifer, who was dealing with a myriad of feelings lately. But the Artiméans had solved big problems before, and they'd have to figure out how to do it again.

By now they had several finished obliterate components from Florence's team in Artimé. She'd procured a limited number of them and had put each one in its own tiny protective box that had to be magically opened with a whispered password, so that if anyone dropped one accidentally or if it fell into the wrong hands, it wouldn't leave an accidental mass grave behind. But would they be enough?

Sky, who stayed quiet most of the time as she observed and assisted, returned to Aaron one day. They'd talked once before, shortly after Thisbe left, about Eagala's inner workings, and Sky had been thinking about it ever since. "I keep coming back to what Thisbe said," she told Aaron.

"About what the Revinir's weaknesses might be?" asked Aaron.

"Yes."

"I've been mulling that over too. Do you have an idea?"

"I'm not sure. But I want to go to Warbler and see if I can find anything she might have left behind that would give us better insight into how to beat her. I feel like there might be something to the idea, you know? Since her magic and this ability is mental, perhaps we need to approach the solution in that way too."

"Yes, I agree. But how?" asked Aaron.

"I'm hoping Warbler will tell me her secrets."

Aaron nodded slowly. "Do you want company?"

"It might be wise to ask Fifer to come along with me if you can spare her."

LISA McMANN

Aaron tipped his head slightly. "Why Fifer?"

Sky glanced at the girl, who was sitting with her head down not far away. "She could stand to get away from here for a little bit," she said lightly. "She's been through a lot of confusing things lately—going from leading the group after Alex's death to basically sitting here not being heard. I think she could use a break."

Aaron studied Sky's expression, then looked at his sister. After a moment, he nodded. "I see what you're saying. I . . . I'm afraid I hadn't noticed."

"You've been overwhelmed. But she's intuitive and has a lot of good ideas. She was a really great leader after Alex died—I'm sure you remember Simber saying so. And I think she has a lot more to give than what we're asking of her right now, which is frustrating her. A challenge might be just the thing to snap her out of this funk, or whatever it is."

"Yes, of course," said Aaron. His expression turned weary. "I'm afraid we've all brushed her away lately. I'm still trying to get used to thinking of my sisters as contemporaries rather than wards."

"It's understandable," said Sky. "Something to work on."

She got up and dusted the sand off her pants. "If it's okay, I'll see if she'll join me, and we'll be off straightaway."

"I think that's a great plan."

"Excellent." With a nod, Sky walked to Fifer. "Could I have a word with you?" she asked.

Fifer's eyes were dull from lack of sleep and general annoyance at everything that was happening. She narrowed her gaze suspiciously. "Are you mad at me or something?"

Sky laughed. "No, of course not. I have a mission for you, if you're interested. I think you're just the person for this very intriguing job. Will you join me on an adventure in the deepest, darkest caves of Warbler Island?"

Fifer stared at Sky as if she'd just given her a new lease on life. "You bet I will," she said. "Whatever we're looking for, I'm all in."

Catching Up

T hisbe and Rohan found one another once more in the
tunnel between their rooms. Both were tired from a
long day and from not getting enough sleep the night
before. And despite the setback with Dev throwing out
the ancestor broth, they were motivated to keep moving. There
was something about this plan to overthrow the Revinir that
gave them hope against all odds. Maybe it was because they'd
both separately gone into this with a plot to trick the Revinir
into thinking they were under her spell. They were so in sync. It
had to be a good sign that they were doing this right.

Thisbe handed Rohan the remaining ancestor broth vial.

"Will you drink this?" she asked. "I want you to be stronger in case the Revinir somehow makes you take the dragon-bone broth." She paused, then turned to face him, looking puzzled. "Wait a minute. Did the soldiers give you a vial to drink today?"

"No," said Rohan, puzzled. "I didn't run into anyone today—I spent most of it sorting dragon bones in a new crypt I hadn't been to before. Nobody goes down that hallway, because there's only one crypt way at the end that's been closed up for years. Sounds like I lucked out."

Thisbe frowned at the vial, thinking hard, then handed it to Rohan. "Maybe just . . . Don't drink it now. Save it. Then, when they force you to drink the other kind, you can switch them out without them noticing and drink this one instead while they're watching you."

"Sure," said Rohan, nodding. "That's a great idea. The last time they gave me a vial was before you were here. I held the stuff in my mouth and pretended to swallow it, then walked around the corner and spit it out after they were gone. It was pretty disgusting—I was gagging, but I wasn't about to drink that stuff. I had to turn away and start working so they wouldn't suspect."

Thisbe remembered how the Revinir had scrutinized her

every move while forcing her to drink it. "You're lucky the soldiers don't care as much about this as the Revinir does."

"I am lucky," Rohan said solemnly. He knew what Thisbe had gone through. "And now I've got a better solution. Thank you." He slipped the bottle into his pocket and frowned. "But what are you going to take when they force it on you?"

"I'm just hoping we have a new batch of ancestor broth ready by the time they come around again."

"That would be ideal. How, though? I'm so angry that Dev threw out the last batch of it."

"He didn't know any better," Thisbe said. "It would almost be funny if it weren't so horrible—he's following every rule the Revinir lays down. It's annoying, actually." She paused, then asked, "Where is the Revinir? I haven't seen her since she sent us down here."

"She can't fit through the hallways in the catacombs anymore, so she stays at the castle. It's quite nice. Until she sends for you, that is—then it's a long, life-sucking journey to find out what trivial thing she wants."

"I was wondering if she was too big now," said Thisbe. "That works in our favor too."

"She doesn't have to worry about us like she did in the past, because she thinks she's controlling us. I've actually felt very free down here since my return. The soldiers don't check up on us as frequently, and Mangrel has relaxed exponentially. It's much better, compared to before. Though I'd rather be out of here, obviously."

"That's the goal," said Thisbe. "How quickly can you get me more ancestor bones? The sooner I can make that broth, the faster we can get the other black-eyed slaves on board with our plan."

Rohan glanced out of the tunnel at his door. "If you want to take a risk and blast me out of here, I can go right now and leave them for you in the kitchen, hidden in a sack."

Thisbe eyed him and saw how tired he was. "We need a good night's sleep for once, or neither of us will be at our best. Besides, how will you explain your broken lock?"

"Good point. Perhaps we should save the explosions for the final stages so no one becomes suspicious about us."

"That seems wise." Thisbe grinned. "Though, if they're not onto us after I blasted this tunnel, I imagine they never will be." She still thought Mangrel must have at least suspected

LISA McMANN

something—the explosions had rocked the walls. Unless he'd been sound asleep in another wing of the catacombs, he would have felt it. "Where does Mangrel sleep?"

"Closer to the river."

"Oh. Maybe that's why he didn't come when I blew the tunnel open."

"Maybe." Rohan rested his eyes and let out a long sigh. "I hope Maiven is okay."

"Me too. What is she doing while you're here?"

"She told me not to worry. That she had plenty of things to do."

"She's so old and frail. How can we help but worry? She could die any minute."

Rohan lifted his head and shifted his weight on one elbow, facing Thisbe. "You don't know who she is, do you?"

Thisbe shrugged. "I know she's important somehow. Who is she?"

Rohan cast a guilty look down. "I've been meaning to talk to you about this, but I . . . waited. It's kind of big news, I guess, and I wasn't sure how to say it."

Thisbe stared. Her voice faltered. "Big news?"

Rohan looked up. "Maiven was the queen of Grimere. That castle that the Revinir took over? It's *hers*."

Thisbe's heart thudded, and she sucked in a breath. The actual queen?

"She was also the commander of the military. She's not as frail as she seems. You should have seen the difference once we got some decent food and she could move around again and get exercise. As soon as she was able, she took her weapons out of storage and started working with them. Within a week she was a different person. I can only imagine how strong she's gotten in the time I've been away."

Thisbe stared at him. She'd been in a prison cell with a *queen*. And not just any queen—the queen of the land of the dragons. Thisbe's own land. And the woman had been the commander of the military! "Wow," she breathed. "Queen, commander of the military . . ." She shook her head in awe and then said jokingly, "Is that it?"

Rohan eyed her carefully as if considering his words. "Thisbe, she's also your grandmother."

Astonishing Revelations

R ohan," Thisbe said, sitting forward. Her eyes were wild. "What? How? Are you sure?"

"I'm sure," said Rohan. "She told me herself. Maiven is your grandmother."

"How does she know that?" Thisbe sat back, bewildered and shocked.

"She figured it out. After the dragons were forced out of the land by the usurpers, her daughter was taken away by pirates to your world. I gave her all the details about your vision of the girl being taken away and someone shouting for Maiven Taveer. She was struck by the description—she said that was a true scene from her life. The person shouting was her assistant. Maiven was with the army, too far away to reach the pirate ship in time. She watched helplessly as it went barreling into the roiling sea, heading for your part of the world with her daughter in chains."

"That's incredible," Thisbe whispered. "So that *was* my mother. I . . . I've wondered."

"Yes. Maiven immediately organized her ships to go after her. The fleet was setting out when the meteors struck our world and caused the earthquake. Some of the ships capsized and were lost. With her people in peril, Maiven called the rest of the ships back. A day later the ground split and the sea fell into the gorge between the worlds. The dragons that hadn't already been driven off fled. In the chaos, the rogue group of bandits, one of which was Shanti's father, took over the castle and ousted Maiven and the rest of her family. The queen was imprisoned in the dungeon and left there, forgotten."

Thisbe was silent for a long time. "But surely there were other girls who were kidnapped or driven away. How does Maiven know for certain that the daughter she lost was my mother?"

"She said you wouldn't have had that vision if you weren't a direct descendant of the girl being taken away."

"So since the assistant was screaming for Maiven because her daughter was being taken . . . and because I had the vision, that means I'm a descendant of the girl. . . ." Thisbe closed her eyes and focused on the scene, which now stayed forever on the edges of her mind. "That makes me the granddaughter of a queen."

"Yes."

"My grandmother," Thisbe said, repeating herself, "is a queen."

"Yes," said Rohan again.

Thisbe leaned forward and pressed the palms of her hands against her eyes in disbelief. "My mother is dead."

Rohan nodded. "I remember. You told me. I—I shared that with Maiven. I hope that's okay."

"She was a . . . what? A princess? My mother?" Thisbe dropped her hands into her lap and shook her head slowly. "She was a *princess*. And nobody ever knew."

"She knew."

"And she somehow landed on Quill and became a Necessary,

doing the work the Wanteds didn't want to do. Never saying a word about it. And dealing with people like Frieda Stubbs saying she was a pirate."

"You said once that she died saving your life—yours and Fifer's."

Thisbe nodded slowly. "I've always wondered about something. Why didn't she try to save Alex when he was sent to his death? But when the wall in Quill was about to fall, she saved us, apparently without hesitation."

Rohan frowned. "Perhaps her instinct was to keep the black-eyed ruling line alive at all costs." He paused. "Then again, I guess it could have been what any mother would do in a situation like that."

"It's strange she never told anyone who she was."

"She might have been afraid to. And in your land, it seems like they wouldn't have believed her if she'd told them. Or they'd send her to the death place for old people for telling stories."

"I don't really consider Quill to be *my* land," Thisbe said, correcting him. "That's the north side of the island, where I was born. But Artimé, where I grew up, is much different— that's the magical side. It's a good place."

LISA McMANN

Rohan nodded as if he were making a mental note of it, his penchant for learning evident. "I'd love to see it someday—see where you grew up."

Thisbe smiled. "Maybe you will." Then she shook her head in wonder, remembering everything Rohan had just told her. "I still can't believe it. I want to talk to Maiven."

"And she wants to talk to you. She wanted to before but didn't wish to take you away from your people or conflict you in any way after all you'd gone through. Especially since she wasn't sure of anything at that point. Not until I described your vision to her in detail after you were gone did she know without a doubt."

Thisbe kept shaking her head in disbelief, though the truth was becoming easier to see now that she had all the information. But the granddaughter of a queen? Thisbe looked up sharply. "So I am from the line of Taveer."

"I believe we have established that." A smile played at the corner of Rohan's lips, but he refrained from further pointing out the obvious.

"And you? Are you also from the line of Taveer?"

Rohan shook his head. "I'm from the other line of black-eyed rulers. The Suresh family. We spent more time in the land beyond the crater lake, where Ashguard ruled. Much of that land is destroyed now."

Thisbe sank back, still feeling dazed. "How did she take it?"

"Who? What?"

"Maiven. When you told her my mother is dead."

Rohan was quiet for a long moment. "She was sad."

A lump rose in Thisbe's throat, and she blinked back tears. "What does this mean for me?" Thisbe asked quietly, more to herself than to Rohan. "Who am I?"

Rohan lifted his head. "If we get our world back, I suppose that would make you a princess too, *pria*."

Thisbe's face warmed at the familiar nickname he'd given her, though she had no idea what it meant. "Why do you call me that?"

"Are you upset that I do? I'll stop if you wish."

"No, but I just want to know what it means."

But Rohan closed his eyes, a small smile on his face. "One day I might tell you," he said. "And hopefully by that point it will be accurate."

"*What* will be accurate?" Thisbe demanded. It was the only

LISA McMANN

time Rohan had ever annoyed her, and he wasn't giving in.

"It's just an affectionate nickname." Rohan slid to his side and got into a more comfortable position. "Do you hate it?"

"No. I—I like it. What shall I call you?"

"You may call me whatever you want, and I will answer to it." Rohan smiled and yawned, then rested his head in the crook of his arm. "I'll collect ancestor bones as soon as Mangrel lets me out. Then I'll rush to get them to you in the kitchen. So if you can stall a bit before starting your batch tomorrow, I'll have them for you fairly early on. I found an ancestor crypt that's much closer to the kitchen than the one I used to go to."

"That's perfect, Rohan," said Thisbe. "Thank you. We'll figure out a way to get this done without Dev messing things up. I've got ideas." She checked her pockets for components and shifted a few specific ones to the top so she'd have them handy in the morning if she needed them.

After that Rohan went to sleep, leaving Thisbe to ruminate over his latest revelations. Including the part about the affectionate nickname.

A Lucky Guess

Once Mangrel opened Rohan's door the next morning, Rohan sped as quickly as he could without being seen to the nearest ancestor crypt for bones. Thisbe went to the kitchen as usual to bottle up the dragon-bone broth that had been simmering overnight. She waited for Rohan before starting the next batch, puttering about the kitchen and throne room, organizing the existing bottles, wasting time.

Dev arrived and went about his work meticulously. Thisbe tried to get a good look at his face to see if his glazed expression had changed at all after drinking the ancestor broth, but he

LISA McMANN

kept his back to her so she couldn't tell. She kept fidgeting as she waited, wanting to get started, so that if the soldiers came again with orders to collect broth for the slaves, Thisbe would be able to provide them with the ancestor kind again.

Finally Rohan arrived and beckoned to Thisbe. She went to the doorway where he stood. "The halls are clear of soldiers," Rohan whispered, handing her a heavy burlap sack. "I'll keep watch while you handle Dev."

Thisbe glanced over her shoulder at Dev, who hadn't turned to see Rohan enter. He was making it easy for her. Not even needing to use up her precious components, she pointed at him, whispering "Freeze." Immediately Dev froze in place in front of his cauldron. Hopefully, no soldiers would come for at least fifteen minutes while the spell was active. But Thisbe could release the spell if she needed to once she was finished.

She dumped the ancestor bones into her empty cauldron. Then she fetched buckets of water and poured them over the bones. Once they were covered, she threw in a hearty bunch of herbs to float on top and hide the bone shapes so Dev wouldn't notice they weren't from dragons. By the time Thisbe had the fire stoked, Dev's spell had worn off. He continued his actions

LISA McMANN

as before with no apparent realization that anything unusual had happened to him.

Thisbe went to the doorway and nodded to Rohan to let him know all was good. But as Rohan turned to go, a beastly roar echoed throughout the caverns, making everything shake. Dust sprinkled down from the ceilings. Thisbe and Rohan froze and stared at each other. Thisbe could feel the haunting roar calling to her inside her head, echoing between her ears. It wasn't coming from the castle—it was coming from Dragonsmarche, and the sound spurred Thisbe toward the elevator. Thankfully the pull was even more muted after her latest dose of ancestor broth, and she resisted it.

Dev came out of the kitchen as if on a mission, with the same destination in mind, though he hesitated momentarily when he saw Rohan and Thisbe just standing there. A confused look flickered on his face, but then it was gone. Thisbe quickly checked her cauldron to make sure the ancestor broth was going strong, then fell in step with Rohan, a few paces behind Dev. They kept their glazed looks and didn't speak or acknowledge each other. But somehow the walk was easier with Rohan beside her.

Along the way, other black-eyed slaves emerged from where they were doing their various jobs. Prindi and Reza were there, and others whose names Thisbe still didn't know. They piled into the elevator and waited as one of the Revinir's soldiers counted them. When the last black-eyed slave arrived, the soldier used the controls to raise them into Dragonsmarche.

Thisbe stared straight ahead. She wanted to look around as they surfaced to see if anything had changed in the months since she and Rohan had flown through here on a ghost dragon's back. But she couldn't risk it. All she could see was the scaly underbelly of the Revinir. Thisbe took the opportunity to search the front side of the dragon-woman's body for weak spots, not having had a good look from this angle on her ride here. The scales were a little sparser on the woman's elongated neck, but there were no clear spots that looked as though a weapon could penetrate.

The black-eyed children filed out of the elevator into the market square. Thisbe purposely stayed away from Rohan, even though she knew the Revinir had no reason to suspect them of communicating. She stood in the back row, and as she turned, she swept her eyes over the others, counting them. Dev, Rohan, Prindi, Reza, and four others. That made nine of them altogether, including Thisbe. One day soon, if everything went according to the plan, these nine would no longer be slaves. They'd be the new rulers of this land.

Thisbe couldn't concentrate on that right now, though. She was busy acting as if she were under the Revinir's mind control. And that task became especially hard when the dragon-woman put her snout directly in front of her face. For the first time Thisbe could see that the Revinir had developed sharp dragon teeth, and her face had elongated to look more dragon-like. Her scorching, rancid breath was enough to make Thisbe flinch, but she fought it and held steady as the Revinir studied her stare and inspected her scales.

"Hmmm," said the ruler, sounding dissatisfied and suspicious. She moved on to the next slave and checked that person. And then the next. When she got to Rohan, Thisbe's vacant gaze flickered. His scales weren't real like everyone else's. Would she notice this time?

"Why aren't there more?" the Revinir mused. "There should be noticeably more scales after the last dose. I don't understand." She came to Reza and studied him carefully and seemed satisfied this time. Perhaps he'd been the one to get the

LISA McMANN

actual dragon-bone broth. It made Thisbe more determined than ever to not only stop the horrible practice of making her fellow slaves become more controlled, but to reverse this terrible, intentionally administered disease.

When the Revinir had inspected everyone, she stood back and towered over them, looking highly dissatisfied. Smoke floated up from her enlarged nostrils, and her suspicious gaze kept tracking to Thisbe and Dev. Thisbe tried hard to ignore her and held her blank stare.

"Thisbe and Dev, where did you get the broth that you gave to the soldiers?" asked the Revinir.

Dev remained silent—he hadn't done it.

Thisbe said evenly, "From the throne room table."

"Did you choose vials from the right or the left side of the table as you were facing it?"

Thisbe's heart skipped a beat. Why was the Revinir asking this? In the back of Thisbe's mind, she could sense what she should answer. "Left," Thisbe blurted out. It was a lie, and she wasn't sure she knew why she had said it.

The Revinir seemed satisfied with the answer. "The oldest bottles?"

Again Thisbe got a strange premonition of what to say, though she had no idea if they were still the oldest after so much time away from the catacombs. "Yes, Revinir." Those bottles on the left might have been the first that Thisbe had placed, back when she was making broth before her and Rohan's escape.

Then, inexplicably, Thisbe thought, *We should throw them out.*

"Perhaps there's a limited shelf life," the Revinir mused. "The old ones have gone bad. That would explain it. Thisbe, did you do anything to that broth before you gave it to the soldiers?"

"No, Revinir."

"Dev, did you?"

"No, Revinir."

"Hmm." Everyone remained silent as the Revinir seemed to come to a satisfactory conclusion as to why most of the slaves didn't have visibly more scales than before.

The phrase popped back into Thisbe's head. *We should throw them out.*

"Everyone, go back inside," the Revinir said. "Kitchen staff, pour out all the old vials of broth and start fresh. When your first batch is done today, bottle it up and deliver it to the soldiers for dispersal."

Thisbe's heart pounded. It was obviously a coincidence that the Revinir had said what Thisbe was thinking. But this new development of dispersing the broth later today could actually help things along a great deal.

"Yes, Revinir," said Dev.

"Yes, Revinir," echoed Thisbe.

"All right. Back to work."

The slaves filed back into the elevator. As Thisbe waited for her turn to enter, she caught sight of Drock at the far end of the square with a few other dragons, including Arabis and Hux. All three stood perfectly still, even Drock, staring blankly at the Revinir as if waiting for her to tell them what to do next. Thisbe's heart sank, but she kept moving. Drock was either a surprisingly good actor, or he had somehow succumbed to the Revinir's recent call. All Thisbe knew was that Drock never stood perfectly still. So this was a bad sign.

On the walk back to the kitchen, Thisbe's expression was vacant, but her mind was anything but—she couldn't stop going over the conversation that she'd just had with the Revinir. What had prompted her to lie about the broth? And more importantly, how had she known what to say? Thisbe had never had premonitions like that before. But they'd been perfectly accurate. She'd appeased the Revinir's suspicion. And she'd even somehow gotten her to say what Thisbe had wanted her to say.

It didn't seem possible that Thisbe had orchestrated that, but it had been a pretty big coincidence. And as much as Thisbe wanted to assert her own version of mind control on the Revinir, she knew deep down that the dragon-woman had probably already been thinking all along that the broth had spoiled. And Thisbe had simply made some good guesses in confirming it. Maybe Thisbe had had an accurate feeling about what to do for once. And maybe things were just finally going her way. After all, she'd had a lot of unlucky things happen lately. She was bound to get one thing right eventually. Perhaps today was just her lucky day.

An Investigation

Fifer and Sky took a boat to Warbler, with Fifer's birds accompanying them overhead, carrying the empty hammock. When they arrived, Copper met them in the marina, which was located in the small inlet on the east side of Warbler, a quarter turn from the beach. Dozens of beautiful handmade ships floated around them—the Warblerans had a knack for shipbuilding, and Sky had practically grown up working on boats. To their great shock, one of the ships was a charred skeleton of its former self.

"What happened there?" Sky asked her mother.

"The Revinir and her dragons sent a fire shower down on

our island as they passed overhead," Copper said. "That one caught and quickly became a full-on blaze before we could put it out."

"What a horrible thing to do!" said Fifer.

"She wanted to spite us. She knows she'll never run this island again."

"It doesn't surprise me that she'd just try to destroy it," said Sky. "She's been on a rampage lately." Sky tapped her lips thoughtfully. She'd feared the Revinir coming to fight Artimé but knew Warbler was just as vulnerable. Maybe even more so because of the dragon-woman's history. "I think you should prepare for more attacks, Mother."

Copper nodded her head solemnly. "We've already begun to do that."

Fifer swept her gaze over the ships. They could all be gone in a matter of minutes if the Revinir and her cursed dragons returned. "At least she won't be able to fit into your tunnels."

"Her own protective design is flawed in a way that hurts only her," said Copper with a rueful smile.

The three didn't linger outside. As they walked toward the back entrance to the warren of underground passageways where the Warblerans lived and worked, Sky quickly explained to her mother why she and Fifer were there.

When she was through, Copper nodded thoughtfully. "I think everything belonging to Queen Eagala has been preserved and stored in her old living quarters. Any journals, maps, and keepsakes will be there. You're welcome to all of them." She led them in through the opening and down the long passageway.

They popped in to say hello to Copper's assistant, Phoenix. He sat at a desk in the room outside Copper's throne room—which no longer had a throne in it. Copper thought thrones were ridiculous, not to mention uncomfortable. In place of the throne was a simple desk and chair, with a small sofa for constituents who came in to speak with her.

Sky and Phoenix, who had grown up together, chatted briefly like old friends. Fifer watched them. It was nice to see Sky laughing again. Then, leaving Phoenix to his work, Copper led them down another hallway, past rooms where Warblerans were making sails or creating hardware to repair their fleet. The three weaved farther into the heart of the island until they reached a gilded door. The handle and hinges were encrusted with sparkling jewels.

"I would have never guessed this was Eagala's old room," Fifer said sarcastically. Copper unlocked the door and swung it open, letting Sky and Fifer inside. Then the woman left them to rummage around as they wished. "Good luck," she called on her way out.

Fifer and Sky looked around. There were shelves loaded with books and wooden boxes filled with notebooks and loose papers and maps and other drawings. There was also a crate containing gold rocks like the kind that Dev treasured.

Fifer knew from reading Lani's books and hearing Sky's stories that the gold had once been used to create long, thin needles with sharp thorns. The thorns were weaved into necklaces that were then embedded into the necks of the people of Warbler to silence them. Fifer knelt beside the crate and ran her fingers through the gold rocks. In their world the gold was worthless. But in Dev's, this stuff would make a person rich. "We could have used some of this in Dragonsmarche," Fifer murmured. She picked up a few rocks and examined them.

"Might not be a bad idea to take some with us," said Sky, picking up a curious-looking book. She opened it and saw it was filled with diagrams and mathematical equations. She

LISA McMANN

turned the book sideways, squinting to read handwritten notes in the margin.

"Are you sure Copper won't mind?" asked Fifer, scooping up a handful.

"She has no use for them." Sky put the book down and picked up a second.

Fifer pocketed the rocks, then closed the crate and opened the one next to it.

"The Revinir is definitely greedy," Sky said. "It seems strange, living in a world like ours, to be so transfixed on making money. But she and the pirates were trading with other worlds secretly for many years before we learned that other places even existed."

"So going to the land of the dragons and understanding the monetary system wasn't such a shock to her."

"No." Sky read aloud a few equations, then frowned and searched for a pencil. She started working some figures.

Fifer watched her curiously. "What are you doing?"

"I'm checking her work. She's got a number of chemical formulas written down here that I'm familiar with. She's actually quite smart. No wonder she figured out that the whole dragon-bone-marrow-and-broth thing would alter her body's chemistry."

"So she already knew she could become a dragon when she lived here?"

Sky wrinkled her nose. She turned a few pages and studied them. "I don't know about that. Maybe. I wonder if she'd been trying to trap Pan's young for a long time. I knew the dragons were worried about the pirates capturing and trading them. But maybe they were also worried about Queen Eagala getting her hands on them." She read a few more pages. "I doubt we'll ever know. But it's so interesting, isn't it?"

Fifer nodded. She rummaged through the second box and pulled out a notebook with a tattered cover and opened it. "What's this?" said Fifer softly. She gazed at the first page. The date was written in a childlike scrawl. "This is from when she was a child. It's like a journal or something."

Sky looked up and went over to Fifer so she could see.

"It's dated sixty years ago," said Sky. "I can't believe she still has this."

"She was nine," Fifer said, blowing dust from the brittle pages and beginning to read. "The journal begins on the day that Marcus and Justine sailed away without her."

"Wow," said Sky, reading silently alongside Fifer. "And look how she signed the entry. Is that her real name? Emma?"

"That's, like, so normal. Her name can't be Emma."

"Why not?" asked Sky.

"Because Emma is a nice name. Not like Eagala or the Revinir. Those sound sinister. Emma sounds like the name of your best friend's mom."

Sky laughed. "None of my best friends' moms were named Emma. I don't know anyone with that name, actually."

"Me either," admitted Fifer. "I just . . . Maybe I read it in a book."

"Anyway," said Sky, "it makes sense that when she decided all of Warbler needed nature and animal names she picked Eagala—it starts with the same letter." She went back to the books she'd been looking at.

"I guess." Fifer turned the page. "My, she was angry about Justine and Marcus leaving. She's got a full-on rant here." Fifer read on, then lowered the journal. "I feel weird reading this. Is it wrong?"

Sky glanced over her shoulder. "I can see why you'd feel

that way. With anybody else, I'd pause and think that through too. But the Revinir has abducted Thisbe and our dragon friends. She set one of Warbler's ships on fire and destroyed it. She's taken a world of dragons and black-eyed children as her slaves by putting a mind control spell on them. And she intends to keep manipulating and stepping on others as she stomps and claws her way to the top of everything with no regard for anyone else." Sky took a breath. "I say, as a citizen of Warbler and Artimé, that she has waived all right to privacy. We need to fight her however we can, and this might just give us a clue as to how."

Fifer thought that through, then nodded. She sat down and read further. Every now and then she reported something out loud to Sky. "Emma feels abandoned." And: "Emma is extremely angry at her parents for not letting her go after her brother and sister." And: "Emma is determined to get re—" Fifer stopped short and stared at the page.

Sky looked up. "To get what?"

"To get revenge against the island of Quill," Fifer said slowly. She turned her head. "And that's exactly what she's been trying to do for sixty years."

"Even long after her siblings died," said Sky. "She's still paying them back."

"And hurting us."

Sky nodded. "Does she say anything else about her parents? I don't think we know anything about them. I certainly don't remember them, and I don't think my mother does either."

"She talks about her father being away at sea. And her mother, who was the ruler of Warbler, often spoke about missing her homeland and her family."

"Interesting," said Sky. "So her mother was from somewhere else. I wonder if she came through the Dragon's Triangle like Kaylee. How many journals are there?"

"This whole crate is filled with them," said Fifer.

"We should take them home with us so we can read everything."

Fifer nodded. "We're not going home yet, though, are we?"

Sky looked up. "Why not? Don't you want to?"

Fifer shrugged. "I don't know. It feels kind of nice being here, just us. I like talking with you."

Sky smiled. "I like talking with you, too. And even though

we're in a hurry to figure this out, you know you can come to me whenever you need me, right?"

Fifer nodded.

Sky tilted her head. "Do you need me right now?"

Fifer's eyes filled. She nodded again. "Things are just weird."

Sky set down the book and went over to the girl. Fifer reached her arms around Sky, and without knowing precisely why, started crying into Sky's shoulder. There were so many things. Alex's death after they'd finally become friends. The demotion from leadership just when she was starting to feel so attached to Artimé and its future. Thisbe growing distant, having newfound purpose in the land of the dragons, and having new friends like Rohan who seemed closer to her than Fifer was these days. Simber ignoring her and her quarrels with Seth. And none of the others seemed to be affected by these things that meant so much to Fifer. It made Fifer feel like she didn't belong anywhere. Like she and her goals and desires weren't important at all. "I'm sorry," Fifer sobbed, even though she wasn't sure why she said it.

Sky patted her on the back and whispered, "There, there," to her and let her cry. She didn't ask what was wrong. She remembered being thirteen, and she knew that Fifer would tell her whatever it was when she was ready.

After a while they separated. Fifer thanked Sky and apologized for getting her shirt wet with tears.

"I think my shirt is glad to be of help," Sky said with a crooked grin. "It has seen a lot of tears lately."

Fifer sniffed and wiped her face, feeling better just to let it out, even if she didn't have any solutions to her problems. At least Sky was there, and it gave Fifer comfort to know she could go to her whenever she needed to. They went back to sorting through the books and crates and packing up the things they needed to study further.

By the time they were ready to head back to Karkinos, they were already getting a better idea of who Emma-Eagala-the-Revinir was. And what had led her to become such a bitter, power-hungry person. They loaded everything up in the hammock, and Fifer sent the birds to Karkinos. Then they took the boat and followed, eager to continue their studying.

But once they neared Karkinos, they abruptly realized that

something was amiss. Because Karkinos was deserted, and they could just make out that Artimé's lawn was covered with people and statues and creatures. And they all seemed to be fighting each other. The magical world had gone mad.

Great Strides

By the end of the day, Thisbe had coerced Dev into dumping out and rinsing the old bottles of dragon-bone broth while she tended to her secret ancestor broth. When it was ready, she scooped out the steaming ancestor bones and threw them away so they wouldn't be discovered. She started filling the clean vials with her new batch of bone broth. Once she had several dozen bottles poured, she stopped Dev and gave him his dose to drink, then set one aside for herself. She picked up seven more, then hesitated as a thought struck her. She grabbed an additional seven and brought all fourteen to the outer chamber to give to the soldiers to disperse.

"Why so many bottles?" asked a soldier.

"The Revinir wants two doses for each slave," Thisbe said smoothly. "To make up for the spoiled dose last time."

"Oh." The soldier seemed to accept the explanation, and since she hadn't gone out to Dragonsmarche when the slaves had, she wouldn't have known what was said. Because the slaves all told the truth now while under the Revinir's control, she didn't need to question the girl.

The soldier headed out. Thisbe heard her explain the reason for two doses to her partner. Satisfied, Thisbe went back inside the kitchen to finish filling bottles and putting them in the throne room, starting again from the left as before. Then she built a new batch of dragon-bone broth, deliberately making sure Dev saw her hoist the large bones into her cauldron in case he ever got questioned about what Thisbe was doing. Once she had it going, she helped Dev finish bottling his dragon-bone broth, and she brought it into the throne room. She examined the bottles carefully, memorizing the ones that she'd made: more golden in color and even a little thicker in viscosity. There was definitely a difference, and Thisbe was determined not to confuse them.

As Dev started his next batch, Thisbe pocketed a few extra vials of ancestor broth to bring back to her crypt in case she and Rohan needed them as an antidote. She hesitated. She wanted Dev to ingest two vials like everyone else, but she didn't want to tell him to take two—he'd been with her this whole time, so he knew that the Revinir hadn't actually given that order. She didn't think he'd accept the directive from Thisbe—not the way he'd accept it from someone in authority like the Revinir or a soldier. So she kept quiet and made sure he'd finished his single vial.

She rinsed it out and saw that Dev was acting strange again, like he had been the previous time. He was leaning over the counter, his face tinged with gray.

"Are you all right?" Thisbe asked him. She checked for soldiers, then went over to him. He stood up, a bit shaky, and turned to face her.

This time he seemed to focus on her for a moment. His brow furrowed. "Thisbe?" he said softly.

Thisbe froze. "Dev!" she said in harsh whisper. She grabbed his arm. "Do you know me?"

But then his eyes glazed over again, and all recognition was gone. Thisbe dropped her hand, and he turned away to his station, methodically stoking the fire.

That evening, when Thisbe and Rohan met in the tunnel between the crypts, they felt a renewed sense of urgency.

"Dev had a moment of recognition after taking one dose today," Thisbe reported. "I wonder what's happening to the others. We're going to have to get to them somehow before the Revinir notices."

"She already noticed the first time," said Rohan grimly. "She's definitely going to notice this time too. Especially since she ordered us to take two. I actually had to swallow one of them while the soldiers watched, because I didn't have anywhere else to go with this first dose before I had to down the second bottle. Please tell me it was the ancestor broth. It looked golden like the other one you gave me, and I didn't get any scales."

"It was! And this new batch has lots of dried herbs floating in it, so that should help you tell the difference too. Future bottles should look the same." She paused, then said sheepishly, "It

LISA McMANN

was me who told the soldiers to give the double dose. The idea just came to me as a way to speed up the process. I figured the soldiers would believe anything I say, and it worked."

"Be careful, *pria*," Rohan warned. "If that gets back to the Revinir, she's going to know something's wrong."

"I didn't think it through," said Thisbe. "You're right—that was a mistake." They were both silent for a moment, wondering if there would be any ramifications. Then Thisbe brightened. "But I feel good about how our meeting went with her in Dragonsmarche this morning. I felt like I was on my game."

Rohan tilted his head. "On your game? I'm not familiar with that phrase."

"Oh—sorry. It's a thing Kaylee says sometimes. Anyway, it means I was really confident about how I answered the Revinir, and she totally believed me—it was like I had a gut feeling about how to answer her questions. And I got them right."

"I assumed you were just answering truthfully," said Rohan. "You tricked me as well."

"And then she said to dump the old broth out, which was what I was thinking and concentrating on. I wonder if I sort of . . ." Thisbe stopped and laughed quietly. "Never mind."

"What?"

"I just wonder if I sort of, somehow . . . I don't know."

"Sort of somehow what?" said Rohan, truly curious.

"Planted that idea in her head."

"Um . . . ," said Rohan, frowning slightly.

"I know, I know. It sounds ridiculous when I say it out loud."

"Yes. It was probably just a coincidence. It must've felt nice to have a day that went right for once, though. You deserve it."

"It did. It felt great." Thisbe pressed her shoulders against the tunnel wall, then stretched, feeling the ache after a hard day of slinging bones and cauldrons around. "But now things are going to get complicated. The others are at various levels of broth saturation. We don't know how close they are to snapping out of the mind control. Do you see the slaves in the hallways regularly? Can you keep an eye out for them?"

"Yes. I know more or less where they are all stationed. I've already been altering my travel routes to make sure I see each of them every day. And you're with Dev, so you can monitor him."

"Right."

"And then?" Rohan asked. "What happens once the others are back in their right minds?"

Thisbe tapped her lips thoughtfully. "We're going to have to move fast."

"How exactly?"

"I'm not sure yet. All I know is that we have to convince the other slaves to help us get out of here once their connections to the Revinir are broken. And we'll have to do it before the Revinir figures out what's going on. Before she has a chance to get a good look at any of us."

"I expect that'll have to happen very soon, Thisbe."

Thisbe glanced up and saw him gazing earnestly at her.

He touched her fingers. "It's not just two of us this time. We've got others whose lives we're endangering by doing this."

Thisbe pressed her lips together. "I know. I don't think she'll try to hurt us."

"I think she will," said Rohan.

"You do?"

"While we're under her control she won't—we're very useful to her. But if she realizes you duped her, well . . . I'm afraid of what she'll do to you."

"You duped her too."

"Yes, but you're the one making the antidote to her dragon-bone broth right under her nose. She's going to feel very angry about that, and I doubt she'll spare your life after something like that. Or mine, if she figures out what I've done."

Thisbe grew silent. After a minute she nodded. "Again you're right."

"I've had a lot of time to think about this," Rohan said, almost apologetically. "My day was a lot calmer and quieter than yours."

Thoughts swirled around in Thisbe's mind. Things were happening faster than she'd expected. How were they going to get everyone out of here safely?

It wasn't like Thisbe hadn't thought about it—she'd spent plenty of time musing back in Artimé before the Revinir came. She'd talked with Florence about it too. And in addition to all the strongest spell components, Florence had given her some of the most basic magical components that many Artiméans had trained with long ago, but that they no longer carried because they weren't terribly useful in combat situations. Florence had thought Thisbe might be in a unique situation, though, and being stuck down here in the catacombs again made Thisbe feel certain Florence had been right. Absently Thisbe checked her pockets, identifying the items by touch. They would come in handy when escape time came. "We need a meeting spot," Thisbe said. "And a way to communicate. Do you still have my . . . my gift? The one . . ." She felt her face grow hot.

"Of course I do," said Rohan. "Shall I practice my seek spell to make sure I can do it?"

"Yes. I'll send one to you first, so you can watch my technique." She reached into her back pocket where she kept the tiny birch-bark diorama that Rohan had constructed for her and unfolded it. "First, think about the person who gave it to you." Holding it in her hands, she closed her eyes and concentrated on Rohan, picturing the moment he'd given it to her. It made her feel wistful even though he was right next to her. "Seek," she whispered.

A ball of light shot out and stopped abruptly inches away in front of Rohan. It exploded into a picture of the diorama.

"Okay, I think I can do that," said Rohan confidently. He reached for the poem that Thisbe had written for him. "I've been wanting to try this out for so long."

"Well, why didn't you?" said Thisbe.

"I—" Now it was Rohan's turn to feel heat rushing to his face. He stumbled over his words. "I didn't want to intrude into your life."

Thisbe caught his gaze. A pang of longing went through her chest, and she grasped his sleeve. "Please don't ever feel that way," she said quietly.

"I also didn't want you to think I needed you." Rohan frowned after he said it. The words hadn't come out sounding right at all.

"Oh."

"I mean, I do, though," said Rohan.

"Do what?"

"Need you."

Thisbe looked up. Words caught in her throat, so she said nothing at all.

Rohan swallowed hard, making his Adam's apple bob in his throat. He turned back to the gift in his hands. After opening the paper, Rohan read the poem that Thisbe had written for him. He mouthed the words but didn't say them out loud, as if saying them would break the spell of their beauty or release

LISA McMANN

them to the world for others to steal. He wanted these words for himself and no one else.

He closed his eyes, thinking only about the girl who'd given him the gift. And then he whispered, "Seek."

A bright ball of light shot from his hands and stopped in front of Thisbe. It exploded in front of her, a picture of the poem.

Thisbe grinned and grasped Rohan's forearm in delight. "You did it!"

"I did!" Rohan turned to face her, and then, before he could change his mind, he leaned forward. "May I . . . ?" he asked.

Thisbe's breath caught. Then she moistened her lips and nodded. She leaned in, and their lips met in a soft, clumsy peck.

After the Kiss

T hisbe and Rohan both felt a little strange—in a nice way—after sharing their first kiss together. But the strangeness faded quickly when they continued talking about their plans. Knowing the Revinir couldn't get to them in the catacombs anymore because of her size, they felt relatively safe establishing Thisbe's crypt as a meeting place. They paused momentarily when they remembered the last time an altercation had happened in that crypt. But not one to be superstitious, Thisbe waved off the possibility of something terrible like that happening again just because they were in the same spot. Besides, they both agreed that having the tunnel as a second exit was crucial in case soldiers came charging after them at the Revinir's command.

Rohan fell asleep holding Thisbe's hand but woke sprawled sideways with Thisbe's shoe in his face. Both had to scramble to their normal sleeping areas when Mangrel's keys rattled outside Rohan's door.

They went their separate ways as usual. While Rohan walked to collect bones for the broth, he tried to hide the little smile on his face so he wouldn't be seen as suspicious. But he had the memory of the kiss to dwell on, which helped him through the day.

As he worked, he made a point to locate all six of the other slaves. Of them, Reza seemed the most glassy-eyed, and he ignored Rohan completely. But the others seemed to be teetering on the edge of lucidity. Prindi wore a puzzled expression, and her eyes tracked Rohan's movements—definitely an improvement. "Prindi," he said.

Her expression flickered.

Rohan said her name again, and this time she nearly focused her gaze on him. But then she blinked and turned away, and the connection was lost. Another dose might put them at an equal level of the broths, like how Thisbe had been for much of the time. He wondered if there was a way to get the slaves to drink more of the ancestor broth. Not just to equate the levels so they'd be functional except when struck by a paralyzing roar, but to give them an extra edge to be able to withstand the dragon-woman's roar completely, like Thisbe had after her second dose. It would take perhaps two more vials for most of them. But Reza, who'd no doubt taken in one more dragon-bone broth while the others were taking the ancestor broth, was two vials behind the others. So he would need four.

As Rohan left Prindi's station and started toward the kitchen to deliver dragon bones, two soldiers approached Prindi.

"You're to go to the castle tomorrow," one of the soldiers said. "The Revinir has a job for you there. Start walking at dawn. Mangrel will let you out of your crypt early."

"Yes, soldier," said Prindi.

Rohan slowed his pace in case there was anything more to hear, but the soldiers were finished. As he continued steadily, his heart began to race. If the Revinir saw Prindi tomorrow, would she notice the girl was more aware of her surroundings than before? Would she notice that she still didn't have more scales, even after the most recent dose? Would she ask Prindi any questions that could incriminate Thisbe? Or might Prindi tell her that Rohan had tried to speak to her?

He had to let Thisbe know so they could figure out what to do. Could they risk Prindi going to the castle and spending time with the Revinir at this point? Or should they try to do something . . . tonight? Before she left?

Rohan wanted to pick up his pace, but he could hear the soldiers coming behind him, and he needed to plod along at the usual mind-controlled speed. Moments later, the same woman who'd spoken to Prindi called out. "Rohan, stop."

Obediently Rohan stopped. He set his expression and waited until the soldiers came up to him. "Yes, soldiers," said Rohan in a monotone voice. He stared straight ahead.

"Are you going to the kitchen with those bones?"

"Yes."

"And then returning this way to get more?"

"Yes."

"Great." The woman glanced sidelong at her companion.

LISA McMANN

"Get another dose of broth for everyone and pass them out along your way."

The second soldier snickered. "You're so lazy."

"I'm resourceful," corrected the woman. "It's lunchtime." She turned back to Rohan. "Do you understand me?"

"Yes, soldier," said Rohan.

"Make sure everyone drinks their vial."

"Yes, soldier."

Rohan waited a beat to hear if there was anything else, then continued plodding.

The other soldier, sounding slightly nervous, called after him, "Let us know if anything goes wrong."

Rohan smirked but answered without looking back. "Yes, soldier."

When Rohan reached the kitchen, he deposited his sack of bones and beckoned to Thisbe. Thisbe glanced at Dev, then sidestepped through the doorway and around the corner.

"How is *he* today?" Rohan asked, meaning Dev.

"He had another moment when he recognized me. I was just getting up the nerve to tell him to drink another dose, but I worry that he'll tell the Revinir I said it."

"Well, you can stop worrying. She's ordered another round, and I've been commissioned by the guards to do their job for them."

Thisbe stared. "That's great!"

"There's only one problem."

"What is it?"

"Prindi has been called to the castle tomorrow to work there. That means she'll start walking at dawn."

"And . . . how is she?"

"She seemed to recognize me for a brief moment, and her eyes are less glassy. I think the Revinir will notice, especially with how much she scrutinizes us every time."

"Oh no! She'll only become more lucid with this dose," said Thisbe, a worried look on her face. "We could give her the dragon-bone broth this time—that would put her back to the same level as Reza. Ugh, but I hate to do that. Can we risk giving everyone two like we did before? And try making a break for it *tonight*?"

"You read my mind," said Rohan. "Can we? Do we have anything to lose?"

"Only everything," said Thisbe, trying to smile. She reached up and touched Rohan's cheek.

Dev appeared in the doorway behind them. He stared. "What are you doing?"

Thisbe and Rohan whirled to face him. Dev's eyes were clearer than they'd been in ages. "Dev!" whispered Thisbe.

"Why are we down here again?" Dev demanded.

Rohan and Thisbe glanced at each other, and Rohan nodded. "Dev," Thisbe said again, and reached for his hand. "We have to take another dose of broth."

Dev pulled away, and in an instant his eyes were glazed again.

Thisbe went into the throne room and picked up a vial of the ancestor broth, then brought it out to Dev. "Drink this. The Revinir ordered it."

Dev seemed confused, but he took the vial. Obediently he uncorked it and took a swig, swallowing it all down.

"And . . . ," said Thisbe, watching him carefully. "One more." She handed him another, making sure it was the ancestor broth.

Dev's face looked pained, but he took it and sipped this one. When he finished, he held his stomach. Thisbe and Rohan helped him to sit on the floor.

"Keep an eye on him," said Thisbe. She went back into the throne room and gathered up a dozen more vials of ancestor broth for Rohan to distribute, plus two for him to pocket. But how was he going to handle everyone by himself? Surely some of them would be defiant once they came to realize what was happening.

She set the broth on the counter and knelt next to Dev, peering at him.

Dev belched. Thisbe backed off, worried he was going to vomit.

But Dev merely swayed in place, eyes closed. Rohan and Thisbe stayed nearby, watching him anxiously.

Finally the boy opened his eyes and took in his surroundings. He blinked a few times. He looked Thisbe in the eye and held her gaze, then wound up like he was going to punch her in the nose. "What are you two looking at?"

Thisbe backed off before he could throw the punch, though she thought ruefully that he probably owed her one. "Sorry for staring," she said. "We can explain."

"How did you manage to get me down here?" Dev said with a sneer. "I told Fifer you were still here. She wouldn't believe me."

"Shh," hissed Thisbe, glancing over her shoulder and realizing that now she had the soldiers to worry about, especially if Dev was talking like his old self. "Be quiet and I'll tell you."

"What is going on?" Dev said louder. He struggled to his feet, still a bit weak in the knees.

Rohan went to help him stand. "There you are," he said lightly. "You've been through a lot, but you're on the other side of it now. We just need you to stay a bit quiet so the soldiers don't come."

The explanation seemed to get through to Dev.

"You were being controlled by the Revinir through the dragon-bone broth she fed you," Thisbe said quickly, still throwing glances at the door in case random soldiers strolled by. "The antidote is this other . . . concoction that I made. You've been under a spell for months."

Dev seemed exhausted and dubious, but he let Thisbe continue. She told him everything she could to convince him they were telling the truth.

Finally, when Dev seemed to be coming around to believing them, Rohan picked up the vials of ancestor broth. "I have to get moving if I'm going to find everyone before the end of the day."

LISA McMANN

Thisbe turned, looking torn. She needed to stay with Dev to coach him on how to fake out the soldiers. But she wanted to help Rohan with the others. "Can you get them to come here?" she pleaded. "This isn't going to be easy. Especially if everyone is as belligerent as Dev."

Dev snorted.

"What about the soldiers?" whispered Rohan. "If they come through here, they'll know something's up."

"I can handle the soldiers," said Thisbe grimly. "And besides, it doesn't matter now. They're going to know something's up tonight, one way or another. We're breaking out of this jail. For good this time."

A New Team

Okay, Thisbe," said Rohan cautiously. "But assuming we convince the others about what's really happening, and you somehow stop the soldiers, and we really do manage to break out of here . . . then what?"

Dev lifted his head. "I know where Fifer and Simber are in the forest."

Thisbe rolled her eyes. "They've been gone for months. Dev, I'm telling you I went all the way *home*, and I was there for weeks and weeks before I came back here to try to save you."

"This is all really confusing," Dev said, sounding defensive.

"Are you sure you're not just playing a trick on me?"

"I give you my word. But we'll need you to help with the others. Do you trust me? I promise everything I've told you is true."

"But . . . ," Dev said, his face pained, "why would you even care to save me?"

Thisbe felt like punching him. "Shut up, Dev. I'm not going to go into everything right now. We have stuff to do. Are you going to help me or not?"

"I guess I don't have a choice. I want to get out of here too."

"Great." Thisbe blew out a breath. "Once we're out, we'll worry about where we'll go from there. With any luck, Drock will be around to help us. Though . . . ." Thisbe trailed off, not at all sure if Drock was still on her side. "Anyway, we can all be thinking of what to do next and discuss it on the way out."

"That sounds sketchy, but I'm in with the plan." Rohan shoved the two extra vials into his pocket, then stepped toward the door with the armload for the other six black-eyed slaves. "I'm taking these with me in case I can't get them to come here. How about extra for Reza?"

Thisbe ran to get more and handed them over. "But you'll try to return here with everyone?"

"Of course." Rohan stopped and flashed Thisbe a reassuring smile. "We've been through worse things. We'll get through this."

Thisbe grinned back. "That's the spirit. Best luck. See you soon."

"That's the plan." Rohan disappeared from the kitchen wing.

"Are you two, like—" Dev began.

"Like why don't you shut it and pay attention," Thisbe snapped. "I need to teach you how to be a good actor in about three seconds."

"Okay, okay," said Dev, but he seemed a little annoyed.

"Rest your face."

Dev let his expression go slack.

"Good. Now cross your eyes, then relax them and stare off into space so it's blurry. Like this." Thisbe showed Dev how to appear like he was under the Revinir's spell.

"That is not how I looked," said Dev.

"You want to bet on that?" Thisbe challenged. "You looked exactly like that. You were being controlled."

"I don't remember any of it. Did I do anything . . . horrible?"

"You . . . you spit fire at Seth and burned him."

LISA McMANN

"What?" Dev exclaimed. "Is he okay?"

"Shh!" said Thisbe. "He's fine. Pay attention and do what I told you. You look totally shocked right now."

"Stop telling me shocking things, then." Dev struggled to compose himself. He worked his facial muscles again until he relaxed, then crossed his eyes and focused on a random spot on the wall, letting the edges blur.

"That's pretty good," Thisbe said. "Keep practicing. Try to do it while you stir your broth."

"Ugh," said Dev, looking at the cauldron. "Have we been drinking this? Look at my arms—they're covered in scales!"

"Focus," Thisbe said in a low voice. "I hear footsteps. If they ask you to do anything, just go along with it."

"Help us all," Dev muttered. He froze, then, with his back to the doorway, went through the method Thisbe had given him. A minute later a soldier came in.

"Did Rohan collect broth from you to pass out to the others?" she asked.

"Yes, soldier," said Thisbe. Dev echoed her.

"Good." She peeked into their pots and wrinkled her nose. "Dev," she said, "the Revinir just sent word that she needs you tonight. She's trying to find the king's personal treasures in the castle, and you're the only one who knows where everything is. Finish up here and go up the elevator—she's sending a dragon to take you. She's in a hurry to find them."

Thisbe nearly choked. This wasn't part of her plan.

Dev nearly choked too. After he hesitated a second too long, the soldier peered at him.

"Did you hear me?" she said.

"Yes, soldier," said Dev, his voice squeaking.

The woman narrowed her eyes and studied him. As he stirred, he tried to keep his gaze set on the wall. After a moment she shrugged, then turned and left the room.

When her footsteps faded, Dev slumped over the counter. His face was gray. "Now what?"

Thisbe was thinking frantically. If Dev didn't go soon, the dragon would report it, and the Revinir would find out much sooner than if Prindi didn't show up tomorrow.

"Thisbe!" whispered Dev.

"Quiet. I'm thinking!"

"She'll figure it out if I go! I can't do this fake thing like you can. I'm miserable at it."

They stood in silence as their plans crashed around them. They weren't ready to make a move yet. Rohan was probably still rounding up the other slaves. They'd have to get here, and then they'd require at least as much time as Dev had taken to understand what was happening—and even longer for Reza to drink the extra broth. Dev couldn't wait that long, or the Revinir would know something was up.

Thisbe turned to her friend, desperation written all over her face. Could Dev pull off the biggest acting job ever? Could he fake his way through a direct meeting with the Revinir just to give Thisbe and the others the time they needed? And maybe even the chance to escape without the Revinir finding out for at least a day?

Even if he could, how would he get away from the castle?

Minus One

Thisbe and Dev stared at each other. "You have to do it," said Thisbe in a low voice. "You have to go to the castle. Or else the Revinir will know something's happening down here, and we'll all end up in the dungeon."

"Thisbe, no!" Dev gripped his hair in his fists and turned to look out the door. The hallway was empty. "What if I mess it up? She'll kill me!"

Abandoning all pretense and not caring about soldiers, Thisbe took Dev by the shoulders and turned him to face her. "Listen to me," she said, trying to be calm. "This is going to

LISA McMANN

be easy." She nodded firmly to convince herself of that. "Just do the face I taught you. Speak in monotone, and don't say much—yes, Revinir. No, Revinir. Nice and steady, no emotion. Find the stuff she needs as quickly as you can. When the dragon returns you to the elevator, don't go back down into the catacombs. Instead, run away. Go to Maiven's house in the village."

"Who? You mean Maiven from the dungeon?"

Thisbe dropped her hands. "Ugh, that's right. You missed absolutely everything, didn't you?" She turned to glance out the door, trying to think. "Okay, new plan. Go to Alex's grave. You know where that is, right?"

"Yes."

"Okay, good." Thisbe breathed a bit easier. "Great. One of us will find you there."

"If the Revinir doesn't kill me."

Thisbe's eyes went wild. "Dev. You have to pull yourself together. You can do this. You just convinced the guards that you were still under the Revinir's spell. Just do that exact same thing. She's not going to kill you."

"Easy for you to say." Distraught, Dev turned to the

soothing familiar action of stirring his pot of broth. "Can't we all just escape when Rohan comes back? What happens if I don't go?"

"She's expecting you to leave immediately, and you're traveling by dragon. She'll figure out soon that something's up. If we can't get out of here before then, it'll ruin our chance of ever helping everyone escape. And then . . . she might kill us. Some of us, anyway. Like me. All of this is on me and Rohan."

Dev sighed and started pacing. "What if . . . ," he began. "What if I drink more dragon-bone broth so that I really *am* back under her control? Then I wouldn't have to fake it."

Thisbe considered that for a moment, then shook her head. "You wouldn't remember to escape. And you'd come back here and be stuck down here all alone."

Dev stirred the broth. "This stinks."

Thisbe wasn't sure what to do. "Please, Dev," she said. "We need you to do this. You're saving eight black-eyed slaves from the Revinir's tyranny. You'll be an even bigger hero than you already are."

Dev stopped stirring. "You don't think I'm a hero. You're just saying that to get me to go."

"That's not true," Thisbe insisted. "I know you, Dev. And I heard all about what you did when you were with my sister and the rescue team. You knew to save the king, which stalled the Revinir's takeover."

"Fat lot of good that did," said Dev. "Does anybody know if the king is dead?"

"We don't know," Thisbe admitted. She studied her friend. "But I do know you can do this, Dev. I believe in you. And we'll be waiting for you by Alex's grave. You can do this. We'll all be together by morning, and we have a safe place to hide out."

Dev grimaced. He stirred a few more times around the pot, staring into the cloudy broth.

"Please," Thisbe said again.

With a deep sigh, Dev pulled the wooden spoon out and set it beside the fire. "All right," he said. He wrinkled his face, trying to get the blank look happening, then turned and stared past Thisbe's shoulder, crossing his eyes slightly to blur the spot and letting his mouth relax. "How's this?" he said in a monotone voice.

Thisbe brought her arms across her chest and pressed her

lips together, pleased. "It's perfect. You've got it exactly right."

With a final sigh and a slight shake of his head, Dev moved to the doorway.

"Go straight to the grave when you're done with her. And if we're not there yet, wait there until someone finds you," Thisbe whispered. "We'll be starting our escape within hours, so we should get there before you." She ran to the throne room and grabbed a vial of ancestor broth, then returned and handed it to Dev. "Take this if you need it to help you be even stronger against the Revinir's roar."

Dev moved to slip it into his money pouch and realized he wasn't wearing it. "Hey!" he exclaimed, breaking character. "Where's my pouch?"

"Fifer has it, I think. She's keeping it for you—you left it at their camp when you went to follow the Revinir's roar. I didn't think to grab it for my return. I'm sorry."

Dev narrowed his eyes.

"I promise you'll get it back with everything in it."

"All right." Dev slipped the vial into his pocket instead. He let his face slack and his sight blur once more. "Here I go."

"Thank you," Thisbe whispered. She watched him leave.

When she heard a noise from the other direction down the hallway, she snapped back into her mind-controlled character and turned slowly. With relief, she saw it was Rohan coming with Prindi and Reza, all of them dragging bones toward the kitchen.

Breaking Out

Rohan, Prindi, and Reza reached the kitchen, and Rohan hurried the other two inside. "Thisbe will finish explaining everything," Rohan told them, then said something in the common language. The two nodded. Rohan turned to Thisbe. "I've given them their doses. They know the basics and know they can trust you. I'm going after the rest of them now." He glanced inside the steaming kitchen. "Where's Dev?"

Thisbe told him everything. "He's on his way to the castle now. We need to move."

Rohan cringed, then nodded. "Okay. Let's make it work."

LISA McMANN

He blew out a breath and shored up his resolve. "These two don't speak much of your language. They understand it better than they can speak it, though, so you can try to explain more if you like. I'll be back as soon as I can." He checked the hallway for soldiers, then sprinted in the direction of the crypts where the others were working.

Thisbe tried explaining to Reza and Prindi everything she could to help them understand what had happened to them and what was about to go down now that they were free from the Revinir's spell. She gave them each a vial of the ancestor broth as she'd done for Dev, then stuck the remaining vials of ancestor broth inside a small sack and handed it to Prindi.

"You're in charge of these," Thisbe said. "This is the antidote to the Revinir's mind-controlling dragon-bone broth. When she roars, you'll still feel a pull, because you are part dragon. But the ancestor broth is strong, and as long as you've had more ancestor broth than dragon-bone broth, you will be able to resist the Revinir's call. Understand?"

The two shrugged uncertainly.

"Okay." Thisbe nervously checked her pants pockets for the collection of magical components she'd need later. Then, wanting to keep the two busy with work so they would look less suspicious if caught, she pointed to the fires and the buckets of water. "Can you put the fires out?"

Prindi said something to Reza, perhaps translating, and they reached for the buckets. Thisbe went to the main hallway and peered down it anxiously. She desperately wished for her component vest. The vest made it so much easier to organize her components, rather than stuffing them all into her front two pants pockets. Plus the vest offered a magical degree of protection. But as she had pointed out to Aaron, the Revinir knew all about the vests that Artiméans wore, and Thisbe couldn't risk wearing it and tipping the dragon-woman off.

Seeing no one in the passageways, Thisbe returned to the kitchen. She picked up a couple of canteens that the soldiers had left lying around and filled them with water, then handed them to Reza to carry. Reza and Prindi spoke quickly with each other. Then Prindi asked Thisbe if the dragons outside were dangerous.

Thisbe assured them that as long as the dragons were being mind-controlled by the Revinir as the slaves had been, they were not dangerous unless the Revinir told them to attack.

"But . . . if we leave?" asked Reza. He seemed doubtful about escaping. "We have everything here."

Thisbe stared at him for a long moment. "How long have you been down here?" she asked softly.

"Always."

Prindi nodded—she too had been there as long as she could remember.

"And . . . you don't remember being out of here? At all? Ever? Not even recently while the Revinir was controlling you? You don't remember fighting me and my friends in the castle? Or flying to my world to find me and Drock? None of it?" Thisbe was astounded. They didn't know what the world was like. It was beyond Thisbe's comprehension.

Suddenly Prindi's eyes widened in fear, and she pointed. Thisbe whirled around and saw two soldiers on their rounds coming in to check on them. Reaching for her pocket, Thisbe found a few components.

"What are you two doing in here?" shouted one of the soldiers. "What's going on? Where's Dev?"

"Something's wrong," said the other. "They're acting different."

Thisbe didn't hesitate. "Freeze!" she shouted, pointing at them. Then she sent shackle components, securing them to the wall in their frozen state.

Prindi and Reza stared.

"We need to hurry," Thisbe said to Prindi, hoping she'd understand. The shackles would hold the soldiers for hours, but the freeze spell would last only fifteen minutes or so—they'd be able to call for help after that.

Prindi and Reza gaped at the frozen soldiers, unable to comprehend what Thisbe had just done. Then they looked at Thisbe fearfully, as if she might do the same to them.

"Come on!" said Thisbe. "Let's find Rohan." Now that she'd started with the magic, she couldn't stop—the soldiers had seen her and Prindi and Reza talking and acting like normal. They knew something was up, and Thisbe wasn't about to let them tell everyone else. Word could get to the castle before Dev had a chance to get out of there.

Thisbe hurried the other two into the hallway, then sealed the doorway with a glass spell. She sprinted in the direction that Rohan had gone, with Reza and Prindi close behind her. Whenever they reached a hallway branching off, Thisbe peered around the corner, then called out for Rohan. She knew it was a risk, but she had to find him fast. And she was ready with her components for the next soldiers who got in her way.

She didn't have to wait long. As they rounded a bend, they came upon a group of soldiers. When Thisbe saw why they were gathered, her heart sank. They surrounded Rohan and the other four slaves. Rohan was facedown on the ground, his arms held behind his back and his cheek against the stone floor. The other four looked bewildered and scared.

"Thisbe!" Rohan shouted. "Help!"

This time Thisbe pulled heart attack spells from her pocket, sending one at each of the three guards who were closest to her. The soldiers flopped to the ground, writhing and helpless. Thisbe ran closer.

The remaining two guards charged at Thisbe, one behind the other. Thisbe flung a handful of scatterclips at the front man. The force of the magic sent him flying backward, slamming into the soldier behind him and propelling them in a stack all the way down the lengthy hallway to the end. They smashed into the wall and hung there by the magical clips.

"Let's go!" Thisbe said, running to the others and trying

to encourage them to come. "No time to stop at my crypt to regroup—we'll just barrel right out of here."

Rohan shouted instructions in the common language and scrambled to his feet. Soon they were all heading toward the elevator, where there were sure to be more soldiers to contend with. As they went back past the kitchen wing, Thisbe stopped. She removed the glass spell, hit the guards there with another blast of freeze spells to keep them quiet for a while longer, then replaced the glass barrier. Then she rejoined the others, and they continued fleeing.

They went past Rohan's hallway and rounded the corner to take them by Thisbe's crypt and to the elevator. There were three guards lounging by the exit. When they saw the size of the group coming at them, they jumped to their feet. "Help!" they called out, pulling their swords. "They're escaping!"

Thisbe dug into her pockets as more guards and Mangrel came running onto the scene. She sent two of the soldiers sprawling with backward bobbly head spells, and a third screaming in pain with the pin cushion spell. One of the soldiers, whom Thisbe had fought once before by the river, dove at her feet, tripping her and sending her sprawling. He pulled his sword and slammed the hilt into her shoulder, causing shock waves of pain radiating through her.

"Get into the elevator!" Thisbe yelled to the others as fury rose in her throat. Every one of the slaves were defenseless except for Thisbe. If something happened to Thisbe, the black-eyed children would suffer greatly. It was up to her to protect them and show the soldiers that they were picking a fight with the wrong person. Trying not to cringe, Thisbe pointed at the guard who'd attacked her and yelled, "Boom!"

His body exploded into pieces, which rolled around on the floor of the catacombs. The remaining soldiers and Mangrel stopped and stared.

Thisbe mentally rammed through her emotions, refusing to feel regret, and reached for her components. Choked up but knowing she had to prove her dominance over the soldiers, she shouted, "He didn't have to die! And neither do you! So stay back and leave us all alone, or I'll do the same to you!"

Rohan reached the button that opened the elevator's glass door, and the others scrambled inside. "Come on, Thisbe!"

Mangrel stepped forward, arms above his head. "Thisbe! Do your magic on these two in front of me! They're not to be trusted. Then get out of here, all of you! I hope you all make it to safety."

Thisbe's mouth fell open in surprise. Was the crypt keeper trying to trick her? But his face was earnest, and he kept his arms raised. She frowned, contemplating killing the two, but she'd done enough to show them what they were up against. One death was one too many, and Thisbe didn't want to add anything else to her list of regrets. Instead she used shackle and silence spells on the remaining soldiers. She left Mangrel unharmed.

"Good luck!" he called to them as Thisbe hopped inside the elevator. Rohan closed the door and hit the button to bring them up to Dragonsmarche.

"Quickly," said Thisbe, bringing out a handful of tiny paintbrushes and handing them all around as the elevator churned slowly upward. "This will make you invisible. Just do what I do." She took one and held it up, then painted herself with broad strokes until she was nearly invisible, leaving a small piece of her shirt untouched. "Make sure you leave a bit of clothing visible so we can find you."

Rohan translated the instructions, and they all started to paint themselves too.

LISA McMANN

"This invisibility won't last long," Thisbe said. "Once we're out, hold on to each other and stay close to me. I'll run for an open area where we have lots of room. We're going to need it."

The elevator surfaced. Standing all around the square were dragons and soldiers. Townspeople scurried with their heads down. There was no market today. For the first time Thisbe could take in the state of the square. Pavers were cracked, and weeds grew between them. Nobody had taken care of it. The place looked horrible and desolate.

The outside soldiers crowded around the elevator, but when they saw no one inside, they looked around behind them to see if anyone was coming to use it to go down. In the confusion, Thisbe whispered, "Follow me!" She grabbed on to someone's hand and led them all through a break in the soldiers to an open area in the square. Once they were safely away from everyone, she counted tiny bits of clothing to make sure there were seven besides hers, remembering that Dev wouldn't be among them.

Then Thisbe called for eight invisible steeds. One by one the horses came to exist in front of the slaves. "Just feel around for them. Jump on their backs and follow me," Thisbe explained, and Rohan translated. A couple of the slaves seemed frightened and began to argue, but Rohan said something to those who were frightened to calm them down. Soon the entire invisible group was cantering through the neighborhood around Dragonsmarche, with nobody following.

As the group's invisibility began to fade, they reached the neighborhood where Maiven Taveer's family's house stood. Maiven, who'd lived in the castle for years before she'd been imprisoned, had spent time here as a child, Rohan explained. When things had begun looking dangerous, Maiven had hidden weapons and gold here. Rohan hurried everyone to the vacant alleyway behind the house so they wouldn't be seen. One by one the steeds vanished, depositing each black-eyed teen onto the ground.

Once they were all there, Rohan told them to wait by the back door. He snuck around to the front of the house, to the spot where Thisbe had said good-bye to him not so long ago. He found the key and opened the door, then dashed through the house and went to the back door to let the others inside. He ushered them all into the den.

A noise made Thisbe turn. Coming through a doorway was

a tall, beautiful, regal woman. She entered the den and moved to the center of the room to greet them. Though Thisbe could scarcely tear her eyes away from the woman, something shiny caught her eye in the corner of the room. It was then that Thisbe realized the walls were covered with the shiniest, most bejeweled, and deadliest-looking weapons she had ever laid eyes upon.

Waiting for Dev

My dear Thisbe!" cried the woman, catching sight of her. "I wasn't expecting you to be among this group."

"Maiven?" Thisbe replied. "Is that you?" The woman hardly resembled the half-starved prisoner Thisbe had known. She was strong and muscular and . . . freshly bathed. Her light brown skin glowed, and her shiny white hair was coiled around her head like a crown with a string of delicate flower-shaped jewels weaved into it. The woman's wrinkles made her even more stately and beautiful. And she carried herself with great dignity.

LISA McMANN

"Do I look different?" asked Maiven Taveer with a small smile. The queen. Thisbe's grandmother.

Thisbe gazed at the woman until her eyes blurred. She rushed into Maiven's arms and began to cry. She couldn't pinpoint what had started the tears, but they were bubbling over now. There were so many emotions going through her: fear surging from the fight and the escape, regret about the soldier she'd had to kill, worry over Dev, and love for this family member she hadn't realized that she had until recently. And the realization of the enormous task still before them was making her feel like what they'd just accomplished was merely akin to a drop of water in a sea. She'd gotten most of the slaves out of the catacombs and to safety. But there were still dragons everywhere under the control of the evil Revinir, who seemed invincible. And Dev, currently at her mercy.

Getting her fellow black-eyed slaves to freedom had felt huge. But it paled in comparison to overcoming the monstrous Revinir. And this tiny part wasn't even over yet. Maiven patted Thisbe's back as the girl sniffed and pulled herself together.

After a moment, Thisbe looked up. "We need to meet Dev by Alex's grave," she said. "I'll go. I can take down anyone who tries to fight me . . . except *her*. Or . . . dragons. But they won't be looking for us."

"Not yet, anyway," said Rohan. "Not until the Revinir finds out what we did. Hopefully we have a few hours before the remaining soldiers can alert her. And then we'll be sneaking around a bit until we figure out how to take down the Revinir once and for all. Maiven, what have you discovered while I've been away?"

"I've done a great deal of studying," said Maiven, pointing to a stack of books and several others open and spread around on a table. She said a few things in the common language, then turned to Thisbe. "You see, Thisbe, our people have never had to fight dragons or dragon-people before—they've always been our allies. But while you were gone, I made a trip to the old curmudgeon Ashguard's ruins on the other side of the crater lake, where the ruling family of Suresh once lived. There, in the palace library, I found some old texts and scrolls. They're written in the ancient language of our people, which no one has made use of since I was a child—and even then it was saved for high-court proceedings and the like. So it's a bit stiff and formal, and difficult for me to decipher. But I brought the items back with me, and I've been working at it, hoping to find something that will give us a clue how to defeat the Revinir."

One of the slaves, whose name Thisbe didn't yet know, spoke up haltingly. "Is Ashguard living?"

"I don't believe so," said Maiven, studying the girl with concern. She spoke rapidly in the common language, then repeated it for Thisbe's sake. "The land across the lake is deserted now. But the buildings, though precarious and mostly ruined, still remain. Did you know Ashguard?"

The girl's eyes, so much more expressive than Thisbe had ever noticed them, brimmed with tears. She nodded. "I am named for him."

"What is your name, dear?" asked Maiven.

"I am called Asha from the line of Suresh."

Maiven was quiet for a moment. "Perhaps I am wrong about the old curmudgeon," she said gently.

Asha nodded and didn't say anything more.

Thisbe glanced at Rohan. "I should go out to the forest now."

"I'll come with you," said Rohan. "All right, Maiven?"

"Yes. Be careful. Once the Revinir learns what happened,

the skies will be swarming with dragons looking for you."

"Do you have any more of those invisibility components?" Rohan asked Thisbe.

"A few," said Thisbe. "We'll use them only if we need them." She quickly took stock of her remaining spell components, sorting them out on the table. She'd used up a fair number of them. The others, recognizing some of the familiar items she'd employed to take down the soldiers, backed away carefully. But Thisbe didn't notice. She divided up the components and put them back into her pockets, which were decidedly less stuffed than before their escape.

After a hurried snack and something to drink, Thisbe and Rohan left the house, taking the back alley again so as not to be seen. They didn't want to become familiar to anyone nearby in case the time came that people were out looking for them as well as dragons.

Things seemed normal, which indicated that the Revinir hadn't heard of their escape yet. They sped through the town with their heads down, talking quietly. "Is there a book on the common language?" Thisbe asked. "I'd like to learn it so I can communicate better with the others."

"I'm sure there is. Maiven has thousands of books in her back rooms. I can teach you some phrases as well."

"I'd love that, if you don't mind."

"We've got some time on our hands."

"You mean as we wait for Dev?"

"I mean as we wait for Maiven to learn more from the ancient scrolls so we can try to figure out what to do."

"I see." Thisbe glanced at him. "Days? Weeks? I'm not sure how we proceed from here."

"We don't have a solution to the Revinir problem yet, so we need to stay in hiding until we figure it out and know we can beat her. I'm sure Maiven will want to train the other future rulers to fight too. She doesn't want to hurt any dragons but the Revinir, for obvious reasons—they are co-rulers of this land. Once Maiven comes across something of use, we'll have to work out a plan. It could take several weeks."

Thisbe sighed, feeling impatient. "I wish my people and your people could all work together. Maybe it's time. . . ."

"Do you have anyone you could summon from your world to help us? Perhaps the rescue team is itching for some more excitement?"

"I've been thinking about that," said Thisbe. "They've had some difficulty lately, though. My brother Aaron was the head mage, but before I left, he was ousted."

"What? You didn't mention that!"

"It didn't come up," Thisbe said. "We had enough to figure out when we actually had time to talk." She filled him in on all that had happened politically during the time she'd been in Artimé. And she mentioned how there were people pitted against her and Fifer, too. "I'm sure things have settled down by now, though. And even while those things were happening, Florence and Aaron and the others were working on new magic to help us destroy the Revinir. I'm hoping by now they've come up with something. Once we get to a secluded spot in the forest, I'll send Florence a seek spell. That'll signal her that I'm ready for them to come."

"That sounds promising," said Rohan. "Perhaps things are looking up for us after all."

After a while they came to the forest. They worked their way down the sickeningly familiar path they'd taken the night they and Sky had discovered Alex's grave. As they ventured farther in, Rohan began teaching Thisbe a few useful phrases. By the time they reached the mound of dirt that was Alex's grave, which was now covered in fresh growth, Thisbe could recite several greetings from memory and give simple commands like "Hurry!" and "Follow me!" and "Watch out for that dragon!"

They settled in, not sure how long Dev would be. While they waited for him to arrive, Thisbe fired off the seek spell to Florence, then started learning words for their surroundings.

The evening wore on, and there was no sign of Dev. Thisbe wasn't too worried—their spot in the forest was a bit of a trek from the market square. But then she started thinking things through and doubting their plan. With a start, she turned to Rohan. "Once the Revinir has the treasures, do you think she'll she give Dev the luxury of another dragon ride? Or would she have lost the sense of urgency and sent him back on foot? That could take significantly longer."

Rohan didn't know the answer. "She doesn't have much regard for us," he said. "I wish I'd thought of that earlier."

Thisbe pressed her lips together. "Let's just sit tight. Even if she tells him to walk back, she won't accompany him down to the dungeon. He could figure out how to sneak out of the castle—he knows his way around that place like no one else."

"Let's keep up hope," said Rohan. "If he's stuck walking, it'll take him a good while longer."

Thisbe and Rohan talked about everything that came to mind. Rohan filled Thisbe in about what he expected Maiven to do with the other black-eyed future rulers while she searched for answers. He believed she'd start immediately teaching them to use weapons as she'd learned them, rather than haphazardly, as they'd been forced to do under the Revinir's control. And telling them the history of their people as rulers, as most of them had been captive since they were very young and wouldn't know much about it.

"I want to learn that too," said Thisbe.

"We're all learning our own history at least a little through this ancestor broth," said Rohan.

Thisbe rolled over to face him. "I've been meaning to ask you for days. What images are you seeing?"

Rohan stared at the sky and chewed on a piece of grass. He didn't answer right away. "It's troubling, to be honest," he said, sitting up. His black eyes shone, and his expression was anguished.

LISA McMANN

"Why?" Thisbe asked. Her heart twisted, and she took his hand.

He looked down. "Like you, I see my mother as a girl."

Thisbe propped herself up on her elbow. "You do?" she asked. "What is she doing? What's so troubling? Was she taken away too?"

"No." Tears sprang to his eyes. "She's . . . she's helping . . ."

Thisbe sat up, alarmed, and reached out for Rohan to comfort him. "What is it?"

"She's helping pirates," he said, his voice cracking.

Thisbe's eyes narrowed. "What?" she whispered.

"Helping pirates . . . steal your mother away."

Waiting...
and Waiting

Thisbe recoiled, pulling her hand away from Rohan's. She didn't know what to think. It was strange that his historic visions showed something so similar to hers. But it was terrible that *his* mother, a black-eyed ruler, was helping to shove Thisbe's mother onto the pirate ship. "What?" she said again. "What kind of person . . . ?"

"I know!" said Rohan, sitting up. "Don't say it. I'm trying to make sense of it. I even drank more of the ancestor broth to see if, perhaps, there was an additional scene for me to learn from, like what happened with you. And . . . it's true. My mother was helping the pirates kidnap your mother." He blew

LISA McMANN

out a breath. "And I guess I'm not really all that surprised."

"How—what do you mean?" Thisbe knew virtually nothing about Rohan's past except that his family was dead. He'd always seemed reticent to talk about it, and Thisbe had never pushed him.

"She's younger than your mother was. A few years younger. So . . . maybe only eight or nine. A child."

"Are you absolutely sure it's her?"

Rohan nodded miserably. "There was a painting of my mother as a child that hung over our hearth. The picture is nearly identical to the image in my mind. I don't understand it—I don't understand why any nine-year-old girl would be anywhere near the sea, helping pirates steal away fellow black-eyed rulers."

Thisbe's head whirled. In the image in her mind, there were pirates around the girl—which was her mother at age twelve—dragging her onto a ship. She closed her eyes and conjured up the scene, listening to Maiven's assistant yelling for Maiven Taveer and watching the scene in motion. This time focusing not on the main girl or the pirates or the assistant, whose back was to her, but on the other people around. And then she froze.

There was another girl, scrappy and barefooted, scared and angry and yanking on a rope that was tied to Thisbe's mother's wrist. Trying to pull and then shove her toward the pirates.

"Why?" Thisbe whispered. "Why was she fighting against her own people?"

"I don't know." Rohan was quiet. "She was a terrible person to me, too. That's why I'm not surprised she did this as a child. I'm . . . I'm sorry, Thisbe."

"It's not your fault." Thisbe didn't know what else to say about it. After a while Rohan stood up, and they both realized how dark it had gotten. Neither had any more answers—or at least, if Rohan had them, he wasn't saying them out loud.

Thisbe's thoughts turned to Dev. "I'm getting worried."

"About Dev?"

Thisbe nodded.

"Me too. Finding the king's treasures shouldn't take long if he knows where they are."

"What if he couldn't escape, and he's actually walking back through the dungeon?" said Thisbe. Her throat tightened. "He'd be going back alone and defenseless, stuck in the catacombs."

Rohan sighed and pinched the bridge of his nose. "That would be just awful."

Thisbe cringed. "We made a big mistake. I didn't have time to think all of this through before I sent him there!"

Rohan shifted. "Do you think we should go down through the elevator and look for him? Do you have enough magic left to fight the soldiers if we do?"

"That seems dangerous." Thisbe blew out a contemplative breath. "Let's wait a little longer."

They settled back down in the darkness, but Dev didn't come.

Just as Thisbe opened her mouth to suggest they'd better go back to the catacombs to find him, a shattering roar pierced their eardrums and tugged at their souls. Thisbe cursed under her breath and clapped her hands over her ears, gritting her teeth as she fought off the pull of the Revinir's call.

Rohan, who still hadn't ingested any dragon-bone broth, held on to Thisbe's shoulders in support and watched the ancestor images flash before his eyes without having to deal with the effects of the roar. He'd heard it, though, echoing like thunder in a canyon. She sounded furious. "She knows," he said.

Thisbe nodded. She could feel it in every muscle and nerve, and she knew with certainty in the back of her mind. "Oh yes. She definitely knows we escaped. The question is, did she find out from Dev? Or after he left the castle? What if she's got him?" She closed her eyes, a strange sensation lingering after the roar, and an odd, dreadful feeling washed over her.

Thisbe tried to shake it off, but the feeling held for a while before fading. Slowly she opened her eyes. "She's got Dev."

Feelings and Premonitions

Should we go to the catacombs and look for Dev anyway?" Rohan asked. "Are you sure he won't be there?"

"I'm . . . pretty sure," said Thisbe, sounding terribly grim. "I got one of those feelings again—one of those premonitions like I had before, regarding the Revinir. She's got him. I feel . . . ugh. Terrible." She got up and wiped the dirt and leaves off her pants, then started tromping back to the path into Grimere. "Let's go. Maiven will be wondering about us, and the others might not know how to handle the roar now that they've got the effects of the two broths competing in their minds."

Rohan hopped up and trotted after her, and together, with a magical highlighter glowing to help them stay on the path, they went back toward Grimere. Once they broke out of the forest, they could see dozens of dragons soaring overhead on their way to the castle, heeding the Revinir's call.

Thisbe's mind worked overtime as they stumbled across the road. Her heart was torn in two over Dev. What a terrible mistake she'd made! She'd asked him to do this—and he'd done it to save eight others. What had happened? Had he broken character? Did he focus on her when she peered at him, or say something not quite right? Had she discovered he was faking it? Or had the soldiers from the catacombs gotten to her and captured him along the way? Whatever the case, Thisbe was certain Dev was caught, enduring the Revinir's wrath. What would she do to him next?

"I should have dumped out the dragon-bone broth," Thisbe lamented. "Now she'll get some and feed it to him."

"No one thought of that," said Rohan, trying to comfort her. "It was very rushed."

"I messed up. Poor Dev—this is all my fault. Why did I think he could do it?" She muttered under her breath. "Maybe he did it just fine, but the soldiers got to her before he could get away. Ugh! I'm a terrible friend!"

Rohan stumbled in the darkness and caught himself. "Listen. You got the rest of us out of there unscathed and without being seen. I'd say you did a lot right."

"I failed Dev. He didn't want to do this."

"But if you hadn't pushed him, none of us would be free right now."

Thisbe scowled as they ran behind some bushes, trying not to be seen by villagers or the dragons overhead. "What's more right?" she asked. "Sacrificing Dev so the rest of us could be safe? Or staying together and risking us all being caught? Is one life less important than several lives?"

Rohan was silent as he contemplated it. "I don't think there's a correct answer to that."

They ran across the road and entered the more familiar neighborhoods of Grimere. Breathless, they wanted desperately to get to Maiven's house before the dragons were given instructions by the Revinir. Once that happened, all hell would break loose as they went on the hunt for Thisbe and Rohan and the others. None of them would be safe outside.

When they reached Maiven's neighborhood, they went through the back alley as before. With great relief they made it inside the house. There they found Maiven teaching her new subjects how to use a shiv and a dagger to kill an attacker. Things were getting very serious.

Maiven heard them enter and went to the door to secure it after they came inside. "Where's Dev?" she asked in a low voice. "Didn't he come to meet you?"

They told Maiven what had happened. Thisbe shared that the roar had seemed to trigger a premonition, which made her certain that Dev had been discovered and captured. Whether the Revinir had determined Dev was faking or she'd found out from the soldiers that the other black-eyed slaves had escaped, Thisbe wasn't sure.

"At least you're safe. I'm not sure what we can do for Dev at this point." Troubled though she was over the news, Maiven also seemed deeply interested in what Thisbe had to say about premonitions. "Tell me more about your premonition, Thisbe. Have you ever had that happen before?"

"They started after I had my most recent dose of ancestor broth," Thisbe said. She shared the feelings she'd had in

Dragonsmarche when the Revinir was questioning her. And the sense of dread when she knew Dev had been discovered and captured.

Maiven clasped Thisbe's hand between her hers. She glanced around as the others were putting away their weapons and getting settled for the night. "I get premonitions too. I've been feeling them on and off for years. That's how I knew the great evil person existed from my dungeon cell, though I didn't know her name. So I believe you when you say you have these feelings. And I hope you'll always tell me about them, even if the feeling is small. Chances are you have had other premonitions in the past but didn't understand what they were or view them as a forecast for the future. The ancestor broth has made them more obvious to you. The more aware we are of these things, the more you and I can help guide our people to make the right choices as we move forward. Between us we can be doubly sure that we're right in our way of thinking."

"That's so strange," murmured Thisbe, while marveling over how Maiven so naturally included her as a leader here. "Why do you suppose it happens?"

"I believe I'm receiving them because I am the eldest

remaining ancestor," said Maiven. "You are noticing them because you've taken in enough of the ancestor broth. And perhaps because you are my granddaughter." She was quiet for a moment. "Since your mother is . . . gone," she said, her eyes involuntarily closing and a wave of pain washing over her face, "you and your sister are next in line for the throne."

"What?" whispered Thisbe.

"If you wish to have the position, of course," said Maiven, recovering and offering a wan smile. "The others here would do as fine a job as you, I'm sure. All black-eyed people are entitled to the position, but many are unwilling to make the sacrifices necessary to rule."

Thisbe sat back, the wind knocked out of her. "I don't think I'm ready for something like that," she said.

"Well," said Maiven grimly, "you won't have to be unless we can overthrow the monster who has taken up residence in my castle. But how? I still don't have the slightest clue."

A Message from Home

It was unsettling to Thisbe to hear Maiven Taveer, queen and commander of the military in the land of the dragons, express that she had no idea how to defeat their biggest enemy. And even more frightening to think back to her Artiméan friends and family, who also were clueless in how to fight this dragon-woman. But it made Thisbe even more determined. The Revinir was taking control of Grimere, and Thisbe believed that she wouldn't stop with the land of the dragons, especially since she still wanted Fifer under her control. Artimé might be safe for the moment, but as soon as the Revinir figured out that Fifer was nowhere around this world, she'd venture back there.

Thisbe and Maiven stayed up talking after most of the others turned in for the night. "Do you suppose the ghost dragons would know how to defeat her?" Thisbe asked Maiven. "I didn't ask them that before, exactly. All I know is that they are unable to kill her."

"That seems like a good route to investigate," said Maiven.

"But they're so forgetful—they may not remember anything. Maybe you and I could meet with them to find out. They might remember you."

"I'd like that," said Maiven. "But how do we get them to meet with us?"

"We might have to go in search of them." Thisbe tapped her lips thoughtfully. "The last time they came to help, Gorgrun told me that I called to them somehow. But I don't know how I did it."

"Really?" asked Maiven. "Gorgrun said you called to them? That's fascinating. I wonder how you did it too, and if you can figure out how to do it again. I worry about traveling there. We'd be in danger of being seen on the road."

"There's a dragon path through the forest that will take us most of the way—at least that's what Fifer told me."

LISA McMANN

"If it's a dragon path," said Maiven, "the dragons will know about it. That seems a rather embarrassing way to be captured, don't you agree?"

Thisbe grinned, feeling wonderfully at ease with her new-found grandmother despite the seriousness of the situation. "That's a good point. No wonder you were commander of the military."

"I earned my stripes the hard way," Maiven said mirthfully. "No more dragon paths for this queen."

"Maybe we'd think more clearly after some sleep." Thisbe looked around the living room and saw that everyone else had found cots or blankets and a place to lay them out on the floor. Rohan lifted his head and waved good night sleepily.

Thisbe waved back. Then she cringed, thinking about how Dev should be here too, safe and sound with all of them. "I'm worried about Dev."

"I am too," said Maiven. "But I know him from my time in the dungeon. He'll survive this. He's resourceful. And when we have the means to get him back, we will. Patience is also something I've learned the hard way."

Thisbe gazed at her grandmother, feeling better. "Thanks."

Maiven squeezed the girl's shoulder. "I have some blankets for you," she said. "Let's get some sleep and worry about Dev and the ghost dragons tomorrow."

Thisbe nodded. "Oh! By the way, I sent for help from Artimé. So we'll have lots of magical people here in just a few days."

"We'll need them," said Maiven. "I'm so grateful for the generosity of your people. They've done so many things for me and our people already. That young man, Thatcher, is a fine person. Do you know he told me he'd come back for me, and he did."

Thisbe smiled. "Sounds like Thatcher."

Maiven walked around the perimeter of the room checking the windows, making sure they were locked and the drapes fully pulled shut.

Thisbe washed up and went to bed. But tired as she was, she couldn't get to sleep. She just stared at the ceiling, thinking about Dev and getting a stomachache imagining what must have happened. She pictured him alone in the dungeon or locked in his crypt . . . or worse.

Dev might never forgive her. And he might never do another decent thing again after this. If he survived.

LISA McMANN

Thisbe hadn't yet gotten a response from the seek spell she'd sent to Florence. She wasn't sure how long it would take for it to go all the way to Artimé, and then for Florence to send one in response to signal they were coming. Perhaps Florence wanted to be ready and on the way before sending it—they hadn't thought to discuss that, but now it seemed crucial to know.

Idly Thisbe wondered how they'd travel. Simber would fly, of course, but the rest of them could take a ship and have Simber ferry them across the gorge. Or they could go on Spike's back. Or perhaps they'd take the faster route through the Island of Fire volcano. That seemed like an easier way for Florence to get to Grimere, if she was planning on coming. Thisbe hoped she was—Florence would be great against the Revinir, she thought sleepily. If Florence took a ship, she wouldn't be able to be flown across the gorge—she was too heavy for Simber to carry.

Thisbe closed her eyes and turned to her side. Hopefully, Florence and Fifer and Aaron would have come up with a solution to eliminate the Revinir by now. That would leave Thisbe free to figure out how they were going to save Dev.

She drifted off.

In the morning when Thisbe woke up, a strange, small orb glowed in the air above her face. It wasn't a seek spell—it was much more compact, and it hadn't exploded into a picture of anything. Thisbe blinked hard and wiped the sleep from her eyes, making sure it wasn't a dream. She slid out from under the orb, not quite daring to reach out to touch it. It swung lightly through the air, staying an arm's length away at about chin level. Sitting up, Thisbe studied it. Could Florence and the others have improved the seek spell? Or was this not from them? Was it a trick? Had the Revinir somehow tracked her down?

Feeling relatively certain that the Revinir had no means to do this type of magic, Thisbe reached out tentatively with one finger and touched the spot of light.

Instead of exploding like a seek spell, it melted and slid into Thisbe's hand. The light faded, and a brilliant white piece of folded paper remained on her palm, with a thin pencil beside it. Thisbe opened the note, a small smile blooming on her face. Florence had indeed figured out how to improve the seek spell while Thisbe had been away. And she'd sent an actual message!

But her smile faded as she read the words.

Dear Thisbe,

Artimé is in a civil war. I'm so sorry—we aren't able to help you right now. But if you and Drock can return to help us . . . we could really use it.

Your friend,

Florence

PS Use the pencil to reply. The verbal component is "send."

A New Direction

While the other future rulers of Grimere got up to start their day of weapons training, Thisbe sat on her cot and stared at the paper in her hand, trying to comprehend the words from Florence. Artimé was in a civil war? How could that be possible? What did it mean? And Florence had done something Thisbe had never imagined could be possible. It was unthinkable. She had denied Thisbe's request for help. With a sinking heart, Thisbe knew things had to be terrible there for that to be the case.

Granted, Thisbe hadn't sent a double seek spell, which

LISA McMANN

would have indicated she was in grave danger and needed help immediately. Perhaps if she'd done that, Florence wouldn't have said no. And it was true that Thisbe was relatively safe at the moment, hidden in this house. So there wasn't a huge sense of urgency. It was just that Thisbe had been counting on her friends to help her in Grimere. Even if they hadn't been excited about going back so soon, like Thisbe had been, they all wanted to see the Revinir destroyed, and they had a much better chance at succeeding if they worked together.

She tried to push back the hurt feelings, even though this felt a little bit like she was being abandoned again. She tried not to think about how Fifer and Seth had been more interested in staying in Artimé than in coming back here. And she tried not to be mad at Aaron, even though the whole civil war thing probably had to do with him being—or not being—the head mage.

Once she got over the initial shock of Florence's note, Thisbe felt ashamed about her earlier feelings. Then concern for the safety of her family and friends grew in its place. This had to be a very serious situation for Florence to decide no one could come to Thisbe's aid. They needed everyone. Including her. That Florence would even ask for Thisbe to return when she knew how precarious things were in Grimere was shocking.

"Oh dear," whispered Thisbe, picturing a war-torn magical world, family against family, friend against friend. Artimé was the last place anyone expected to be engulfed in war. What was happening?

Thisbe read the note again and hesitated when she got to the part where Florence said they could really use her help right now. That was so unlike Florence—they must be in dire straits for Florence to ask Thisbe for help. Thisbe was just a kid! Though it was true that Thisbe was one of the most powerful mages in Artimé. Especially now that she could control her magic and use Artimé's creative magic too. And she was getting more skilled every day.

But Thisbe couldn't leave here. Maiven needed her! And they had training to do. Plus there was no way to get home, unless Drock was somehow not under the Revinir's influence and she could actually find him. And of course the Revinir would definitely find out if they left—would that cause even more trouble for Artimé in the long run? What would stop her from chasing after Thisbe again? Going back to Artimé just didn't seem possible without causing even more problems.

LISA McMANN

Thisbe read the note a third time. While the request didn't sound frantic, Florence was deadly serious, even though Florence had no idea what challenges Thisbe was facing at the moment. For all Florence knew, Thisbe could be back in the dungeon, and any false move could cause a series of disastrous events.

And what about Fifer and Seth and her other friends? Had anyone been hurt? Was Aaron okay? He was the one that the horrible Frieda Stubbs was after. Had she done something to him? *Killed* him? Was Florence just trying to get Thisbe to come home because she really needed to tell her that she'd lost someone else in her life?

The dilemma was so large it was painful. Thisbe dropped her head into her hands, conflicted.

Rohan popped into the room where Thisbe sat. "We're getting some sword training now. I know you've had it in Artimé, but you're welcome to—" He stopped when he saw that she didn't lift her gaze. "Is everything okay?"

Thisbe shook her head and held the paper out to him. "Apparently they improved the seek spell, and Florence replied to mine with this note."

Rohan came and knelt next to her and read it. "Oh dear," he said when he finished. He turned it over and back and read it again. "That's a blow, isn't it."

"A huge blow," said Thisbe.

"I guess I didn't realize until now how much I was counting on them coming to help us here."

Thisbe nodded. "Me too. I just assumed they'd come when I called them. I mean, I knew they had some sticky things to work out, but Artimé doesn't have civil wars! Artimé is the most wonderful place. It sounds like things just went completely bonkers."

Rohan glanced sidelong at Thisbe and chewed his bottom lip, consternated. "What are you going to do?"

"I don't know." She got up, still holding the tiny pencil that had come with the paper, and took the note back from Rohan. "I should probably reply, but I don't quite know what to say. I'm so disappointed, but I'm also scared for them. All my friends, my family . . ." She shook her head in frustration. "But I have friends and family here, too! I feel like I'm being torn in half. And I can't just leave after what happened with Dev. I did that to him."

LISA McMANN

Rohan didn't argue, even though he didn't think Dev's situation was all Thisbe's fault. Dev had his own will, his own mind, and he'd walked out on his own accord. "Whatever you decide to do, I support you. And you know we'll be glad to help you prepare if you decide to go. We can try to track down Drock. . . ."

Thisbe pocketed the items and pressed her fingers to her temples. "I don't know about Drock. When I saw him the other day, I was pretty sure he wasn't with us anymore. And I'm afraid what could happen if we went out looking for him—the dragons must have been ordered to look for us by now. If Drock is being controlled, he could attack us. And even if Drock isn't under the Revinir's control, I'm sure she'll send a fleet of dragons after us if she finds out Drock and I tried to leave."

"It's *Drock's* absence that would clue her in, though, not yours. She knows where he is. But she doesn't know where you are. If you feel like you need to go, you could take the volcano network like before."

Thisbe thought about that for a moment. "I think Florence was really hoping for some help from a dragon, though. I'm not enough of a help to make much difference alone."

"Interesting. A dragon would end fights in a hurry, wouldn't it?" mused Rohan. He reached out and gave Thisbe a quick hug. "Why don't you get some breakfast and keep thinking. I'll be in the weapons room with the others."

Thisbe nodded. Rohan left, and she went to the kitchen and prepared a meal, thinking deeply about what to do. She wanted to ask Florence for more details, but she wasn't sure how much room she had on the paper or how many words she could send. Was anybody dead? Or hurt? What did a civil war look like, exactly? Was the mansion still standing? Whose side was everybody on?

The more she imagined the scene, the more she felt like she should go. Maybe there was a way for Drock to sneak away without the Revinir noticing. Or . . . what about the ghost dragons? Perhaps they could at least get Thisbe across the gorge and help her find Spike, who could take her to Artimé. If only she could get the ghost dragons to come.

"What a disaster," Thisbe said under her breath. In her mind, the images that had plagued her in the past now seemed like part of her, and the scenes randomly flashed at the edges of her sight. One was of ghost dragons flying and marching together over the market square. When she'd first seen it, that scene had been a vision of the future, Thisbe realized now. Something that hadn't happened yet, as opposed to the other images that told part of a story from long ago. Someday maybe she'd be able to tell the difference between past and future. And maybe understand the premonitions, too.

As she ate, the images of ghost dragons flipped through her mind. Could Gorgrun and Quince help her? And would they? It would be a long, dangerous, and potentially fruitless walk to find them in the cavelands. If only she knew what she'd done before to call to them.

She pulled out the message from Florence and studied it, then held her pencil poised to respond. But she didn't write anything. She still didn't know what to say. Should she stay or should she go? With a sigh, she slid the items back into her pocket and cleaned up her dishes, then went to find the others and learn more about sword fighting. Perhaps she'd have a chance to teach them a few things too.

A Surprise Visitor

L ater, Thisbe and Maiven met again, this time to talk about what was happening in Artimé. Maiven offered Thisbe support in her decision, whatever it was, but agreed that trying to find Drock right now would only serve to antagonize the Revinir and send her chasing after them again. They also agreed that the only viable option to get Thisbe across the gorge, if she decided to go, was if a ghost dragon would take her. But the length of the journey to find them was daunting.

"It'll take two days on foot at least," said Maiven. "And dragons will be searching everywhere for any sign of you. Perhaps . . . *I* should go."

LISA McMANN

"You?" said Thisbe, alarmed. But the old woman who'd seemed so frail after years in the dungeon had regained her strength. Maybe it wasn't such a bad idea.

"No one knows who I am," the former queen pointed out. "They don't remember me. They think I'm dead. Only some of the dragons might recognize my scent, but if they're under the Revinir's control, I doubt they'd do something to an old woman, whether they recognize my scent or not. They're supposed to be looking for young people. I'll glide right under their noses."

"But who will train us while you're gone?"

"I was hoping you'd teach everyone some magic at some point to see if anyone in our group has untapped natural abilities we can nurture. After all, you had something in you—though you might have gotten that from your father's side of the family. But Rohan said you taught him your seek spell, so that may mean there is hope for the others."

Thisbe considered that. It would definitely make her feel better about leaving them if she could teach them a few basics. Things that didn't require components, like invisible hooks and the glass spell, could possibly come in handy. "That's a great idea," said Thisbe. "And worth a try, at least."

"I'll leave after dark, then, unless you tell me otherwise."

They practiced hard all day. Maiven would teach them a move, then, while the future rulers practiced it, she'd go to her ancient books to try to uncover anything that would help them figure out how to take down the Revinir. Then she'd teach another move and go back to her books. Thisbe was glad for the refresher course, as she'd been so focused on magical-warrior training when she'd been home the last time that she hadn't practiced sword fighting at all. She was feeling it too—sore muscles everywhere.

Seeing Maiven puzzle over the books without gleaning any answers was the deciding factor for Thisbe. Perhaps Aaron and Fifer and Florence and the others had made more progress in Artimé. At the very least, Thisbe knew Florence had been working on the obliterate spell, and hopefully this trip home would at least afford her the chance to pick up one of those before coming back.

Because she was definitely coming back. Part of her couldn't imagine Artimé's civil war lasting more than a few days before one side or the other sheepishly surrendered or everyone came to their senses. While the people of Artimé knew how to fight and had done it often, they'd never turned on each other before. And they'd always gone reluctantly into battle, only as a last resort. What in the world had happened there to make things go this far off track? Maybe it wasn't as bad as Thisbe had first imagined it to be. After all, Florence only said they could use some help. She didn't beg or demand. Though that wasn't Florence's way of doing things either.

They broke for the evening meal, and then Maiven went to pack a light bag and get ready for her journey to the cavelands. As night fell without a moon in sight, Thisbe and the others checked the window locks and drew the curtains tightly shut. But when Maiven reappeared, looking ready to go, Prindi let out a scream from the back window.

Rohan turned quickly and gasped. "They've found us! Hide!"

Pressed up against the glass was the horrifying face of a dragon.

Teaming Up

The other future rulers ran and dove for cover behind pieces of furniture, screaming. Thisbe grabbed heart attack components and peered out through the drapes of the front window to see if they were surrounded, while Rohan barred the door—not that any of it would do any good against a dragon.

Maiven drew her sword and stood poised, giving an air of safety to the room, and then she narrowed her gaze and looked closer, scrutinizing the shape in the shadowy alley behind the house. After a moment she strode toward the window, unafraid.

LISA McMANN

"Maiven!" said Thisbe sharply. "Be careful!"

But Maiven kept going until she reached the window. She looked out. And then she unhooked the latch and slid the window open.

The other black-eyed children screamed again, for certainly the former queen had lost her mind. But the woman held her hand out to quiet them. "Well, what a sight," she said through the window. "Are you alone?"

Thisbe's heart pounded. What was going on? Had Maiven known this dragon when she'd been a ruler?

Maiven stepped aside, then went to the door and opened it wide.

"Maiven!" Thisbe said again, feeling frantic. "What are you doing?"

But Thisbe soon realized why her grandmother was acting so strangely. The dragon lumbered down the alley to the open door and pressed his nose inside as far as it would go, then tilted his head downward against the frame so he could see.

"It's Gorgrun!" Thisbe exclaimed. She let out a held breath. "Don't worry, everyone. Gorgrun is one of the ghost dragons. He's safe and not under the Revinir's spell."

Rohan came out from behind the sofa and joined Thisbe to greet their old friend. "We were just talking about you," Thisbe said. She reached up tentatively and patted the dragon's bony snout. "How did you know to come?"

"You called us," said Gorgrun, who didn't seem at all annoyed to be explaining this for the second time to Thisbe, because he'd probably forgotten.

"I did?" asked Thisbe, delighted but puzzled. "So there are more of you?"

"Quince is hiding nearby." Gorgrun's nostrils flared, and smoke filled the living room. The future rulers waved their hands to try to clear the air.

"Perhaps you could take a step back, sir," said Maiven, firmly yet politely. Gorgrun obliged, tugging his face out of the doorframe and rattling the house in the process.

Thisbe coughed and fanned the smoke away. She studied the dragon, wondering if just by thinking about them in conjunction with the images had been what brought them here. "The reason I called you is because I have a huge favor to ask. Will you take me to my world across the gorge?"

"Across the gorge," said Gorgrun, a puzzled look on his

LISA McMANN

face. "Seems to me I've been there before, a long time ago, but I can't recall who I visited."

"Could it have been Pan? The ruler of the sea?"

"Oh—" said Gorgrun with a start. "Oh my. Yes. It was definitely Pan."

Thisbe frowned. "She's not there anymore. She's under the Revinir's spell. I haven't seen her, but she's in this world."

"That's a pity. One of the finest dragons I know. We'll have to do something about her being under the Revinir's control." He cleared his throat, making the dishes rattle in the cupboards. "Take you across the gorge, you say? Of course I can. I'll take you wherever you want to go, if it helps you to someday reclaim this realm for the dragons, so I can die."

Thisbe thought about the obliterate spells that Florence was working on and her desperate need to collect a few of them. "Yes," she said. "I believe it will help significantly. Will you perhaps be willing to help us stop a civil war? Perchance?"

"I suppose I would," said Gorgrun. "Quince and I both would be happy to go . . . where again?"

"To the seven islands. Across the gorge and halfway through that world. Not quite as far as the trip to Pan's island." She had more questions for him about how to defeat the Revinir, but she figured she'd have plenty of time to quiz him on the long ride.

"No problem," Gorgrun assured her. He looked at the rest of the people in the house, most of whom had come out of hiding by now. "We'll take you all if you like."

"Oh, no—that's not necessary," said Thisbe hurriedly.

But Maiven interrupted. "Actually, Gorgrun, that would be nice."

"What?" said Thisbe. "What are you saying? You need to stay here to train and fight!"

Maiven tapped her lips. "We can still do both of those things in transit—and isn't it even better learning to fight on a moving object? Think of the balance skills we'll acquire. With our weapons, books, and a few supplies, I believe we can do everything we need to do from a dragon's back." She paused. "And it sounds like your people can really use some help. It will be good training for our group."

"But I don't want anyone here to get hurt," said Thisbe passionately. "There are so few of us left. We must all be very careful."

LISA McMANN

Maiven put her hand on Thisbe's shoulder and looked into her eyes. "Thisbe," she said quietly. "Our people do not shy away from a fight for justice. That's our nature. And it's partly why so few of us remain—many of the parents of these future leaders died fighting for their rightful land and rulership. To live our lives where we look the other way when something isn't right? That is no life at all."

Thisbe was quiet. She looked around at the other solemn faces and was surprised to see that they all seemed willing and eager to go along with this sudden change of plans. Prindi nodded and stepped forward. "We will help you, Thisbe."

Rohan echoed her. Then the others did the same.

"You are all very noble," Thisbe said, her eyes shining. "I gratefully accept your help. But . . . can we escape here without the Revinir finding out? I can't have her chasing me down again and bringing even more chaos to my land."

"We're way ahead of you," said Gorgrun knowingly. "We haven't used up all of our tricks yet. Our ghostlike qualities allow us to make ourselves appear as fog to all but the black-eyed rulers if we choose to do so. We activated it at the time we left the cavelands. Although all of you can see us as we truly look, no one else has detected us—not even your neighbors. We will float past the castle and across the gorge in the same manner until we are quite out of sight of anyone in this world."

"That couldn't be more perfect," said Thisbe, greatly relieved to hear it.

Maiven smiled. "Then it's settled—you shall be our Trojan horse." She turned to the future leaders. "Let's pack up and go before Gorgrun forgets to look like a cloud of fog."

Thirty minutes later everyone was armed with all the weapons and ancient books they could carry. They slipped out into the alley and climbed Gorgrun's ethereal, skeletal tail and nestled on his soft, cloudy back. With his riders hidden in the foggy folds of his sagging skin, he moved through the neighborhood like a ghost. At the road he took flight, slowly and deftly dodging the cursed, glazed-eyed dragons who were out searching for these very same black-eyed people.

As they passed the castle in the distance, Thisbe sat up and looked at it, feeling a pang in her heart. She hadn't forgotten Dev. Was he there? Or in the dungeon? Or perhaps the catacombs? There was nothing they could do for him right now. He'd have to figure out how to stay alive on his own until they were ready to go after the Revinir and rescue him. "Please be okay, wherever you are," Thisbe whispered, sending the words away on the wind. "We'll be back."

From a castle turret, stuck behind a crisscross of rusty iron bars, Dev peered out into the darkness and waited for the Revinir to bring him the dragon-bone broth she'd threatened him with. It wouldn't be long before he descended into oblivion again. Would Thisbe come to save him in time? Had she figured out where he was?

As he stared moodily into the darkness, a sliver of moon appeared above the treetops. Dev looked closer, then squinted, not quite believing what he was seeing. The moon lit up a pair of ghost dragons who carried a party of riders across the gorge. With a sinking heart, Dev realized who they must be, and that they were escaping without him.

"Thisbe!" Dev screamed through the bars. But the dragons didn't turn back.

He screamed her name again, but to no avail. A rush of

LISA McMANN

air escaped his lungs, and then another, until he was sobbing. Devastated, he collapsed against the cool stone wall and watched them grow small, feeling an ache in his stomach larger than the one caused by Shanti's death. He'd been abandoned by the ones he'd saved.

A long time after they were out of sight beyond the mist, Dev dried his tears and set his jaw, pressing his mouth in a tight, grim line. He was alone against the Revinir. His choices were simple and horrible. He could drink the broth, or die fighting the monster. Either way, there was no longer any hope for him. He closed his eyes and pressed his back against the stone, welcoming the cold.

Once across the gorge, while everyone else settled down to sleep, Thisbe pulled the note and pencil from Florence out of her pocket and wrote:

Dear Florence,

Stay strong. We are coming to help. Please keep Fifer and Aaron safe if you can. I can't bear to lose anyone else.

—Thisbe

With a hitch in her breath and a blunt feeling of fear hammering her heart, she folded the note along the creases, then tucked the tiny pencil inside. Holding it in front of her, she concentrated, then whispered the magical word and sent the message soaring across the sky like a shooting star, pointing the way home.

Acknowledgments

Hello to all the amazing people in my life! If you are reading this, you are one of them. I like you. A lot.

Some of you are in the publishing industry and you worked on this book. From editorial to art, marketing to publicity, library to sales, I want you to know I value you and your amazing abilities that I don't possess. I take comfort in the fact that if creative people get banished from our dystopian world and are sent to their deaths, you will be there with me, along with everyone who reads these books. It's going to be a good time.

I'm confident my family will be banished too. Matt, Kilian, and Kennedy: You have been there through each of these Unwanteds books from the very beginning. Thank you for all of your creative ideas, brilliant suggestions, and helpful feedback for the past many years. I always know I can count on you.

Booksellers, maybe you ordered this book for your store. As a former bookseller, I have the fondest feelings for you and the greatest empathy for your sore feet. I also know shelf space is precious, and I am grateful that you make room for me.

Educators and librarians, you had me at "How many books would you like to borrow?" I spent my Saturdays at the public library as a kid, and my weekdays trying to figure out how to stay in at recess so I could hide from bullies and read whatever you had in your classroom. Today I thank you for putting my books into the hands of young readers who might feel Unwanted too.

Kids! You give me life. Every day someone asks me, "Where do you get your inspiration?" I say it's from you. It's from readers who tell me on Instagram or Twitter or Facebook or in a letter or in person that these books mean something to you. You make me want to keep going. Thank you for your joy and enthusiasm and for making me laugh.

Most of all, thank you to Liesa Abrams and Michael Bourret. I love our little team.